Published by KJC Books

Copyright © 2018 by KJ Charles

Edited by Veronica Vega
Cover art by Lexiconic Design
Layout by eB Format
Image: John Pettie, *Two Strings To Her Bow*
Flourish from Vecteezy.com

ISBN: 978-1-912688-03-6
Also available electronically, ISBN: 978-1-912688-02-9

Chapter One

"*Hist! There! Look!*" *Sebastian whispered, and pointed down into Darkdown Hall's extensive gardens. Araminta knelt by him to peer out through the leaded windows, fearful of discovery yet aflame with the realisation that at last she would learn the secret of Darkdown Hall and its sinister guardians.*

Lord Darkdown stood at the centre of a stone circle lit by flaming brands, his handsome face twisted in terrible pride. Around him stood the men whom Araminta feared more greatly than any others: Sir Peter Falconwood, whose ungodly knowledge had trapped her in this nest of devils, and Darkdown's nameless, cruel-eyed brute of a henchman. The torchlight danced and flickered over these three evildoers, like the hellfire they invoked in the very name of their blasphemous society, and over one thing more. A young lady clad in nothing more than a thin close-fitting white shift, her heaving bosom the sole sign of life, lay deadly still on a stone slab at the centre of the circle.

Araminta's heart stopped as Darkdown took a step forward and raised a knife—

Guy read on frantically, page after close-scribbled page, reached The End in a rush of adjectives and relief, and yelped, "Amanda!"

He didn't have to shout. His sister was on the chair opposite, pretending to sew while carefully not looking at him. Nevertheless, shouting seemed appropriate.

"What?" Amanda enquired, raising her head with an innocent look that fooled nobody.

"This—this—!" Guy gestured at the manuscript he held, for lack of words.

"It's quite long, dearest. Which part do you mean?"

"Which part do you think? What about the part where the hellfire club descends on a virgin in that—that lascivious manner!"

"It's all perfectly decent," Amanda said. "Or at least, if it isn't, the indecent parts are only hinted at, which means they're in your head. I can't be held responsible for your thoughts going awry."

"Oh yes you can," Guy said with feeling. "You are publishing under a pseudonym, aren't you?"

"*Yes.*" Amanda spoke with understandable annoyance, since Guy had asked her that before. He'd asked when she'd announced she was going to send her long-laboured-over Gothic novel to a publisher, he'd asked again when it had been accepted for publication, and the closer they came to publication, the more he fretted. He'd have worried a great deal more if he'd known the incendiary content before this moment, which was probably why Amanda hadn't let him read it until now. "It's just By A Lady, and it's not as if I, or we, have any reputation left to lose so I don't see why you're making such a fuss."

"I am not making a fuss!"

"You are so."

"No, I'm not."

"You're about to."

Guy opened his mouth to deny it and realised she was right. He was about to.

"Well, other people certainly will! The implications are frankly outrageous, and as for the atmosphere, I don't know where you got all those extraordinary goings-on from—"

"My own shocking exploits, where else?" Amanda said, with some sarcasm.

Guy didn't rise to that bait. "It's all very Gothic-romance, I suppose, and that may be what people are reading, but really—" He could hear himself sounding sententious and disapproving, and he felt a stab of guilt as Amanda's mouth tightened. She didn't cry these days, but he knew his sister. "It's not my kind of thing, Manda, you know that. And I'm not saying I didn't like it. It's very good."

"You needn't pretend."

"It is. It gallops along marvellously and you can tell a story." She could, though it was a ridiculous story, full of all kinds of disturbing situations that Guy would strongly prefer he hadn't read. He had a feeling they might stick in his mind, which would be bad enough even if his sister hadn't come up with them. "I'm sure plenty of people will love it, and I really am awfully proud of you, but—"

"But you don't think it's respectable."

"Of course it's not respectable!" Guy said. "You didn't intend it to be respectable. Don't tell me you wrote all those bosoms and unlawful rites and handsome villains chaining people up and leering in their faces in order to be respectable."

That had been one of the worst parts: the youthful hero Sebastian in a dungeon, bound and helpless at the mercy of the dastardly rake Sir Peter Falconwood with his "strange cruelties and velvet tortures" for several chapters before Araminta rescued him. It wasn't entirely clear what the book had meant by "velvet tortures", since the whole sequence was a mass of allusion and implication. That had been both a relief and—in a way Guy had no intention of considering further—a disappointment.

He coughed. "The point isn't the respectability. It's a Gothic romance and I dare say it's a very good one, and if it's By A Lady then it can be as—as unrespectable as you like. But Manda, Sir Peter Falconwood?"

"What about him?"

"The libertine Sir Peter Falconwood, who is fair-haired, scientifically minded, and in a hellfire club with the notorious rake Lord Darkdown?"

"I know he is. I wrote it. What about him?"

"Oh, I don't know," Guy said, with tenuous patience. "Do you think our neighbour Sir Philip Rookwood, who is a fair-haired, scientifically minded libertine in a hellfire club with the notorious rake Lord Corvin, might possibly object to his caricature as a murdering devil-worshipper? Manda, he could sue us!"

"Oh, nonsense," Amanda said, far too airily. "He won't read it, and if you go around belonging to a hellfire club called 'the Murder' and having orgies, you can't complain if people wonder about you. And my publisher assured me they would protect my anonymity. And it's not even meant to be him anyway."

"When you say all that in court, put the last part first."

"Well, it's too late now. The book's about to be published. And probably nobody will buy it anyway, so you're worrying about nothing."

Guy was reasonably sure he was worrying about a glaring case of libel, unless Sir Philip Rookwood had a very well-developed sense of humour. He had no idea about that, since he had never in his life spoken to their neighbour. No Frisby would speak to a Rookwood. He would have cut the man dead if he'd ever met him, although the matter had never arisen since Guy and Amanda lived in seclusion and Sir Philip treated Yarlcote society with a disinterest bordering on contempt.

Sir Philip Rookwood, with his shocking manners and worse reputation and utterly appalling set, was the most thrillingly dreadful thing to happen in Yarlcote since the death of his brother Sir James. Nobody spoke of that business to Guy and Amanda, but their friends and neighbours kept the Frisbys fully informed of Sir Philip's goings-on. In fairness, Guy could see why his sister had been inspired to write a Gothic romance about the man; it would be hard not to.

Sir Philip had peculiar ideas and never attended church on his infrequent visits to Rookwood Hall. When he did come, he brought with him a retinue of foreigners and philosophers and people generally agreed to be of ill repute, attended by their own servants with Yarlcote people firmly excluded. Most of all, he was the closest friend of Viscount Corvin, and everyone had heard of Corvin. The Devil's Lord, they called him: rich, rakish, deadly. He'd killed a man in a duel, or two men, or ten. He ruined reputations; he'd conducted an open affair with an unmarried lady, causing the end of her engagement to marry, then refused to wed her himself. He tampered with forbidden knowledge, and dabbled in strange exotic ways, and when he and Rookwood descended on quiet, respectable Yarlcote, good society would have turned its collective back on them both, if only it had been given the opportunity to do so.

It was not. Sir Philip never hosted balls, or dinners, or made any effort to meet his peers or cultivate his tenants. Upsettingly for the narrative, he was an excellent if eccentric landlord, possessed of a superbly efficient steward. This was deeply resented by landowners who had more moral character but were less prompt in carrying out repairs. Still, they could at least point to his offensive lack of personal interest in his tenants, or his staff, or his neighbours. Sir Philip came to Rookwood Hall for one reason only: to host the Murder, as he and Corvin called their club, or at least that was what everyone said they called it. The Murder. One couldn't belong to a club called that—a hellfire club, no less—and then object to a young lady's Gothic flight of fancy. Could one?

"You're fretting," Amanda said. "I wish you wouldn't. Oh, Guy, please. This is the only interesting thing that's happened to me in five years and if you're all worried and unhappy and hating every minute it will spoil everything. Please don't disapprove."

"I don't disapprove," Guy said untruthfully. "I think it's marvellous that you wrote a book and it's been published, and they even paid you. Ten pounds!" It was a lot of money, although considering how much scribbling and crossing-out and rewriting

Amanda had done, not to mention the eye-watering cost of paper for the fair copy, Guy couldn't consider it a generous hourly wage. But it was money that Amanda had earned fair and square, money for which they weren't dependent on anyone else's goodwill, and far more than that, it was an occupation that had given her pleasure for months. Guy was probably making a mountain out of a molehill with his fears of exposure and public shame, and the least he could do for his sister was keep his endless worries to himself. "I think you're wonderful, and I dare say Rookwood won't read it anyway. Which is his loss," he added hastily. "Only, if you're going to write another one, please don't libel anybody else?"

"I'm sure it isn't libel if I just happen to use a name that sounds a bit like someone else's name," Amanda said, sounding not nearly sure enough. "And I've started writing the next one, actually."

Oh God. "Really? Another Gothic romance? What about?"

"I'm not quite sure. I'm a bit stuck on the plot. Guy?"

"Mmm?"

"What do you think Rookwood gets up to at his orgies?"

Guy choked. "Firstly, they are house parties. Please don't go around saying orgies, people will be appalled, and it's probably not true. Secondly, I've no idea."

"Oh, you must. Aren't all those classics you read full of all sorts of shocking things?"

"They're in Latin," Guy objected feebly.

"You could tell me what they say."

Guy's mind flicked guiltily to his special shelf: a handful of unexpurgated editions painstakingly obtained over several years. "No, really, Manda. Honestly, I've no idea what Rookwood and his friends do. I'm sure it's just drinking and...and suchlike."

"Yes, but *what* suchlike?"

"There might be, uh, female companionship?" Guy hazarded. "Of the lowest kind. Not at all the thing. I really don't know and I'm quite sure you shouldn't try to find out, and if you put it in a book I dare say they couldn't publish it."

"No." Amanda fiddled with her sewing needle. "Guy?"

Guy balanced the pile of pages on his lap and picked up his half-glass of port. He suspected from her wheedling tone that he might need it for whatever was coming. "Yes?"

"We couldn't pay a call, could we?"

"On whom?" He took a sip of port.

"Rookwood."

Guy coughed a fine crimson spray across his legs, the manuscript, and Amanda's sewing. "What? No!"

"He is our neighbour, and what happened really wasn't his fault any more than it was ours. Don't you think—"

"No, I do not! We are not going to pay a call on Sir Philip Rookwood, not ever, and particularly not when he has a houseful of— *Amanda Frisby*." He did his best to sound authoritative while wiping port off his chin. "If you're hoping to spy on Lord Corvin or Sir Philip's orgi—his house party, just to get ideas for a book—"

"But it's such a chance," Amanda said. "A hellfire club on our doorstep! You can't tell me not to be interested. And it is absurd we shouldn't speak to our neighbour because of what his brother did twenty years ago."

"What his—" Guy groped for words. "His brother ruined everything. You can't possibly forgive that!"

"That was his brother," Amanda said obstinately. "We could extend the hand of friendship to Sir Philip—"

"Who's bosom friends with the Devil's Lord and in a hellfire club and has orgies!"

"Ha! I knew it was orgies."

Guy spluttered, without port this time. "Absolutely not. He is not a fit acquaintance for you, even without the—the unfortunate history between our families. He is a disgrace to the neighbourhood and to his old family name, and we are not going to extend any sort of recognition to Sir Philip Rookwood, not ever. That is my final word."

Two days later, Amanda didn't come back home.

Guy hadn't expected her for luncheon. It was a beautiful day and she'd gone up to Mr. Welland's to borrow his hack. She loved riding. Guy tried not to repine about their financial situation—it couldn't be helped, and Aunt Beatrice was really very generous, considering—but if things had been different Amanda would have had a horse of her own. Of course, if things had been different she could be married by now. They were well born enough, they'd been plump in the pocket once, and Aunt Beatrice had married the second son of a marquess, so they'd had the connections for a good marriage. If it hadn't been for Sir James Rookwood, and then the thrice-damned Mr. Peyton—

But there was nothing to be done about any of that, and no point regretting the past. Guy spent the morning in the garden, staking out peas and beans. He had bread and cheese for luncheon rather than put Mrs. Harbottle to any trouble, and settled down with the *Anacreontea* and a Greek dictionary afterwards, with the glow of a day's work done. He didn't even look at the time as the afternoon progressed, reflecting only that Amanda was doubtless enjoying the early summer air, roaming far abroad. In that alternative past where Sir James Rookwood hadn't ruined them, Miss Frisby would never have stirred abroad without a groom, or at least her brother's escort, but as it was, she rode alone. Guy didn't give it a thought until Mr. Welland burst in.

Mr. Welland was a near neighbour, his house no more than a mile away, a retired merchant with a successful career in corn. He'd handed over the business to his son and retired to the country with his wife, and he was a friendly, respectable sort of man although mercantile in his conversation. Now he was red-faced, and his habitual smile notably absent.

"Mr. Frisby!" His voice was hoarse.

Guy found himself on his feet, panic rocketing through him. "What is it? What's wrong?"

"It's Miss Frisby. The hack I lent her, Bluebell, has just come back, exhausted. My man says she's been galloping hard. And Miss Frisby wasn't with her."

"What?" Guy said stupidly. "How can Amanda not have been with the horse?"

"She wasn't ridden. I'm afraid Miss Frisby must have fallen. And she went out at ten, and goodness knows how long the horse has been wandering. I hoped you'd say Miss Frisby had come back here."

Guy shook his head dumbly. Mr. Welland's face tightened. "Do you know where she intended to ride?"

"I didn't ask. She always rides by herself." Guy heard his own culpable carelessness in every word. "We have to look for her. It's—oh, heavens, it's already five o'clock!"

"It won't be dark for a few hours yet," Mr. Welland said. "I've sent my man out to raise the alarm."

"May I borrow a horse?"

"I rode Daffodil over here for that very purpose. I'll walk back. An absurd name but a reliable beast. You'll find Miss Frisby, I'm sure of that. She's probably walking home now, or found a cart to cadge a ride. She's a resourceful young lady."

"Thank you," Guy said, covering the horse, the reassurance, and the lack of rebuke in two heartfelt words. "Thank you, Mr. Welland. I must put on something to ride in— Is that the door?"

It was the door, and Mrs. Harbottle was exchanging words with someone. "News?" Guy asked aloud, and hurried down to the hall, Mr. Welland at his heels. A man in plain black livery stood there. He saw Guy and gave a bow of terrifyingly precise respect.

"Master Guy!" Mrs. Harbottle said. She was wide-eyed. "Master Guy, this man—gentleman—person...he's from the Hall."

"From *Rookwood* Hall?"

"Yes, Mr. Frisby," the man said. He spoke with a smooth, bland tone, just like one of the sinister servants in Amanda's book. "I carry an urgent message from Sir Philip Rookwood."

"Sir Philip?" Guy yelped. "You work for—"

"I have the honour to serve Lord Corvin," the man said with just a fraction of reproach. "The letter, sir, if you will forgive my informality." He bowed again and handed Guy a note.

Guy unfolded it with trembling fingers. It was brief, evidently dashed off in haste.

To: Frisby, Drysdale House

Sir

I regret to inform you that Miss Amanda Frisby has been injured in a fall while trespassing on my land. She has broken her leg and is receiving urgent medical attention at Rookwood Hall. Kindly send suitable attendance for her to Rookwood Hall immediately, and honour me with your presence at the earliest possible opportunity.

Yours

Philip Rookwood

Guy stared at the words. "Broken leg," he repeated. His voice sounded odd.

"I fear so, sir," the servant said. "Sir Philip and Mr. Raven found Miss Frisby in a field, I understand."

"But—is she all right?"

"No, sir. Her leg is broken."

Mr. Welland gripped Guy's shoulder and gave it a little shake. "Come on, young fellow. Your sister needs you. May I—?"

Guy handed him the letter. Mr. Welland read it, brows rising. "The lady is at Rookwood Hall? Well, that won't do from what I hear. No offence," he added, with a nod to the man in black, which was superbly ignored. "But she'll have to come home from that place quick smart."

"I believe Dr. Martelo feels that moving her would be unwise," the servant said, apparently unmoved by the slur on Rookwood Hall and its inhabitants. "He is in attendance on the young lady and will be available whenever you wish to speak to him."

"I'm coming," Guy said. "Mrs. Harbottle, please pack what Amanda might need for the night, just in case. And—can you come with me, for attendance?"

The housekeeper grimaced. "Now, Master Guy, you know there's Harbottle laid up with his rheumatics."

"Jane, then."

"I couldn't ask Jane to go to such a place, Master Guy, not even for Miss Amanda." She gave the black-clad servant a minatory glare, as though he were poised to ravish the maid-of-all-work. "You bring her home, that'll be best."

"I'll see what needs doing when I get there," Guy said, unable to waste more time. "Please, pack now. I need to go."

It was almost four miles to Rookwood Hall. They rode at a brisk canter. Guy would have liked to gallop, but he wasn't sufficiently familiar with the horse or, really, the lanes. They'd gone around by other ways for most of his life.

The servant, who was named Cornelius, rode with him in silence, for which Guy was glad. If he'd talked he'd have started babbling, he knew. *How bad is her leg? How bad is Sir Philip? Is she in danger? What's going to happen now?* Cornelius couldn't answer any of that, or wouldn't, most probably, so Guy concentrated on his seat and tried not to think about terrible things. Amanda in pain. Amanda in the clutches of Sir Philip Rookwood, with his hellfire club and his orgies. Anyone, anyone at all and most especially Aunt Beatrice, finding out that Amanda was at Rookwood Hall, the place from which everything wrong with their lives had sprung. Mr. Welland's reaction had been quite enough, and he probably didn't even know the old story; it would be unthinkable for any gently bred young lady to spend the night at Rookwood Hall with its master in residence.

If he's laid a finger on Amanda… Guy thought, then realised he didn't know how to finish the sentence.

It was still light, though the shadows were long and the evening sun gold. If Amanda was well enough to travel, Guy would have her home tonight, he told himself. It was only four miles, some sort of pallet could surely be arranged. If not, well, he'd stay by her side all night, awake, and get her back in the morning. The Rookwoods wouldn't cast any further blight over her life. He wouldn't let them.

The ride seemed interminable but at last he was cantering up the drive to Rookwood Hall. He had an impression of glowering grey stone wreathed with ivy. The great oaken door gaped open, and two men waited in front of it, both perched with shocking casualness on stone parapets.

A groom came forward as Guy brought Daffodil to an awkward halt. He slid off the horse, feeling the ache in his legs and backside from the unaccustomed exercise, and walked, stiff-legged and ridiculous, up to the house's entranceway, towards the men.

One of them was a lean sort a few inches taller than Guy, with fairish hair and a sneering look, and the other was a black man. Guy had never in his life seen a dark-skinned man except in pictures, where they were clad in outlandish flowing gowns, or lion skins, or beggarly rags. This one wore breeches and a coat like any gentleman might, and was smoking a cigarillo. He pitched it away as Guy approached and said, in a voice that had nothing of exotic shores about it, "Here you go, Phil. Outraged brother. Have fun."

The fair man gave him a scathing look. That would be Sir Philip Rookwood, then, whose family had ruined Guy's life.

"Sir Philip," he said, cheeks feeling rather stiff. "I'm Guy Frisby."

"Thank God you've got here," Rookwood said. "Your sister seems to have taken a very nasty fall while riding uninvited over my east meadow for reasons I cannot imagine. Have you not brought someone to attend her?"

"I'm here."

"I meant a woman," Rookwood said impatiently. "This isn't a female household, hence I specifically told you— Oh, for God's sake. You're going to have to take her home tonight if we can't sort something out. Cornelius! Can you organise a woman?"

The black man snorted. Rookwood swung round to him. "Contribute or shut up."

"Contribute? What else do you want me to do?" He slid off the parapet to his feet, proving to be a little taller than Sir Philip and very solidly built, and nodded to Guy. "John Raven, at your service. Your sister's with the doctor now, so why don't you have a word with him first."

"Because David Martelo doesn't run this house," Rookwood snapped. "If Frisby wants to take his sister home, he shall, and should."

"I do want to," Guy said. "Very much. And I wish to see her at once, and if she has come to any harm—"

"—it is hardly my responsibility." Rookwood spoke over him. "I did mention that she was trespassing, I think."

"Twice," Guy said. "You've made it entirely clear that she is not here at your invitation and the sooner I can take her away the happier I dare say we shall all be. I would like to see her now."

Rookwood lifted a sardonic brow. "This way."

Guy followed him into the house. It was rather bare inside and rather dark, with panelled walls. He could smell wine and cigars and spirits, and as they passed one closed door there was a burst of masculine laughter.

"She's in the Blue Drawing-Room," Rookwood said, walking past. "Here."

He knocked at the door. A man's voice said, loudly and with a slight accent, "Clear off."

Rookwood opened the door, just a crack. "David? The lady's brother."

"Good. Come in."

Rookwood opened the door and waved Guy forward. He went in and saw Amanda.

She lay on a trestle of some sort, white and unconscious, her hair loose. Her skirts had been cut away, baring her legs to the tops of her thighs. One leg was bandaged, the visible skin purple-red and swollen, the bandages soaked scarlet. A dark man stood by her with his hands on her bare skin, and the room stank of brandy.

Guy made a strangled noise and started forward. A powerful hand gripped his arm from behind. "Hoi," Rookwood said. "Frisby, calm down. That's the damned doctor!"

"What the devil—" Guy struggled, trying to wrench his arm free from the painful grip, and failed.

The doctor had his hands up. "Mr. Frisby, is it? Your sister has sustained a bad fracture of the thighbone. If you start a fight in here and knock her leg, you will kill her."

That got through as nothing else might have. Guy said, "What?"

"The bone broke badly," the doctor said. "It tore the skin and came very close to the great femoral vein. She has lost a lot of blood. The leg was not easy to set, and if the bone shifts out of place it will probably do a great deal more damage—perhaps too much for her to bear. So you will calm yourself, or you will leave this room. Do you understand?"

"Why does she look like that?" Guy demanded. He couldn't take his eyes from her white face. Amanda always had a high colour, no need for rouge on her cheeks, and was far more sun-kissed than any conventional lady would be thanks to long walks and rides, and to not caring for her complexion any more. This ashen, unmoving statue wasn't Amanda.

"Pain," the doctor said briefly. "And also laudanum and brandy. Setting the bone was an unpleasant business. She fainted, which was just as well."

Guy moved forward, shaking off Rookwood's restraining hands, and looked down at his sister. She was cold and still and pale, and panic clutched his heart. *She's breathing*, he told himself. *You can see her breathing. Stop.*

"Thank you for—for helping, Doctor," he managed.

"We'll see if I have," the doctor said. "My name is Martelo. I think you have brought an attendant?"

"No," Guy said. "We don't—her maid wouldn't—there's our housekeeper but her husband isn't well. I'm here. I'll do what you need."

"What I need is a skilled nurse. Is there any such to be summoned here? Your doctor?"

"That's Dr. Bewdley." Guy contemplated the man in front of him. Dr. Martelo was very dark, with huge tangled black eyebrows over sloe-black eyes, a prominent nose, extremely black hair, decidedly brown skin. His powerful bare forearms were liberally coated with dark hair too. He was surely no more than thirty, and he looked and sounded foreign, and Guy couldn't begin to imagine Dr. Bewdley's reaction. "Er."

"Send for him and tell him we need a nurse," Martelo said. "In the meantime, can you obey orders?"

"Yes?" Guy managed.

"Good. Summon your doctor, and anyone else you can to make her comfortable. Philip, we will need a truckle bed in here for the nights."

"Wait a moment," Rookwood said. "I think, and I believe Frisby agrees, that the lady should be moved to her own home as soon as possible."

"Naturally," Martelo said. "I'll let you know. Meanwhile—"

"By *as soon as possible*, I meant today."

The doctor made an indescribable noise of mingled incredulity and scorn. He sounded like an outraged horse. "Today? Nonsense. A fortnight at the earliest and only then if I am quite satisfied the bone has knit well enough."

"A fortnight?" Rookwood and Guy said, in horrified chorus.

"At the *very* earliest. Not one moment before I am satisfied. Not one, Philip."

"But she can't stay here," Guy said.

"No, she can't leave. Have you not listened to me?"

"This house is not appropriate for a lady's sickroom," Rookwood said levelly. "It is a bachelor establishment."

"Then bring in some women, if the lady's reputation is at risk while she lies on her sickbed," Martelo said.

"Of course it's at risk," Rookwood snapped. "Her state of health has nothing to do with it."

"And is all that concerns me. Find a way to satisfy the proprieties if you must, but summon me a nurse, and get out of my sickroom."

"It's my drawing-room," Rookwood pointed out.

"It's mine now. Go away, both of you. I need to look at this leg."

Guy found himself standing outside the drawing-room, slightly stunned, with the evicted master of the house, whose expression was distinctly sour.

"Well," Rookwood said, mouth pursed. "This is a cursed business. Naturally you will consider my house as your own until your sister can be removed." That was perhaps the least sincere-sounding offer Guy had ever heard. "There is plenty of space in this barrack, at least. I suppose you will stay in the sickroom, but she must have a woman with her too. Can you send for her maid?"

"She wouldn't set foot in this house," Guy said. It was a statement of fact, not intended as an insult, but when he saw Rookwood's brownish brows shoot up he realised how it had sounded. He opened his mouth to stammer an apology but Rookwood got in first.

"I do beg your pardon, Mr. Frisby. Had I known Miss Frisby intended to trespass on my land and then colonise my house for an infirmary, I should have conducted myself differently."

"Had my father known your brother's intent to—to trespass on *his* land, I dare say we should all have conducted ourselves differently for the last few years," Guy said furiously. "But we all have to live with the consequences of his actions, don't we? I want my sister and myself in your house no more than you do, Sir Philip, so perhaps you will do me the favour of summoning Dr. Bewdley and his nurse now. I should like Amanda examined by someone I have reason to trust."

Chapter Two

"Dear God," Philip said, collapsing into a chair some time later. "The boy is a plank. An utter plank. Possibly the most outrageous specimen of plankhood I have ever encountered. A fortnight! God damn Martelo, and Amanda Frisby with him."

"Have a drink," Corvin said soothingly. He didn't actually get up to pour one, but it was a kindly thought, which Philip acknowledged with an obscene gesture as he went over to the decanter. "That's the way," Corvin said. "Pour me another while you're there."

"What are we to understand by 'plank'?" enquired Sheridan. He was short, sharp, cocky as a schoolboy, and still, after a year's partnership, running rings round Philip's old friend Harry, who constantly looked as befuddled and proud as any bridegroom on his wedding day. Philip felt a vague urge to say something avuncular every time he saw the pair of them.

"Oh, the obvious," Corvin answered on Philip's behalf. "Straight, unbending, wooden, and only suitable to be walked on."

"His sister's in a bad way," John said. "That leg was nasty."

"You don't know anything about it," Philip snapped.

"I helped set it."

"You pulled where David told you to pull. Stop pretending you're a bonesetter. Brute strength, that's what you provided."

"Strength and a bit of common sense, which is why he didn't ask you."

Philip held up a hand in acknowledgement, partly because John had won that round, partly because he was damned grateful not to have been asked. The woman had been screaming and sobbing when she'd been brought in, dress soaked in blood, and David had insisted there was no time to lose. John had acted as his assistant to pull the leg straight without causing any more damage, and emerged from the room with bloody hands, stained cuffs, and his normally rich complexion gone the colour of dry earth. The idea of wrenching a broken leg around made Philip feel queasy, he had not enjoyed John's vivid description of the sound of bone-ends scraping together, and in any case, the woman in the drawing-room was Eleanor Frisby's daughter, and Philip wouldn't have touched her at gunpoint.

The Frisby children, in his house, for a fortnight. "Oh God," Philip said aloud. "Someone tell me David was exaggerating. Tell me she'll walk away tomorrow."

"Her foot was all but pointing backwards," John said. "You're stuck with them. Well, you're stuck with the girl, and you won't get the plank out of here while he's got her virtue to protect."

"I'm not letting the plank out of here," Philip said. "I'll bar the doors if I must. The last thing I need is to find myself accused of compromising Eleanor Frisby's daughter."

John's lips rounded in silent surprise, then he started to laugh. "Oh, my God, I didn't think of that. Oh, that's a good one."

"Hit him, Corvin," Philip requested.

"You have to admit, it has a certain piquancy," Corvin said, but he leaned over to swipe a hand. John ducked sideways mostly as a formality.

"Who's Eleanor Frisby?" Sheridan asked. "The girl's mother? Do you know her?"

"Phil's brother did," Corvin replied on his behalf. "In the Biblical sense, you understand."

"Shut up." Philip looked around the room. They lacked Isabella Crayford, since her Marianne had a theatrical engagement, and David

Martelo was still attending the Frisby girl, but otherwise they were all here. Corvin and John, his lifelong companions and the heart of the Murder, impossibly dear and endlessly exasperating in their very different ways. Harry with that perennially surprised look of his, and Sheridan resting his head against the bigger man's shoulder. George Penn the composer, and Ned Caulfield, deeply reserved and extraordinarily gifted, who played the violin for him. These were Philip's closest friends. They were here for comfort and safety, to think and talk without constraint, to touch as they chose, or sleep in the same bed without worrying about it. That was what the Murder offered, it was a rare privilege for some of them—for all of them, really, except Corvin, who could afford safety—and Philip was furious that the Frisbys had arrived to ruin it.

He sighed. "Eleanor Frisby, the mother of the girl and the plank, was the woman with whom my brother ran away."

That ought to have been a startling revelation. It wasn't, because Corvin and John remembered it all, and the others, not being in Society, clearly had never heard of the great Rookwood scandal. Sheridan glanced around at the other blank looks and offered, "Well, that's...awkward, I suppose?"

"It was a great deal more than awkward," Corvin said, taking over as always where there was drama to be found. "Sir James, as he had recently become, was some five years older than Phil, which made him twenty-one when he distinguished himself by absconding with his neighbour's wife, the famous Frisby. She was thirty if she was a day, and by all accounts merely passable in looks—"

"The plank is well enough," George observed. "If that's the pretty boy who was shouting at Phil in the hall."

"I dare say, but in any case, the mother swept young James off his feet, age and beauty or no, such that he was not content to make it the usual discreet affair. Well, he couldn't if he wanted. Her sister had married extremely well—Easterbury's younger son, a shocking dullard—and that aristocratic connection was all that was needed. The scandal spread like wildfire. James and la belle Frisby fled to the Continent, abandoning on his part an estate—in which we now sit—and on her part a husband and two children. The husband took it poorly."

Philip couldn't help a groan at the memory. He had been just sixteen when James had bolted, and the enraged Mr. Frisby had descended on him for lack of any other living Rookwood, venting his fury in a torrent of threats and abuse. Philip had lived in the Corvin household then, as he had most of his youth. No adult had troubled to step in between the outraged cuckold and the boy, but his best friend had strolled in after some moments, as preternaturally self-possessed as ever, and called for footmen to see the fellow off. At that time it had been perhaps the most frightening experience of Philip's life.

"Yes, he was dreadful," Corvin agreed, correctly interpreting the groan. "I dare say that's how the son came by his own plankishness. Anyway, Sir James and Mrs. Frisby left for the fleshpots of Europe, and lived in carnal enjoyment right up to the point that their carriage fell off an Alp."

"You say that as if it's related," John said. "They didn't drive off a mountain because they were at it."

"How do you know? They might have."

"I suppose it wouldn't be a bad way to go," Sheridan said thoughtfully. "Until you started falling. So that was how you became Sir Philip, Phil?"

"Yes. I was eighteen."

"And Romeo and Juliet only had two years. That's rather sad."

"For them," Philip said. "Whereas it was a damned nuisance at every turn for everyone they left behind."

"I suppose so. It must have been dreadful for the children," Sheridan said.

"I imagine it was, since the humiliated cuckold flung himself to the devil at a great rate. It was not joyous for me, at sixteen, bearing quite so much of other people's notoriety on my shoulders. And it has caused a great deal of awkwardness since. If I wanted to mingle in Yarlcote society—"

"Where's that?" Ned asked.

"Where we are," Philip said patiently. "The nearest—for want of a better word—town. If I wanted to mingle in this society, it would cause endless difficulty, and particularly because one could not ask a Frisby to be in a room with a Rookwood. I've never actually aspired to be in a room with them, needless to say."

"But now they're staying in your house," Sheridan said.

"And one of them an unmarried young lady," Corvin finished. "Which raises the spectre of Philip ruining the daughter as his brother did the mother, only without the carnal pleasure."

Sheridan scowled. Philip said, "I am not going to compromise the woman under any circumstances. Her brother is here. I will send for all the women of Yarlcote to protect her virtue in a phalanx if I must, and if they'll come. I must say, Corvin, it is gratifying to discover quite how well we have destroyed our reputations. I've never laid a finger on anyone within fifty miles of Yarlcote, yet this house is renowned as a sink of corruption."

"Well done, boys. Do you want us to leave?" John asked.

"No. I've a fortnight's work here to keep my steward honest and reacquaint myself with the books. In hell's name don't abandon me."

"Never, dear heart," Corvin assured him. "What's that noise?"

It was shouting, and it came from the direction of the Blue Drawing-Room. Philip said, "Oh God," and hauled himself up from his chair. Nobody offered to help.

Sinclair, his man, stood in the hall. He wasn't actually shaking his head in disapproval, but might as well have been. "What's going on?" Philip demanded.

"Local doctor's arrived. He's not getting on with Dr. Martelo, by the sound of things. They're having a right dust-up."

Philip shot him a glare. Sinclair regarded the goings-on of the aristocracy as a theatrical entertainment laid on for his benefit, and his mask of professional courtesy was tissue-thin at best. Philip kept him on out of a vague sense it would be hypocritical to sack the man for regarding social convention with as much contempt as Philip did himself, and because he was a rather good valet, and mostly because he and Corvin's man Cornelius (christened Albert Scrope, which naturally Corvin found intolerable) shared a bed. It made life a great deal easier when one had the right sort of people around one.

Some aspects of life, anyway. "Has anyone brought a nurse or female attendant for the Frisby girl?"

"Bert's working on it, Sir Philip."

"Cornelius."

"If you say so. In any case, he ain't sent anyone yet. I dare say they're all feared for their virtues. It's a pickle, this, and no mistake."

"Stop enjoying yourself," Philip told him, and went to see what was going on.

The local man, Dr. Bewdley, proved to be white-haired, red-faced, and puffed up with outrage. That still put him slightly ahead of David, who was dishevelled and bloodstained, as well as foreign and thus inherently dubious. The two doctors were nose to nose, leaning in, and speaking at an unnecessary volume. The plank Frisby stood unhappily by his sister's body, now decently covered with a sheet. She seemed to be asleep, or unconscious.

"She is my patient," David was saying. "And if you think, after what I have told you, that you can move her—"

"If you think that Miss Frisby can be left in this house—"

"If that bone slips it could pierce a blood vessel," David said. "We had hell's own job to set it in the first place. She will be moved over my dead body."

"I assure you, sir, a magistrate will take the dimmest view of your efforts at obstruction. I am her family doctor."

"And Mr. Frisby is her family," Philip put in. He sided with David as a matter of principle, but if the plank actually wanted to remove the girl, it would solve all Philip's problems. "Dr. Bewdley, yes? I am Philip Rookwood, I don't believe we've had the pleasure. Please let me assure you that while my hospitality is extended to Mr. and Miss Frisby for as long as is required, we will not hinder the wishes of her brother——"

"Yes, we damn well will," David snapped. "If she is moved she could die. Will you please get that into your thick English skulls?"

"It's not up to me or to you," Philip said. "Or indeed to Dr. Bewdley, although if Mr. Frisby wishes this gentleman to attend the lady, he is most welcome." David made a noise suggestive of extreme contempt. Philip reminded himself to have that talk about tact with him, again. "It is Mr. Frisby's decision," he said loudly. "And if he feels it necessary to remove the lady, I will supply all the assistance required to do so safely."

"There is no *safely*. You cannot put her in a cart with her leg in that state," David said. "The jolting—— I beg you, don't let this happen. Phil, as a friend, please."

Dr. Bewdley's eyes bulged at the informality. Philip took a long, reluctant moment during which he reminded himself that David was one of his best friends, and then met the plank's eyes. Frisby was nearly as white as his half-dead sister, his hunched stance speaking of misery, and he didn't look remotely the pretty boy George had called him. He looked like a man with all his worst fears coming to life around him.

"Mr. Frisby," Philip said, cursing himself with every word. "You will do as you wish, but let me say three things to you. First, Dr. Martelo is an excellent and highly experienced man; if I had a sister I would put her in his hands without hesitation. Second, I quite understand your reluctance to accept my hospitality, but I give you my word as a gentleman that your sister will be treated with the utmost care and respect by me, my friends, and my staff while she remains here."

Dr. Bewdley snorted. It wasn't as good as David's snort, but it was still quite expressive enough to constitute an insult, and Philip made a mental mark accordingly.

"That was two things," Frisby said. His voice was cracked.

"Yes. The third is that I hope you will not allow the idle words of"—he flicked a glance at the doctor—"petty, malicious busybodies and spiteful gossips to influence your decision. Miss Frisby has suffered a severe injury, and Dr. Martelo advises she should be moved as little as possible. You might well consider any other concerns to be trivial until she has made a recovery."

"And certainly not worth risking her recovery," David said. "Thank you, Philip."

"I beg your pardon," Dr. Bewdley said, swelling. "Miss Frisby's reputation is not 'trivial'. Reputation is a woman's crowning jewel, her greatest possession, and I will not stand by to see it tarnished."

"I think her life is a greater possession than her reputation." Frisby's voice shook slightly. "Dr. Bewdley, do you think, as a medical man, that there is any risk—any at all—to Amanda if she is moved?"

"I think this man greatly overstates it."

"Is the risk equal whether she is moved or not?" Frisby persisted. "Absolutely equal? Are you sure that moving her will not alter the outcome, or the dangers, one jot? Whether it would endanger her recovery now or her chances of walking again?"

"Compound fracture of the *fe*-mur," David said in a sing-song sort of way to nobody in particular.

"Perhaps there are some risks inherent to moving her. But if you are asking me whether I should leave her in a sewer because it would be dangerous to take her out—"

"I beg your pardon?" Philip said. "*What* was that, sir?"

"An exaggerated illustration," the doctor said, reddening. "I intended no disrespect."

"Then you should exert more control of your metaphors. And if you are so concerned with Miss Frisby's reputation, you are welcome to supply as many nurses as you see fit. In pairs. With armed men to protect them, if you choose," he concluded, letting the sarcasm drip on the carpet. "Mr. Frisby, a decision please."

Frisby glanced between the doctors. "If moving her is dangerous, then she mustn't be moved until she's better. I shall stay with her, and if you will please arrange for nurses, Dr. Bewdley, then I'm sure Jane and Mrs. Harbottle will come too."

"I cannot approve of this," Dr. Bewdley said. "Not at all, and I shall not oblige any nurse to attend a house about which she feels a very natural discomfort. And I am surprised at you, Guy Frisby. What would your father say?"

The blood drained from Frisby's face. Philip wondered if the man was going to faint, and decided that he'd had enough of this conversation. "Very good, the lady remains. Kindly address your bill to me, Dr. Bewdley. The door is that way."

With the huffing doctor safely off the premises, Philip returned to the Yellow Drawing-Room where the others were making inroads on his brandy. It was almost eight o'clock, he realised. He trusted that dinner had not been too greatly disrupted by the medical drama; he was damned hungry.

"Did you pour oil on troubled waters?" Corvin enquired. "More importantly, have you got rid of her?"

"No to both. I persuaded the plank to stay here when his doctor was persuading him to take his sister and wipe our dust off his feet."

"That was peculiar of you."

"Blame David. He's flying the lady's colours. Blah blah liable to die if moved. Bah."

"You're all heart," John said, grinning. "Still, if David says so, he's probably right. And it would be a bit much to have another Frisby's death on your hands, after James."

"That's what I thought but I don't have to be pleased about it. This house is liable to be rendered hideous by nurses creeping around in pairs, in hourly expectation of rapine."

"What on earth have you done down here?" Harry demanded. "There may be men who pose less of a threat to women than you, but—well, they're mostly in this room. Where did you get this reputation as a ravisher?"

"Corvin," Philip and John said in chorus.

"I am not a ravisher," Corvin said indignantly. "I have never in my life forced myself on the unwilling. It's not my fault if the willing aren't willing to admit they were willing."

"And it's not your fault if they won't form an orderly queue either. It's never your fault. We know," John said.

"My parlous reputation is a combination of Corvin's priapism, my brother's indiscretion, this society's notoriety, and my failure to marry," Philip concluded. "Popular opinion and a lack of alternative entertainment round here has turned me into a sort of Bluebeard without the wives, which, I may say, I have never regretted before, but there's a first time for everything. Ah, the dinner bell. Christ, should I have invited the plank to dine with us?" Surely not, he decided; he would drag David out of the sickroom and leave Frisby in charge there. The man would not wish to mix with their set any more than was absolutely necessary.

He went along to the Blue Drawing-room to communicate that in the most courteous manner at his disposal. Frisby just nodded. He looked worn and pallid.

"Ring for a servant to find me or come to the dining room if you're worried," David told him, while Philip waited at the door. "I won't be long."

"Is there much to worry about?" Philip asked him, once they were all seated. "Presumably it's simply a matter of the bone healing straight?"

27

"I don't know when you became an expert." David was wolfing down his meal with scant respect for the artistry of its creation. They had, of course, brought Corvin's cook. "When her femur—thighbone—broke, one end tore through the leg and pierced the skin, sticking out." He waved his knife, apparently to simulate splintering bone. "She was lucky not to tear any of the larger blood vessels in the leg, and we'll be lucky to avoid infection, fever, or worse. I've sent for whatever medicaments Yarlcote can supply, and cleaned it as best I can, but it's an ugly injury. Thank you for taking my part."

"A pleasure," Philip said. "Or rather, the very last thing I wanted to do, but never mind. Why such concern for the lady?"

"I resent losing patients at the best of times," David said. "I particularly resent it when it's caused by human stupidity rather than Nature's ways. John and I worked hard to put that leg back together, and I will not see it bumped apart on a cart because of some damn fool nonsense about propriety."

"I second that," John said. "What a ghastly job you have."

That led to a spirited debate, in which the relative ghastliness of David's bloody work, Harry and Sheridan's grovelling in mud for old bones, George and Ned's grovelling to wealthy patrons, and John's likelihood of being beaten to death, sued for libel, or both, were addressed in some detail.

"They're all ghastly occupations," Corvin pronounced at last. "Whereas I, as a gentleman of leisure—"

"You work harder than any of us," John said. "When it comes to making yourself a spectacle, getting on people's wicks, and tupping, I've never seen anyone work as hard as you."

That provoked cheers, laughter, and much clinking of glasses and hammering of knives on the table. Corvin attempted a rebuttal, which failed because he was laughing too hard to speak, and the room bore some resemblance to a rowdy tavern when Sheridan twisted round and raised a hand. Philip followed his gaze, as did the others, and one by one, Corvin last, they fell silent.

Frisby was standing by the door. He was very pale, eyes huge and shadowed, and Philip felt a flash of guilt that they had been enjoying themselves while his sister lay in pain, followed by a stronger flash of annoyance that he should be made to feel that by a stranger in his own damned house.

"I'm sorry to interrupt," Frisby said in a shaking voice. "But, Dr. Martelo, I think Amanda is feverish."

David threw his napkin onto the table and rose. He hadn't drunk more than half a glass of wine; Philip wondered if he'd been expecting this. "Don't wait for me," he told the assembled Murder, and strode out.

It put something of a damper on the evening. None of those present knew the Frisbys or had any reason to care what became of them, and Philip felt no obligation to turn any part of his house beyond the Blue Drawing-Room into an infirmary. Yet as the clock ticked and David did not return, the mood became increasingly sombre, and they all retired around eleven rather than making a night of it. Corvin cocked a brow at Philip, who shook his head. He wasn't in the mood.

"Your loss," Corvin told him, unmoved.

"I'll take his leavings," John said. "Come on, you bugger."

That left Philip alone in the drawing room of what would have been his childhood home if he'd ever been invited here. He'd grown up either at school or in the Corvin household, and the five-year gap between himself and his brother might as well have been a century and an ocean. James had never had the slightest interest in making his acquaintance, and when he'd died, Philip had been left to conduct obsequies for a stranger. If he'd been a few years older he wouldn't have bothered wearing black at all, and occasionally still regretted the magnificent cat that would have thrown among society's pigeons.

All of which meant that he looked around at the accumulation of Rookwood wealth and history without fondness. It was a damn fool inconvenient house, and if he were Corvin he would probably raze it to the ground to make way for a new, practical building with servants' accommodations that were less like rat warrens, fewer pointless corridors, windows that kept the heat in, fireplaces that worked, and rooms that weren't panelled till a man felt he lived inside a linen-chest. A modern house, that was what he wanted, amid lands farmed in the modern way. He wouldn't get the former because his wealth, unlike Corvin's, was entirely exhaustible, and because he saw no reason to rebuild a house that he had no plans to live in or pass on, but the latter...he needed to talk to his steward about that.

He extinguished the candles except for one he took to light his way, and headed out. He intended to go to bed, but stopped in the hall, then trod softly towards the Blue Drawing-Room. Light spilled out from the door, which was ajar, and he heard the quiet murmur of male voices and a little whimper, which he assumed was the patient. He hesitated, wondering whether to enquire after his unwanted guest, or whether Frisby would not appreciate the reminder of whose house he was in. He had not decided at the point the door opened.

Frisby emerged carrying a basin, and recoiled with a muffled exclamation on seeing Philip. Water sloshed from the bowl. "Blast it! Why are you here?"

"It's my house," Philip retorted, without thought.

"And I'm so sorry to inconvenience you with my unwanted presence in it!" Frisby snapped. "I dare say you'll be delighted if I'm not here long!" He turned on his heel even before he'd finished speaking, almost as if hiding his face, and hurried off in the direction of the kitchen. Philip stared after him for a moment, shrugged to himself, and went to bed.

Sinclair brought the news with his morning tea. "Lady's in a bad way."

"Lady—you mean, Miss Frisby?" Philip sat up, yawning.

"We ain't got any others. Dr. Martelo was up all night. Bad fever, he says. Not sure she'll pull through."

That jolted him awake. "Are you serious?"

"Not a joking matter, is it? The doctor's that worried. Mr. Frisby's sent for Dr. Whatsisname, you know, the old snot we had yesterday, but Dr. Martelo says if he tries bleeding or purgatives he's going to kick him out so hard he bounces. That's Dr. Martelo kicking Dr. Whatsit out," Sinclair amplified helpfully.

Philip knew all about David's obstinate opposition to bleeding. They'd had trouble with this before, since it was the treatment of first resort for most doctors, whereas David ranted about admitting infection and causing unnecessary damage to an already weakened constitution. He'd lay ten pounds that Dr. Whatsit would want to bleed Amanda Frisby. Any doctor would.

"Oh God," he said.

"I should say so. Oh-oh, carriage on the drive," Sinclair added, cocking his head at the sound of wheels. "That'll be the other quack, I expect."

"Oh *God*. Shut up and get me dressed. Quick."

Even with Sinclair doing his impressive best, it took too long for Philip to be ready. The argument was in full swing by the time he half-ran along the hall to the Blue Drawing-room.

"This woman is in a high fever!" Dr. Bewdley was saying in a kind of subdued shout. "It is vital that we relieve the inflammation by drawing off blood at once!"

"A decoction of willowbark will bring down the fever," David retorted. "Bleeding her will simply drain her body of strength."

"Nonsense. You suggest nothing more than old wives' remedies—"

"She's already weak enough! Why do you want to exhaust her further?"

Philip glanced past the warring doctors. The subject of their disagreement looked, to his inexpert eye, as sick as a dog. She was a nasty sort of colour, pallid and sweating. Frisby crouched over her like a mouse at bay, eyes darting between his sister and the doctors. He was patting her forehead with a wet cloth, and his grey face and dishevelled state suggested he hadn't slept.

"Nonsense!" David shouted at Bewdley. Amanda Frisby moaned, eyelids fluttering, and Frisby's eyes met Philip's just for a second. They were hazel-green, full of fear and misery and, unquestionably, a plea. Perhaps it was a plea to some deity rather than to Philip, but unfortunately none of those were available.

"Gentlemen," Philip said, pitching it loud enough to cut through the doctors' row. "Take this professional dispute into another room, now. And don't come back until you have reached a civil conclusion."

"Sir Philip, I—"

"I said, take it elsewhere. Will I be obliged to summon footmen to remove you both? Get out. And don't let me see either of you until you can speak like gentlemen."

Dr. Bewdley's mouth dropped open. David snarled, "Very well," and marched to the door. Dr. Bewdley, evidently feeling he had gained ground, turned to Philip and opened his mouth.

"*Out*," Philip said. He filled the word with command and contempt mixed, and the doctor went, leaving Philip, Frisby, and the supine woman in a room.

Frisby was staring at him. "What—what will happen now?"

"I expect they'll continue that endless and unanswerable argument," Philip said. "I shouldn't dream of trying to sway you, but I will observe that David kills significantly fewer patients than most doctors of my acquaintance, and he never bleeds."

"He told me about it." Frisby's voice had the vague quality of exhaustion. "He explained why he wouldn't and it sounded awfully convincing but—Dr. Bewdley's always been our doctor. Always."

"The decision is yours. If you want her bled I will remove David from the premises while it's done, although I can't promise he will be polite about it afterwards."

"Why is it mine?" Frisby demanded. "I don't know what's best!"

"Nor do I. I would, myself, leave it to one or the other doctor, but not both."

"I suppose you mean it was foolish to call Dr. Bewdley in."

"That was exactly what I meant, yes. Did you sleep at all?"

"No. I—Amanda—"

"If you don't sleep you'll make bad decisions," Philip said. "Let me order a bed made up for you. You won't be of any use to your sister or to David if you knock yourself up."

"I need to stay with her. You must see. I have to."

"I will have an appropriate attendant come and sit with her. My word of honour." It ought to be inconceivable that anyone would spread gossip about a woman lying desperately sick; he well knew it wasn't. Worse, Philip had a vivid image in his mind: both Frisbys in his house at death's door, needing nursing for months or, even worse, dying in Rookwood Hall, whence the last baronet had set out to ruin their mother. He enjoyed his reputation, but he liked to keep it fictional. "I insist, Mr. Frisby. Make your decision as to which doctor you trust and I will implement it. Meanwhile, get some sleep and you will be better placed to sit with her tonight if her fever has not broken by then."

"I..." Frisby blinked. At the dizzy stage of exhaustion, Philip guessed. "You promise she'll be looked after?"

A Frisby, trusting a Rookwood to care for a woman's virtue. It was enough to make a cat laugh, except that there was nothing funny about the fear and pain on Frisby's face. "I give you my word. I will order you a room and a bite to eat, and then you shall lie down and recover yourself." Philip rang the bell and gave swift orders when the man appeared. "And send me Cornelius once the food is ready," he added. "Very well, that's done. Have you reached a conclusion about the bleeding?"

"I don't know." Frisby's voice was tremulous. "If I say yes and it weakens her—or no and the fever worsens—"

"You can't make the right decision," Philip told him brutally. "You don't have sufficient information. What we need is another patient with a similar injury. Bleed one and not the other, and observe the results in both." Frisby was looking at him with wide-eyed horror, as though he expected Philip to break someone's leg on the spot. "I speak purely theoretically," he felt obliged to explain. "At the moment almost all patients are bled, and some live and some die. In order to see if bleeding is truly effective, we need to ensure more patients with similar ailments aren't bled, and to observe the results."

"But if you deny people the right treatment, that would be murder."

"Negligence, surely. Notwithstanding, I grant your principle, but how else are we to test the thesis?" Frisby gaped at him. Philip sighed. "Never mind. What would you like the doctors told?"

"I want them to do their best," Frisby whispered. "I want them to know the right thing to do, and do it. Only they won't agree what that is, will they?"

"No."

"What would you do?" Frisby asked, and looked startled at his own words.

Philip felt equally startled. "I couldn't possibly make a suggestion as to Miss Frisby. It is hardly my place."

"No. Of course not. I shouldn't have asked."

He looked wretched, and the misery in his big green-brown eyes was discomfiting, and Philip had, as he had often been told, no shortage of opinions. "However," he said, and watched those eyes widen fractionally with hope. "However, were it my decision, I should compare the chance of doing harm through action or inaction, and I should probably choose the latter. And I should also bear in mind that David Martelo is a remarkably intelligent and determined man, with a wide education and varied experience." Frisby looked slightly dubious at that. Philip reminded himself that cosmopolitan ways were not generally considered an advantage outside sets like his own. "I'd trust

David with my life, or my sister's if I had one. You have no reason to. But I would."

"Well," Frisby said. "Uh. Thank you."

There was a knock: Cornelius, as commanded. "Breakfast is served, sir, and the Small Rose Chamber is made up for Mr. Frisby."

"Thank you," Frisby said. "Uh— Sir Philip, could you—that is— no, I should—"

"Would you like me to tell the doctors your decision?" Philip suggested. "It might be awkward for you to offend one of them, whereas I won't care in the slightest."

"I—no. I'll do it." He pulled himself upright. He wasn't such a bad figure of a man, Philip realised: not tall, but compactly built, and his mouth was decidedly well-shaped. He wasn't precisely striking, but he might be presentable under other circumstances. "Where are they?"

"In the study, next door on the right." Philip could well see the rubicund old bully Bewdley reproaching Frisby into a morass of uncertainty. He had no intention of letting that happen, having spent quite enough time on this already. "I will meet you there shortly."

Frisby went off, visibly steeling himself. Philip turned to Cornelius. "Right, where's the female attendance?"

"I regret, Sir Philip—"

"For God's sake! I promised Frisby we'd look after her. How hard can it be to find a woman in this blasted country?"

Cornelius coughed in a manner that made his displeasure clear. "I *regret*, Sir Philip, that an attendant will not be available until the early afternoon. I have secured the services of one Mrs. Fossick, who will arrive once her daily tasks are performed. She is not medically experienced except, she informs me, in the delivery of infants, but I judge her highly qualified to sit on a chair."

"While drinking gin? Marvellous."

"Unfortunately, I was unable to find an alternative candidate willing to visit Rookwood Hall. Sir."

"And we all know whose fault that is. Stick your master with a pin for me when you next dress him."

Cornelius coughed again, this time with a nicely judged tone of breaking bad news. He had what Corvin sourly described as a complete wardrobe of coughs for all occasions. "The female individual demanded a half-guinea for her services."

Philip winced. "It's a tribute to propriety, we'll pay it. Thank you."

David stuck his head through the door. "Philip, there you are. I've left Frisby trying to get rid of that elderly ass. I'm busy, go and help him."

Philip muttered, but duly headed studywards, where he found Frisby stammering miserably as Dr. Bewdley upbraided him. "Excuse me," Philip interrupted without compunction. "Are you the lady's relative, Doctor?"

"No, sir, I am her physician, and have been since her childhood."

"Whereas this gentleman is her brother, so his wishes will be respected. You heard what he told you. Or do you need it repeated more loudly, perhaps with an ear trumpet?"

"I shall wash my hands of Miss Frisby's welfare," Dr. Bewdley said, very red. "If my experience is to be dismissed in favour of this damned foreign nonsense, I shall not return to this house to be further insulted."

Philip bowed low. "If your self-esteem is of greater concern to you than your patient's welfare, then I can only conclude your absence is for the best. Good day."

He waved the gobbling doctor away, packed Frisby off to breakfast, and went back to the sickroom, where David was in place. He gave Philip an absent smile, his focus on the sick woman. "You have done good work. Thank you. Is there news on a nurse?"

"We may have to find one ourselves. It's possible I may have offended Dr. Bewdley."

"You amaze me. Where's Frisby?"

"I persuaded him to take some rest by assuring him his sister would have female attendance."

"Some drunken sot to mumble in a corner? I can't see the use of it, but as long as your damned proprieties don't get in my way... I don't like this, Phil. She's running a very high fever. Will you help me sit her up so she can sip the decoction?"

Philip could think of nothing he wanted to do less than manhandle Eleanor Frisby's half-clad daughter. "Just a moment." He rang the bell and ordered the footman to summon Mr. Sheridan Street. David's eyes were rolled ceilingwards when he turned back. "Yes, I know it's ridiculous," he snapped. "I gave my word, blast it."

Sheridan arrived a few moments later. "Can I help?"

"I don't know," Philip said. "I promised Frisby his sister would be appropriately attended, expecting Cornelius to magic up a woman to sit with her, and she won't arrive till this afternoon."

"Ah," Sherry said. "And you want me to be Mrs. Salcombe? Drat. I'd be happy to, but I didn't bring any of my petticoat wardrobe with me."

Sheridan had inadvertently caused the freethinking but personally conventional Harry a great deal of confusion when the older man found himself falling hopelessly in love with his beardless apprentice. In the end, Corvin had had a quiet word with both parties to clarify matters, following which they had married privately and swiftly. Sherry kept to his masculine identity for professional and personal convenience, was Mrs. Harry Salcombe when needful or desired, and regarded the whole business with indifference. He was a geologist and Harry's partner in life; anything else was, in his opinion, trivial.

"Is it necessary to dress up?" Philip asked. "It's all lip service anyway, her virtue is safe with us. But if you'd be willing to play Mrs. Salcombe at a later date if any testimony is required, then I won't have entirely broken my word to Frisby. Stretched it to snapping point perhaps, but not broken."

"Of course I will. It may be a nonsense, but convention is the last thing the poor woman or her brother should have to worry about at the moment. I shall sit here unmoving until the actual attendant arrives, and I shall Respectable Matron the very hell out of anyone who doubts it after. Can someone send for my book?"

It was a long day. The promised woman arrived, freeing Sherry, and proved to be exactly the bosky, gin-smelling sort of character that Philip had predicted. David relegated her to a corner. Frisby slept through it all, emerging from his room around three, and was persuaded to borrow a hack, ride home, and talk his maid or housekeeper into attending on Miss Frisby during the day. Sherry's tolerance was limited, the exercise would do him good, and David wanted him out from under his feet. The boy was a fretter.

Philip spent several hours going through account books and crop yield reports and tried not to feel that he was shirking something important. Frisby took over from David in the sickroom around seven, which meant that the possibility of inviting him to join them for dinner once again did not arise.

"You'll do it at some point," Corvin said. "I know you. Conventionality will creep up on you when you least expect it."

"It's about the last thing on Frisby's mind, I should think," Sheridan said. "She's awfully sick and her leg is the most horrible colour. Are you sure it wouldn't be better to let the bad blood out, David?"

"Shall we not start that hare now," Philip suggested firmly. He was having second thoughts himself. It had been absurd to put his tuppence-worth into Frisby's deliberations. He'd done it because the poor fellow had looked desperate for some sort of certainty, but now he was having trouble not thinking of the consequences if the woman died on them with the most standard treatment left undone. Amanda Frisby was a damned nuisance and Guy Frisby was worse, and Philip wanted the whole business off his hands.

David went to bed early, getting some sleep in case he was needed during the night. The rest of them played whist, keeping the noise down, and retired around midnight. Corvin let the others go first, then came up and sank down beside Philip's chair. "Hoi, you. Look at me."

Philip did. It wasn't a hardship. He'd known that face from childhood, seen his friend grow from boyish roundness through angularity and ghastly spots into his adult good looks. Corvin had reddish-brown hair, when he would have far preferred a suitably Gothic black, but at least he could boast steep brows, a striking pair of dark brown eyes, and a general appearance of handsome untrustworthiness. He was the very model of a heartless rake, to people who didn't understand. "Very well. What am I looking at?"

"One who loves you. You're taking this all rather seriously, Phil."

"It's the blasted Frisbys. You must see the problem."

"I see their problem. I'm wondering why it's yours."

"Because their mother died," Philip said. "Because James persuaded a married woman to abandon her children and reputation, and then drove off a cliff with her. James's stupidity enriched me and deprived them of everything."

"True, but I don't recall he consulted you about it."

"It's as though the name I bear is a blight on their family. A Rookwood trespasses against them and they lose a parent—two if you count their father, drinking himself to death. They set foot on Rookwood land and calamity strikes. I feel like a curse, V."

Corvin put a hand on his, without comment, and Philip interlaced their fingers. "I'm being absurd. You needn't say so."

"You are, rather. Might I observe that if there were a family curse it wouldn't really be your business anyway?"

Philip used his free hand to bat at Corvin's head. "Rot you. Why aren't you in bed with John?"

"Twice in a row? Please. John wouldn't, and I couldn't."

That was a flippancy, though John undeniably tended to be rough with Corvin: Philip had watched and winced often enough. He wondered if he might like to watch tonight and decided not. He wasn't in the vein, for that or anything else, and in any case it seemed a little bit indulgent with a possibly dying woman in the house.

He let out a sigh. "If you're seeking entertainment, look elsewhere."

"Dear boy, I would, but David's disinclined, the Street-Salcombes are devoted, and nobody in his right mind would step between George and his devil's fiddler. If you want company of any sort I am entirely available." He batted his eyelashes, for all the world as though it were a proposition instead of Corvin-parlay for *Are you really all right? Do you need to be held?*

"I'm very well," Philip said, answering the spoken and unspoken questions at once. "Go to bed. We'll get out of here tomorrow and go for a ride or some such. I can't tolerate this deathb—this sickbed atmosphere."

"Indeed not." Corvin brushed Philip's fingers with his lips. "Goodnight, my dear."

Philip stayed a few minutes longer, thinking about things of no worth, and took up a candle to retire. As the night before, he slipped along the corridor to the Blue Drawing-room first. David had said that fevers worsened at night and had cursed their failure to find a nurse willing to attend the Hall. Philip took a mordant pleasure in the reputation he and Corvin had built for themselves, which confirmed all his beliefs about human nature, but it had its drawbacks.

The sickroom door was open again: David always insisted on fresh air for patients. Philip could hear a low, fretful sound, which he supposed was Amanda Frisby, and a soft voice.

"No, don't, Mandy-may. Your leg's splinted, that's why you can't turn over. I know it's horrible. I know the cloth is cold and I'm sure it hurts but please try not to move. You've an awfully good doctor and he's promised you'll get well soon, and Mrs. Harbottle will be here tomorrow to look after you. Maybe she might make her chicken broth? If you can drink anything but this wretched willowbark. Oh God."

A brief silence.

"Anyway I was telling you about the house. You'll be so cross you missed it all. Serves you right. Everyone's being so kind and generous and helpful. Dr. Bewdley came to see you and he—he sends his good wishes, but we've agreed Dr. Martelo will be in charge. He's awfully kind. He's a Jew, did I say? I don't think he's what I would have imagined, but then I'm not sure what I would have imagined, so I suppose he wouldn't be. And he's Portuguese, though he's lived here for years. He's travelled to any number of places, you know; you have to get better, so you can talk to him. And he's got a lot to say about medicine, but you needn't worry about that now. No, no, Manda, don't move, please. Please. If you thrash about you'll hurt your leg, and if you do that— Oh dear God," Frisby whispered. "Please get better. Please. I can't do without you and you've got so much more to do, and I know it's been—not marvellous for you but we've been happy enough, haven't we? And we can do more. I'll be braver, I swear, and you'll put all the nonsense behind you. You're so brave and so marvellous and so clever, and you aren't going to let a stupid broken leg stop you, are you? Oh God, Christ, anyone, someone help us. Let her get better. Please."

Philip's candle had only been a stub. It guttered now, and went out in a soft sigh, and he stood in the darkness, listening to a sick woman moaning, while her brother wept because he loved her.

Chapter Three

A manda's fever raged on. Guy sat by her bedside talking endlessly in the hope that she'd hear. He helped tend to her bodily needs and slept fitfully during the daytime, and obediently went for rides because Martelo and Rookwood insisted on fresh air and sunshine. He went home for clean clothes on the fourth day and discovered that a box had arrived for Amanda. It was *The Secret of Darkdown*, her book. He took a copy with him, praying she'd one day see it, even hoping that authorial pride might call her back.

He was sitting with her the next morning, exhausted. He hadn't woken Martelo to ask for help; he'd become reasonably expert at giving her the decoction by now and he no longer panicked as her fever worsened in the night. Or, rather, he had become so used to living in constant panic that it felt almost like calm. Martelo was looking fairly grey himself, after the days and nights wrestling with Amanda's illness, and Guy needed him to be well because he'd pinned his fading hope on the dark, intense man, and he didn't know what he'd do otherwise. He didn't want to think about speaking to Dr. Bewdley again after offending him so deeply, and was thinking of exactly that in a distant, exhausted way when he heard a hoarse voice whisper, "Guy?"

He looked down. Amanda looked up. Not the blank creature of pain and fever, but Amanda, with recognition in her eyes.

"Manda?"

"I feel..." She swallowed. "Awful."

"Oh God. Oh, Manda. Just—just stay there." He rang the bell frantically, and turned back to take her hand. It felt noticeably cooler, and so did her head. "Manda."

"Why are you crying?"

"Nothing. I was just fretting a little, you know how I do. No, don't try to move. You broke your leg, do you remember?"

"It hurts."

"I bet it does." A servant poked his head in. Guy rapped, "Dr. Martelo, quick!" for all the world as though it were his house. "You had a bad break and a very nasty fever and, uh...we're in Rookwood Hall."

Amanda blinked at that, her mouth moving slightly. It ought to have been a delighted shriek. "I'll tell you everything as soon as you feel more the thing," Guy assured her. "You need to rest now, and have some of your medicine."

He got her to sip the drink. She made protesting noises at its bitterness, for which Guy couldn't blame her, and at which he was unspeakably relieved. He'd tasted the vile stuff and the fact that she'd swallowed without noisy complaint had been one of the more unsettling features of her illness.

Rapid steps rattled down the hall, and Martelo burst into the room like an unkempt hurricane. "Frisby? What is it?"

Guy swallowed. "The fever. I think it might have broken."

The doctor brushed past him without ceremony, but he took Amanda's wrist with all the delicacy of a gentleman handling a duchess. "Well, now. Well. Good morning, Miss Frisby. My name is David Martelo, your physician. You've given us all a fine scare."

Jane arrived a little later, slipping into the room with an alarmed look, and giving a great sob when she saw Amanda's improved state. By then Dr. Martelo had satisfied himself and Guy that the fever had passed, the swelling in her leg was markedly reduced, and Amanda, though weak and in need of sustenance, was unquestionably on the mend. Guy hovered, smiling through tears of happiness and exhaustion, until Martelo turned and clapped him on the arm. "Go to bed, man. She's going to recover, I'll stake my life on it, and you're burned to the socket. I don't want to see you again until the afternoon. Out."

Guy emerged into the corridor. He ought to have breakfast, he supposed, but he was drained beyond speech with relief and the backwash of days of pent-up fear, and all he wanted was sleep. He made his way into the hall and came up against the entirety of the Murder, the whole gaggle of them standing in the hall, talking in hushed voices.

Guy stopped, abruptly aware of his bedraggled state and tear-stained cheeks. Rookwood met his eyes and strode forward, face tense. "Frisby. What's happened? Is it—? Is there anything at all I can do?"

Guy blinked, and then realised what he meant. "No! I mean, no, it's not, she's not— The fever broke. She's looking better. I think she's going to recover."

Rookwood took that in, and then he smiled. It was extraordinary. Guy hadn't really paid much attention to his appearance, beyond fair hair and an expression that suggested supercilious boredom or mockery most of the time. Now a huge, broad, entirely real smile took over and transformed his face, and suddenly he looked wonderful.

Rookwood grabbed his shoulders. Guy thought for a second he would be pulled into a hug, and wouldn't even have cared. "Excellent. *Excellent.* Oh, well done, the Frisbys."

And then there were men all round him, the short round-faced one yelping with glee, Mr. Raven shaking his hand, Lord Corvin enthusiastically proclaiming Dr. Martelo's virtues—in fact the lot of them rejoicing at Amanda's deliverance with as much honest pleasure as though they weren't a notorious hellfire club at all.

That afternoon, Guy emerged from a sleep so deep it was more like unconsciousness. He lay in bed blinking his way back to full awareness, and remembered. Amanda's fever had broken. It was—surely, maybe?—going to be all right. Though there was still her leg to mend, and the chance of her walking with a limp all her life, probably an ugly scar. And Dr. Bewdley would have to be propitiated since Guy had sorely wounded his vanity, and they had now to think about their sojourn at Rookwood Hall among a group of men who might not be quite as bad as everyone said, but that wouldn't count for anything if everyone went on saying so, and then there was Aunt Beatrice. If she heard that Guy and Amanda were here, the consequences would be unspeakable. Guy could perhaps write to her and explain, but she was not very easy to explain things to, especially where Amanda was concerned. Guy could very easily imagine her descending on them to insist Amanda was moved right away; he found it less easy to imagine himself standing his ground to resist her. It was quite hard to stand up to someone who held your existence in the palm of her hand.

It might be better not to write at all, and hope she never found out. Rookwood clearly understood Amanda's invidious position, and there was no reason the news should spread. But if she did find out and he hadn't told her...

He was fretting. *Stop it*, he told himself. *Amanda is going to get better. Enjoy not worrying for five minutes, can't you?*

Someone had left a jug outside his room, the water still warm enough for him to wash and shave in reasonable comfort. Guy dressed with care, for the first time in several days. He assessed himself in the mirror, ruefully aware that his complexion was rather ashy and the dark smears of exhaustion under his eyes all too visible. Still, he was presentable.

He gave his cravat a last tweak, headed out of the bedroom with a confident stride, and promptly got lost.

It wasn't entirely his fault. The old Jacobean house was a maze; getting from his remote bedroom to the main stair involved four turnings; and he had no recollection of the last few days beyond the constant blurring hum of panic. Nevertheless he'd been up and down to and from this room multiple times. He ought to have known the way, but he hadn't actually paid attention to his feet in the glow of relief. He'd somehow taken the wrong dark, narrow corridor, and now he had no idea where he was.

Well, the house couldn't be that big. Surely walking would bring him to a stair of some kind. He went on past a row of mediocre oil paintings of stocky men with large chins and found himself faced with a narrow spiral stair going up and down, or a corridor off to the left. One room had an open door, and he heard a voice coming from behind it.

He decided he'd poke his head round the door and ask for guidance. It made more sense than wandering, and in any case he was starving hungry and disinclined to waste more time. He went up to the door, hand poised to knock politely, and his intended *Excuse me* stuck in his throat.

Rookwood and Corvin were there. Corvin was leaning back, one knee on a couch, and Rookwood was standing over him, very close, far too close. He had one hand cupping the back of Corvin's head. The other, Guy saw numbly, was unfastening his own breeches.

Corvin was looking up at Rookwood with a truly Satanic grin—the Devil's Lord, they called him, and that grin was all the reason anyone needed—and as Guy stared, unnoticed, he said, "I've missed your cock, my lovely."

"That must make a change," Rookwood said. "After all, you haven't missed many."

Corvin laughed, open and unashamed. "I adore you."

Rookwood leaned down and kissed him. It was a deep kiss, open-mouthed but very tender, and then he straightened, gave Corvin a gentle but authoritative shove to the shoulder, and pulled the front flap of his breeches open and down. "Right. Let's have you."

Guy stepped back, away, managing somehow to remember not to make a noise, not to run, not to panic. If they thought he was spying, that he'd seen—seen—

What had he seen?

He wasn't entirely ignorant. He read the newspapers with their breathless denunciations of abominable offences and he read Greek and Latin literature, a lot of it, in his unexpurgated editions, carefully obtained without thinking too much about why it was important they should be unexpurgated. He knew his Petronius and Suetonius, his Catullus and Lucretius and Martial, very well indeed. But that was printed words, the pictures only in one's head. It wasn't two flesh and blood men smiling into one another's eyes, kissing, planning to do heaven knew what in the filthiest language.

He'd thought the hellfire club's reputation was a nonsense. How wrong had he been? How could he not have even noticed that he found himself amid such... *Depravity*, his mind supplied, and that must be the word, except for that kiss.

My lovely. I adore you.

Guy wanted to leave the house. He wanted to wipe it all from his mind. He wanted not to be aware of the uncomfortable, squirmy feeling in his gut and the heat in his face and the fact that he hadn't walked away at once, or raised the roof in moral outrage. The fact that he'd been momentarily transfixed.

Startled, he told himself. He'd been startled. Of course he had. Anyone would be.

He hadn't even noticed where he was going as he hurried away, cursing Corvin and Rookwood and their outrageous, immoral, unforgivable leaving-open of doors, and it seemed a cruel irony that he found himself at the main stair without even trying.

He wanted to go back to his room and hide, but there was Amanda. He came downstairs in a rush and went straight to the sickroom. She was awake, with Jane in the corner, sewing, and the short one of the Murder sitting by the bedside, reading aloud from a book.

"'The cold of the flagstones seeped through her thin shoes, but it was nothing to the chill at her heart. For that night, Araminta had seen evil.' Hello, Mr. Frisby." The man put a paper in the book to mark the place, as Guy gaped in horror. "I was just reading to your sister. I'm not sure we've been introduced? Sheridan Street."

"Guy Frisby," Guy said numbly. "Uh, that book..."

"It's awfully good." Street was a few inches below Guy's height, with very boyish looks and a beardless chin. "I'm dying to know What Araminta Saw." He emphasised the capitals dramatically.

"You can borrow it," Amanda whispered. "If you like. I've read it."

Guy turned to her, pleasure at hearing her voice warring with a desire to scream. "I'm really not sure—"

"He brought you something you'd read before? Brothers," Street said with contempt. "Don't worry, I've got the new Mrs. Swann with me. I'll leave you to it," he added to Guy. "I just popped in to say good afternoon."

Guy looked after him as he left, then turned to Amanda. She gave him a weak smile. "Hello, you."

"How are you feeling?"

"Awful. My leg hurts and my head hurts and the medicine is vile." Amanda sounded petulant; it reminded Guy of his father, once the drink had weakened his constitution past repair. He'd spent months dying at home, in such a querulous, fretful way that the house had felt like a conspiracy after his death in the shared guilt of relief.

He shook off the thought. At least the self-absorption of the invalid meant Amanda hadn't read any distress on his face. She was cursedly acute in good health.

Guy rang for something to eat and drink, and settled down to sit with her, chatting lightly until she slept again. She was still incurious as to their company. He doubted that would last.

It was past four once he'd had tea, bread and butter, and cake. He went out, intending to take the fresh air and exercise on which Dr. Martelo insisted, and bumped into Sir Philip Rookwood.

"Ah, Frisby. Congratulations again on your sister's improvement." Rookwood looked more relaxed than usual: satisfied, even, and Guy was not going to think of what sort of satisfaction he'd found at Corvin's hands. "I trust her health continues to improve?"

"Uh," Guy managed. He couldn't look Rookwood in the face; he didn't want to look any lower. He fixed his eyes on the man's neck instead. He was casually dressed, his cravat in a loose knot—or, perhaps, pulled loose from its original arrangement, revealing a bit more of his throat than usual. He was well shaved, not as smoothly as Street, but without a hint of stubble. His lips were curved. He was smiling. He was smiling *at Guy*, with a slightly puzzled air.

"Frisby?"

"Yes. Thank you. Sorry, sorry, I mean—"

"Good Lord, stop. I only asked how she was."

"Yes. I mean, well. I was just going for a walk."

"Right," Rookwood said. "I'll just come with you, shall I? Wouldn't want you to get lost in the grounds. Still less to step in a rabbit hole and break your leg; we've had enough of that."

Guy should have refused. He should probably have turned from Rookwood with disdain, except he'd been accepting the man's hospitality for days, and also that casual reference to getting lost sent him into a flurry of panic over whether Rookwood knew he'd been lost in the house. By the time he'd realised that didn't make sense, he was walking down the drive with his host, who'd been kissing Viscount Corvin and doubtless worse not an hour earlier.

"Are you interested in the history of the Hall?" Rookwood asked. "I ask with the reservation that it has none of note, and no architectural merit either. And also that I know nothing about it. Other than that I'm sure I could speak fascinatingly on the topic."

"You must know about your own house," Guy protested, without thinking.

"It wasn't meant to be mine," Rookwood said. "As you probably remember."

That was a startling thing to hear. Guy opened his mouth and found himself unsure what to say.

"It has occurred to me that I ought to apologise," Rookwood went on. "Not that I had any part in James's actions, but I can't help feeling his responsibility has descended upon me along with his house. For what little it's worth, I regret the wrong done by one whose name I bear to your family. I imagine the consequences were unpleasant."

"Unpleasant. Yes, it was rather *unpleasant*," Guy said. "He ruined my father. He tainted our name beyond repair and made us all the objects of contempt and mockery. He took my mother away."

"How old were you?"

"Eight. Amanda was five. We never saw her again."

"No," Rookwood said. "Again, I am sorry. There's not much more to be said than that, but if my regret for the part James played in this is of any use to you, you have it."

They were walking as they spoke, around the maligned house. Rookwood Hall didn't have much in the way of gardens, no tended flowerbeds. All the cultivation Guy could see was fruit trees and what looked to be a kitchen garden.

"The part he played," he said. "What does that mean?"

Rookwood shrugged. "He didn't abduct Mrs. Frisby. She made a choice."

"What do you mean by that?" Guy demanded furiously.

"Exactly what I say; it wasn't an insult. I hold that women ought to have the same right and duty to self-governance as men, for good or ill. They don't, legally, but that doesn't make them any the less moral beings."

Talk of moral beings and self-governance from a pleasure-seeking rake was so ludicrously unexpected and hypocritical that Guy lost his breath. Rookwood went on unawares. "I can't apologise for your mother's decisions because they aren't mine to account for, even by proxy. I should prefer to put the bad blood between the Frisbys and the Rookwoods to rest if I can. That's all."

As if he'd intended anything of the kind; as if any olive branch could stretch over the abyss between them. "I see. Is that why you offered us your hospitality when you very clearly didn't want to?"

"Oh, dear. I had hoped it wasn't too obvious."

Guy swung round to face him and was stopped in his tracks by Rookwood's smile. It was real, and amused, and relaxed. He looked— Guy crushed back the memory of the smile when he'd bent to kiss Corvin. He couldn't find anything to say.

"Quite seriously, anyone in such a plight would have had a claim on my hospitality," Rookwood said. "I'm not a monster. And David Martelo wouldn't have permitted any other course of action."

"I must ask," Guy said stiffly, one of the ongoing worries he hadn't considered rising up like bubbles in a stew. "The doctor, and the woman you hired. Their fees—"

"I should take it as a personal favour if you would allow me to account for that."

"Certainly not." Guy fervently wished he could accept. Heaven knew what extortionate prices a London doctor like Martelo could demand. He and Amanda lived within their allowance, but not so far within that they had guineas to spare. He prayed Amanda's ten pounds from the publisher would cover it.

"My house, my responsibility," Rookwood said. "And if you want David paid at all you'll let me do it. He's far too involved now; he won't take a penny from you."

"But he will from you?"

"I can manage David Martelo."

Manage. Guy shoved down thoughts of that, and the commanding *Let's have you.* Oblivious, Rookwood went on, "And you wouldn't even have needed the woman were it not for the need to safeguard your sister's reputation in my house. An attendant's fee is cheap at the price if the alternative is offering my hand in marriage."

Guy's mouth worked for a moment while the outrage rose up inside him like a pot boiling over, and then it erupted. "Of course you would rather anything but that! I suppose you think my sister is beneath you because of—of what happened? Well, she isn't, and if she was it would be your damned brother's fault, but she's not and let me assure you," he said furiously, ignoring Rookwood's efforts to get a word in, "she wouldn't dream of stooping so low as to a man of your reputation and—and vile habits. And you may keep your bribes. I don't want to owe you anything!"

"Hoi!" Rookwood almost shouted. "Will you please calm down?"

"No! Your family is an affront to decency and your coven here is even worse with your murders and disgraceful goings-on, and— Just stay away from my sister!" Guy turned on his heel and stormed off, ignoring Rookwood's, "Frisby..." because he could hear the amusement in it. The damned swine was laughing. Laughing! How dare he laugh? What made him think he could ridicule Guy?

It took him about five minutes' walk off the grounds and down a country lane to conclude the answer was: because he was ridiculous. Coven? *Murders?* He'd read Amanda's book again the previous night in the intervals while she'd slept, and the spirit of the damned thing had apparently seeped into his brain.

He attempted to tell himself that he'd been justified in his fury, if not his words, and walked on fuming, but a mile or so in the afternoon sun sucked all the anger out of him and left him feeling nothing but foolish. Rookwood's remark had been extraordinary, yes, not the kind of thing anyone would say, but he seemed to make a habit of shockingly blunt remarks. Guy had taken it as a caustic dismissal of Amanda's suitability as a bride, because he'd heard that too often, and between the days and nights of terror and that quivering sensation in his belly at what he'd seen, it had all become too much to be borne.

It wasn't remotely unreasonable, if one was fair about it, that a man would prefer not to marry an inconvenient invalid with whom he'd never exchanged a word. And that went double when he had Lord Corvin murmuring his adoration. Lord Corvin was a very attractive man, or at least Guy supposed he must be, with a smile that would doubtless be devastating if that was the sort of thing one wanted. It was quite clearly the sort of thing that Rookwood wanted, law or no.

And Rookwood had let Guy and Amanda ruin his party, and he'd apologised for his brother and even offered to pay the bills that had been nibbling at the edges of Guy's tenuous calm. And in return Guy had taken the first opportunity to shout at him for no reason except that his nerves were red raw and he couldn't stop picturing Corvin on the couch, and Rookwood smiling down at him.

"Oh Lord," he said aloud. What could he do now? What if Rookwood's mood went from amusement to offence? What if he demanded Amanda should be removed and her leg was injured, or he turned Martelo against them, or he forbade Guy the house and left him unable to care for his sister?

"Stop it!" he said aloud to the teeming thoughts in his brain, and walked faster, as though he could outrun his own stupidity.

He'd been walking for an hour or so, and was on his way back, when he heard hoofbeats. A rider was approaching at a quick trot, and Guy recognised the lean build with a dull sense of inevitability.

Rookwood reined in his horse, approaching at a walk, and looked down from his superior vantage.

"Mr. Frisby. Could we, perhaps, speak? I seem to owe you another apology."

Guy blinked up at him. "What?"

Rookwood swung down off his horse, a graceful movement. His riding breeches were evidently of excellent manufacture, and stretched well over his long, muscular legs. "An apology. I am prone to flippancy, and I feel you detected disrespect to Miss Frisby where none was intended. Nevertheless, the misunderstanding arose from my misplaced sense of humour, and for that I apologise."

Guy gaped like a fish. "But— I was awfully rude to you."

"You were," Rookwood agreed. "But you have a duty to Miss Frisby's name, so it was quite correct to take up arms, whereas I have John Raven and Lord Corvin as bosom friends, and thus barely notice insult, much as a beekeeper no longer feels the stings. And you have also had a rather trying few days, so perhaps we might simply agree to put that exchange behind us."

"That's very generous of you," Guy muttered, face burning.

"Think no more of it. Now, I spoke to David. He assures me that Miss Frisby's progress is excellent and, even better, we have finally secured a capable nurse who will take the night watch, assuming that meets with your approval. If you would like a second truckle bed made up downstairs, say the word, but David does not think it necessary, and begs that you will have a proper night's sleep. Before that, I hope you will join the rest of us for dinner."

"Dinner?"

"The evening meal," Rookwood explained with great gravity. "We really are quite civilised, and not as bad a set as popular opinion holds. Except Corvin, but one can't help that. Don't dress." He lifted his hat, mounted with effortless elegance, wheeled his horse, and set off back down the path, leaving Guy gaping.

He trudged back to the house and sat with Amanda for an hour. She mostly dozed, and Guy watched her, the natural sleep, the better colour in her face. If everything else was a calamity, he could still not regret that she had come to this house and Dr. Martelo's care.

The prospect of dinner loomed over him like shades of the prison house. He was not looking forward to this and felt a dreadful certainty that it was some joke at his expense, some opportunity for mockery, as when the bigger boys invited one to play and then it turned out one was to be the ball.

Surely not. *Rookwood apologised*, he told himself, and *They were pleased for Amanda, truly.* It did no good, because he couldn't stop thinking, *What if Rookwood knows I saw him?*

Guy was well aware that he could march to the local magistrate and lay charges. Possibly some people in his position might feel that made them powerful. He didn't. For one thing, the idea of bringing charges against one's host was repugnant. For another, he was well aware that if Rookwood felt threatened, he could all too easily retaliate. Guy's mind was as fertile as Amanda's in its own perverse way: he could come up with infinite paths leading to disaster. The things the Murder could say, destroying Amanda's reputation all over again, making Guy look a weakling or a pander, making them talked about. Guy loathed being talked about; it made him nauseous even to imagine people gossiping and whispering and sneering.

Well, if Rookwood had offered this olive branch because he was aware Guy knew his secret—or because he feared it after the stupid accusations Guy had flung—Guy would take it. He would give Rookwood no reason to consider him a threat. He would do his best to be polite and go unnoticed, and Rookwood's companions would doubtless forget about him quickly because Guy was eminently forgettable.

He just prayed he wasn't seated next to Lord Corvin.

He came down to dinner at the gong, wondering if everyone else would appear in the correct black garb despite Rookwood's assurances, and was relieved to see they did not. The very opposite, in fact. The stocky man with a Northern accent was frankly rather shabby and Mr. Raven's cuffs and wrists bore smears: not dirt, but bright colours. Rookwood and Corvin both looked admirable, but the balance of the gathering was entirely normal.

Rookwood made the introductions, for those whose names Guy hadn't previously grasped. George Penn, a composer, was the other black man in the group, slightly older than the rest of them, with skin of a markedly lighter shade than Raven's. The quiet fellow with prematurely greying hair was Ned Caulfield, another musician. Guy had heard the piano and violin distantly over the last few days and was glad to express his admiration.

The Northerner, introduced as Harry Salcombe, said he worked with Mr. Street. "I'm a geologist," he explained.

"You study the Earth?" Guy hazarded.

"And its formation, yes."

"Oh." It sounded rather dull, but Guy knew what was required. "That's fascinating. Could you tell me more?"

"Oh dear," Corvin said, from the top of the table. "On your own head be it."

"Well, Mr. Frisby," Mr. Salcombe said, visibly settling in. "How do you imagine the Earth came to be?"

Guy blinked. "Well, Creation. The Bible tells us—"

There was a chorus of hisses, as though everyone present had inhaled sharply, and Mr. Street said, "Be gentle with him, Harry." Mr. Salcombe flashed him a grin, turned back to Guy, and began to explain the beginnings of the world.

The next hour was a blur. Guy had no interest in modern science whatsoever, still less in rocks, and preferred the classics to the Age of

Reason in which they supposedly lived and of which he saw little evidence. But Mr. Salcombe's enthusiasm was matched only by his imagination. He started by dismissing the Book of Genesis as a goatherders' fairy tale and, while Guy was still reeling at the blasphemy, went on to assert that the earth had been created not six thousand years ago, as proved by Bible genealogy, but millions, and not by a benevolent God but in lava and flood and fire. He spoke of creation and a painful birth, of land emerging from chaos and destruction, until Guy could take no more.

"All this is just wild speculation. We've thousands of years of scholarship, and Biblical research, which tells us the age of the world."

"Aye, six thousand years old if you add up the generations in the Book of Genesis." Mr. Salcombe rolled his eyes. "On the one hand, one old book, translated from Hebrew to Greek to Latin to English. On the other, the evidence of stone and earth and our own eyes. What do you think your God gave us eyes for, and minds too, if not to look at things and think about what we see?"

"But you *don't* see it," Guy protested. He wasn't generally argumentative, and certainly not with strangers, but this was too disturbing to be borne. "You may draw certain conclusions from looking at rocks, perhaps, but how does that constitute more than a theory? How does that allow you to dismiss thousands of years of scholarly thought? What proof have you?"

"Hold on," Street said, leaping up, and almost ran from the room.

"There's plenty of scholarly thought behind geology," Salcombe said, entirely unruffled by Guy's challenge. "Avicenna, who was a Persian scholar of eight centuries ago—"

"I know who Avicenna is," Guy said, somewhat nettled.

"You should read him on the formation of mountains, then. And James Hutton, too, *Theory of the Earth*, same thing. Six thousand years, indeed."

Street hurried back into the room, something in his hand. "You wanted to see something? Try this."

"For God's sake," Rookwood said. "You bring those things around the country with you?"

"I found that one." Salcombe spoke with a note in his voice Guy couldn't interpret.

He wasn't really paying attention anyway, because Street had handed him, of all things, an oval stone split along its length. Guy cautiously took the two halves apart and saw a *thing*.

It might have been a carving, except that the other half of the stone fitted it too perfectly, and the thing seemed to be in a different sort of orange rock which was nevertheless of a single piece with the grey stone. It was some sort of insect, over three inches long, with a great helmeted head and antenna and far too many legs, depicted in startlingly clear detail, and Guy had never seen anything that resembled it in his life.

"What is it?"

"*Pediculus marinus major trilobos.* Lyttleton found a great number in the limestone pits at Dudley."

"But what *is* it?"

"That's what it is," Street said. "It's a kind of sea louse, what we call fossilised, preserved in stone. They've been gone from the earth for thousands and thousands of years. Specimens have been found all over the world, and they can reach a foot in length."

"A foot?" Guy tried to imagine what this flattened, leggy thing might have looked like in life and at the length of his forearm. He failed. "How is it so big, when lice are so tiny?"

"Many creatures were huge then. We've found thigh-bones of creatures larger than elephants, the teeth of unimaginable predators. The remnants of a world before ours." Street's eyes were distant, seeing a vista Guy couldn't imagine. "A world of life gone to dust, or to stone, before humans were thought of. And there are so many more creatures like this, so many different species. Plants, animals, insects. A whole dead kingdom under our feet."

"Cheery, isn't he?" Corvin said.

Rookwood sighed theatrically. "Knowledge is the highest pursuit of man and the spur to all progress, and you treat it as drawing-room entertainment."

"But," Guy said. The stone louse sat cold in his palm, an alien, terrifying thing. How could it be this old? He had a book in his possession that was a hundred and fifty years old, and barely touched it because of the crumbling edges of the paper. Human achievement gone to powder, while this mindless thing of stone lasted millennia. He felt peculiar just thinking about it. "Entire species?"

"Animals the like of which you've never seen. Far, far more than this." Street held out his small, callused hand for the stone.

Guy gave it back reluctantly. "It's an extraordinary thing, I grant you. But—but really, how *does* this square with the teachings of the Church?"

"Well, it doesn't," Salcombe said. "That's all."

"Or you could suggest that the book of Genesis might be read as an extended metaphor, or perhaps that our translations from the original Hebrew lack nuance," Rookwood said. "There are many great minds attempting to reconcile the new learning with, ah, revealed truth. But I'm afraid you won't find any of them here. This is for the most part an irreligious gathering. Atheistical, even."

Guy's jaw dropped. He wasn't quite sure if atheism was legal; it certainly wasn't acceptable in decent company. He'd never met a self-confessed atheist in his life until this bizarre sojourn. He'd also never met a black man, a Jew, or a geologist. Or a viscount, come to that. He wasn't sure exactly how his quiet rural existence had brought him to this point, but Amanda would be wringing every detail out of him for months.

He cleared his throat. "As a Christian, I cannot approve."

Corvin rolled his eyes; Rookwood sighed audibly. Guy flushed. He'd sounded intolerably prissy even in his own ears, and worse, he was being cowardly. He ought to do more than disapprove: he should defend his faith in the strongest terms against these atheists with their wild theories that cut at the heart of everything he'd ever been taught. But he'd held a dead stone monster in his hand and he couldn't find anything to say.

Raven opened his mouth. Penn said, mildly, "Every man is entitled to his beliefs."

"Yes, any man has a right to his beliefs, and a duty to question them too," Raven retorted. "If you don't take out your beliefs for washing now and again, they're just bad habits."

That started a discussion among the company in general, greatly to Guy's relief. He ate and drank and watched his tablemates as the conversation swerved like a drunkard in the road. They went from the need to abolish the offence of blasphemous libel and separate church from State into a discussion on the system of elections. Martelo and Salcombe argued that every man over the age of twenty-one should be entitled to a vote and representation in the House; Raven and Street suggested women's opinions should be canvassed equally; and Corvin spoke, with languid wit that might even have been seriously meant, about the desirability of abolishing the House of Lords. "After all," he said, "I have a seat and a voice there, and you wouldn't put *me* in charge of the country, would you?"

It was beyond argument, for Guy: he couldn't begin to formulate answers to questions he'd never even considered asking. He just listened, in a slightly wine-flown haze, to a debate that felt like some sort of lengthy hallucination, each proposition more destructive and extreme and simply not done than the last.

This, then, was a hellfire club: a debating society for alarming ideas. Guy could well understand why one would need a private room; a zealous magistrate could prosecute some of these opinions if aired at a public meeting. But this was Rookwood's home and thus, since he was an Englishman, his castle. The Murder could say what they wanted in their own company, and Guy, who hardly ever said what he wanted, had nothing at all to offer this meeting of lively, informed, well-travelled people saying unimaginably bizarre things. He simply watched and listened, with the sense of being caught in one of those fiery upheavals that Salcombe said had made the world.

He was so absorbed that he didn't notice the food he consumed, or the wine from his ever-filled glass. He just listened, baffled, disturbed, and oddly exhilarated by a conversation the like of which he'd probably never hear again. He looked between the speakers, from one to another, and his gaze came to a stop at Rookwood.

Sir Philip was listening to Caulfield, who was making a point about the American constitution in a quiet, hesitant voice. Caulfield had barely spoken, and it was noticeable that the voluble gathering, most of whom habitually talked over one another, all paused to listen to his few contributions. Guy didn't know if that was because he was more worth listening to than the rest or because they were simply being kind to a shy man, and he didn't find out because he didn't hear a word. He was entirely caught by Philip Rookwood in the candlelight.

Rookwood's hair, a mix of brown and blond strands, was shot with gold as it caught the reflection of the many flames; his blue-grey eyes, the colour of a summer squall from a clear sky, were intent on Caulfield with a look of deep absorption that brought his encounter with Corvin to Guy's mind and shortened his breath. The baronet was toying absently with a biscuit, elbows on the table, cheekbones shadowed by the dancing light, lips just slightly curved, not in amusement, but, Guy thought, in unconscious happiness. Sir Philip Rookwood was where he wanted to be in this atheistical, democratic gathering, among his friends, and those who were more than that, and there was no trace of the habitual mocking smile or the lifted brow.

He looked painfully handsome when he was happy. He looked like someone Guy would have dreamed of calling friend and never dared ask. Like someone who kissed a man, pushed him back with confident certainty, and smiled into his eyes.

Guy didn't realise he'd been staring at that half-smiling mouth until it curved—a slow, sure movement—and he looked up and met Rookwood's gaze.

He couldn't breathe. He had no idea how long he'd been staring like an ill-mannered gapeseed. He shouldn't have been staring at all, at anyone but particularly not at Rookwood, and he had to stop now but he couldn't look away from those eyes. He was sure Rookwood's smile was all mockery, but he was pinned by that grey-blue gaze that refused to drop, and Guy had never felt so nakedly *seen* in his life.

"If everyone's finished," Raven said, "are we going to listen to George's new piece?"

"Of course," Rookwood said. He kept Guy's helpless gaze an endless second longer, then leaned back with a slow blink. "George's composition, Frisby, and Ned will grace us with his playing. We can wait if you and David wish to visit the fair invalid first." He smiled. Guy shivered. "Don't be long."

Chapter Four

They gathered in the drawing room to listen to the musicians. Philip had made a small wager with himself as to whether Frisby would use his sister as an excuse to run and hide, and was pleasantly surprised to lose. The man didn't look precisely confident as he slipped in behind David, but he was there, even if he didn't quite manage to meet Philip's eyes.

"Not scared him off yet, then," Corvin breathed in his ear. That required standing extremely close, so Philip turned, gave him a fond smile, and ground his heel in a slow emphatic movement on Corvin's toes.

"Touchy," Corvin said, with a provocative grin, extracted his boot from under Philip's foot, and went to take a seat. Philip cast him a look and turned back to see Frisby was now looking at him with the sort of shock that suggested Philip had slapped him in the face.

What on earth—? He couldn't have heard Corvin unless he had ears like a bat, and a man standing on his friend's foot was surely nothing to get upset about. One would hardly be shocked by the informality after that exchange of looks earlier.

He considered that as they settled to listen to the new sonata, George on piano and Ned playing the violin. Philip liked music well enough, but he lacked whatever sensibility it was that caused people to go into raptures. Ned's face as he played was that of an angel on the verge of spending, and Corvin could sit entirely absorbed through concerts that lasted hours; Philip tended to find it a reasonably enjoyable background noise while he thought about something else.

Frisby was evidently one of those who liked music properly, because the slapped look and the self-conscious awkwardness had both fled. He sat and listened to the musicians with wide eyes and slightly parted lips, and since it was, for once, possible to watch him without sending him scurrying, Philip did.

He wasn't in the habit of approaching unknowns. Corvin and John had been there since he was ten for the needs of body and soul, and Philip counted himself one of the luckiest men in Britain on that account alone; if he wanted variety, he could rely on Corvin's supernatural ability to discern on sight if someone might like to share his bed. Asking the wrong man risked violence, denunciation, extortion, or a panicked flight to the nearest magistrate, and Philip did not like any of those prospects.

He was as sure as he could reasonably be about Frisby, and absolutely sure Corvin would have told him if he was barking up the wrong tree, but that didn't exclude the possibility of the aforesaid panicked flight. That might even be more likely if the man was one of those terrified to acknowledge his own nature. It would be a glaring stupidity on Philip's part to do anything but ignore the fellow until he took his sister home, never to pass Rookwood Hall's threshold again. The man was nervy, under a great deal of strain, doubtless inexperienced, and a Frisby. Each of those factors suggested Philip should leave the fellow well alone; together the conclusion was inarguable.

And yet.

He kept thinking of what he'd heard that first night. The way Frisby had sat by his sister and spoken to her, never stopping or giving up. The way he put her first and stood for her in the face of his own obvious fears. Perhaps other people would shrug and say that was natural in a family, but Philip had no experience of that, direct or indirect. His own family had hated the sight of him and said so; Corvin's parents had been so uninterested in their offspring that they made stray cats seem nurturing; John couldn't name his country of origin, far less any relative.

He would, he thought, sit by John or Corvin's bedsides, were such a thing required of him. He didn't believe that family love was of a superior kind to the affection one gave by choice. But still he'd stood in the halls of the home where he'd been loathed for existing, and listened to Frisby weep for his sister, and his heart had twisted like wet washing with a childish, agonised longing for something he'd never have.

He'd thought for several terrible moments this morning that Amanda Frisby had died. He'd been sure of it, and startled by his own distress at the thought of Frisby's bereavement. Nobody who loved another person so much should lose them so cruelly. And then the man had said, "She's going to be all right," and his face had looked like Ned's when he played, or Corvin's when he fucked.

Because it turned out that Guy Frisby was in fact rather more than just pretty when he wasn't grey with worry and exhaustion; that there were fires banked under that unassuming polite-to-a-fault exterior; that his eyes widened at new ideas even while his lovely lips pursed. And that he looked at men, because Philip had rarely been so looked at. Corvin hadn't needed to kick his ankle to alert him to Frisby's fascinated stare, although he'd done so anyway. Philip had felt that gaze on his skin.

And he ought, he really ought, to leave Frisby well alone, but when a man made it so clear what he wanted, it seemed rude not to offer.

Frisby had a compact form, not lean or gangly. Habitually rounded shoulders of the type one saw in men who spent their days bent over a desk, although not in the way Philip might like to see him bent over a desk. Dark brown hair, straight and short and cut with competence rather than flair. Dark brows too, over hazel eyes of that flecked green-brown type that looked like nothing much from a distance but rewarded close inspection. A pleasant face, of the sort with which one became comfortably familiar rather than the sort that left one breathless, except for the mouth. That was beautifully shaped, with an elegantly curved top lip and a full bottom lip. A sensitive mouth that moved apparently without the man's conscious awareness, as though he were used to reading aloud or speaking his thoughts to himself. It had moved silently while Sheridan and Harry had spun pictures of their monstrous ancient world, and Philip had wondered what Frisby saw in his mind's eye.

He was sitting rapt now, upright, as the violin soared and trilled. George wrote for Ned's playing, pushing him harder with every piece, and Ned's bow seemed to flicker with the speed of its dance. He was almost on his toes, rigid with physical tension as he controlled the bow, and Philip wondered why, if you loved a man, you'd make his life so difficult. George gave Ned's gift no quarter, forcing him to live up to the music of his partner's imagination and the outer limits of his own skill, increasing the tension every time until the surely inevitable day a string would snap.

Doubtless they made better music that way; doubtless it suited them. It would not have suited Philip. Corvin had never asked him to be more than himself. He'd simply loved, warts and all, without hesitation or qualification as he always did, since the day ten-year-old Philip had been deposited in the Corvin household to spare his parents the sight of him. He'd lived by his friend's generous affection, the first he'd ever known, gulping it like a thirsty man plunging his face into sweet water.

Perhaps he and Frisby had more in common than met the eye, in fact, when it came to mothers who cuckolded their husbands and abandoned their children, and fathers who didn't care if one lived or died. Not that Philip knew much of the deceased Mr. Frisby as a parent except that he had drunk himself to death while wasting his substance at the gaming tables, but that didn't suggest a deal of consideration for his offspring. Doubtless people had clucked disapprovingly and thought the less of the children for the father's selfishness; they always did. No wonder the brother and sister were close. No wonder Frisby preferred not to be looked at.

Then again, Philip had once wished with all his heart to go unnoticed, and then Corvin had seen him and refused to look away. Perhaps Frisby needed to be seen the right way too.

Why, it's all but an act of charity, he imagined Corvin saying, and found he was smiling as the musicians finished and they all broke into applause. Those who knew about music clustered round to offer superlatives; the rest of them gave congratulations. Frisby hung back a little, looking uncertain, and Philip drifted over.

"Don't feel shy about saying you liked it," he remarked, and saw the man twitch at his voice. "And don't feel shy about saying if you didn't, come to that. George prefers intelligent criticism to ignorant applause, which is why I'm keeping back."

"Don't you like music?"

"I like it well enough but that's all," Philip said. "It doesn't transport me in the way it does some. You, perhaps?"

"I, uh, I don't know about *transport,*" Frisby muttered. "I thought they were very good."

"I think you thought more than that. Or, if you didn't, you ought to rent out your face for the benefit of artists, because you looked enchanted."

Frisby went delightfully pink. Philip took his shoulder, feeling the muscle tense, and gave him a gentle push toward the musicians. "Speak your thoughts, that's the purpose of our gathering. George, our guest appreciated your work."

"It was marvellous," Frisby managed. His manners clearly forced him on when his preference would have been to flee. "The melody line was remarkably beautiful. Thank you for letting me hear it. And the playing—it was exquisite."

George bowed, starting a response. Philip stepped away and found himself knuckled hard in the back. That would be John.

"Something to say?" he enquired.

"Just wondering what you're playing at. If even Corvin's letting something lie, shouldn't you?"

"The day I measure my behaviour by Corvin's standards, you may begin to rebuke me."

"I'll rebuke you when I please." John slipped an arm through his and dragged him to the window. "Don't be an idiot. You've enough bad blood with that one for a lifetime, and if you give him grounds to make an accusation—"

"I think you're too severe."

"I think you'd be a fool to foul your own nest. It's a bloody stupid way to go on, and if I want to see my friends being bloody stupid—"

"—you'll have no trouble finding examples," Philip completed for him. "Yes, all right. I grant your argument has some merit."

"Good. Oh, and while I remember, sitting tomorrow."

"I've my steward all morning, but the afternoon is yours."

John let him go with a nod. Philip turned back to the room, and was somewhere between relieved, unsurprised, and unreasonably annoyed to see that Frisby had gone.

He normally rather enjoyed his meetings with his steward. Lovett was not an original thinker, but he made up for that in practical intelligence, competence, and obedience. Philip had read a few recent works on theories of agriculture after he'd succeeded to the title, decreed that repairs were to be done promptly and tenants treated as knowledgeable partners, then not come back for three years. He'd returned to discover that Lovett had obeyed him to the letter and was generally considered to be robbing his master for the benefit of his tenants, who would therefore appreciate it if he remained an absentee landlord all his life. He'd gravely displeased the other local landholders by failing to sack Lovett and double the rents, but confirmed his reputation as an eccentric by introducing various modern ideas in the way of equipment and crops, leaving Lovett to deal with the actual business of arguing the farmers into it.

The latest idea, thanks to an enthusiastic agriculturalist of his acquaintance, was new to the point of madness: the extraction of sugar from beetroot. A factory had been established for the production of beet sugar in Silesia, and Bonaparte had decreed that France too must begin growing the crop, to reduce his nation's dependence on imports and guard against the possibility of a British naval blockade cutting off supply.

It could be done in England, and should. A domestic sugar industry would surely be able to beat the prices of sugar imported from the West Indies, and reduce the profitability of slave sugar, and while Philip didn't delude himself that would be the end of the plantations, it would be something. So Corvin was funding the construction of England's first beet sugar extraction factory, Philip had set aside several fields to grow the latest strain of Silesian white beet, and the sense of limitless possibility was thrilling. Or had been.

"They all think you're mad," Lovett said. "The stuff's useless."

"It's not useless, it's the future. Tell them Bonaparte's growing sugar beet."

"I'd rather not, Sir Philip. It wouldn't help."

"Then tell them I'm a violent eccentric and their very lives depend on doing this properly."

"Mmm," Lovett said. "Perhaps there's a middle way?"

Philip sighed. "Tell them whatever you like as long as I get my beet. Why they must be so hidebound…"

"People like the old ways, Sir Philip. They like what they know."

There was an explosion of laughter from up the corridor, sufficiently loud that they both turned instinctively towards it. Evidently Philip's friends were enjoying a joke. "In ten years' time sugar beet will *be* the old ways that they know. Then someone will discover a new means of extracting sugar from sea water and the farmers will cry, *But beet was good enough for our forefathers!* It's how progress works. The printing press was a modern innovation once. So was fire."

"Yes, Sir Philip," Lovett agreed, in a tone that very clearly meant, *Please stop talking.*

Philip sighed. "Look, just assure them that this is my idea and as such I'll bear the consequences if it's a stupid one. If the factory doesn't work and the beet rot in the fields, that's my problem."

"And a year or two of their lives and hard work for naught," Lovett said. "It makes a difference, Sir Philip. To put your labour into something that will, as you say, rot in the fields and you know it as you work…" He tailed off, searching for words to articulate the concept, and concluded, "They don't like it. They don't want to do it, paid or no. They won't refuse…"

"But they won't be enthusiastic. Or attentive."

"Well, if a man's asked to do a pointless task, he doesn't generally break his back over it, that's all."

Philip opened his mouth to reply, but was distracted by another roar of laughter, this time even louder. Lovett glanced at the clock. "I will ensure the men know your mind, Sir Philip. Unless there's anything else, you will want to return to your party."

Philip forbore to smile. He was aware that his steward considered his infrequent visits an irritating obstacle to the smooth running of the lands, and didn't resent it since he had no desire to take on the day-to-day tasks himself. "Thank you. I shall see you on Monday."

He showed Lovett out himself, then hesitated in the hall. He hadn't seen Frisby at breakfast as the man had been with his sister. It would be courteous to drop into the sickroom and offer a belated welcome to his lady guest. Then again, his interest in her might well be misinterpreted, so he should ask Frisby to make the introduction himself. Pleased with that as a neat solution to two issues, he headed for the drawing room to find out what the noise was about.

Sheridan was on the settee, Harry next to him, legs out and head thrown back, laughing like a drain. Corvin and John were both leaning on the back of the settee. Sheridan held a book, which he was pulling out of Corvin's reach. "Get *off*, I'm reading it. Phil! Oh, listen, listen!"

"What on earth has caused this riot?" Philip demanded.

Sheridan flipped through the book. "Just a moment... Here we are." He cleared his throat and began to read aloud. "'Sir Peter Falconwood was a fair man to look upon, yet thus we see how fairness may be outward only, for his character was as vile as his features were pleasing, and his flaxen hair and blue eyes hid a cruel, cold heart. Though handsome, Sir Peter was no rival to his bosom friend Lord Darkdown in his pursuit of the gentler sex—they might consider themselves blessed by his abstinence! Instead he devoted his energies to strange sciences, cultivating unknown crops on the advice of philosophers rather than that of honest countrymen steeped in English soil'—"

"Excuse me, *what?*" Philip demanded. "What was this fellow's name again?"

"Sir Peter Falconwood," John said. "He's not the main villain though. That's Lord Darkdown, his best friend, a disgraceful rake, and, wait for it, red-haired."

Corvin scowled dramatically. "This is a damned libel. My hair is russet. At most."

"Oh my God," Philip said. "What is this book? Let me see it."

"Mine," Sheridan said, snatching it away. "Well, Miss Frisby's, but she lent it to me. Buy your own."

"I'm going to buy hundreds." Corvin was bright with glee. "*The Secret of Darkdown*. I adore everything about it."

"I hope you know you're all going to die," John said. "Poisoned by mistake, or stabbed by a ghostly nun, or falling off a cliff into hell."

"Well, so are you, if that's who the swarthy henchman is," Sheridan pointed out.

"The— You're sodding joking."

"Sorry," Sheridan said, unapologetically. "You're six feet tall and devoted to Lord Darkdown."

John gave a hiss of exasperation. Corvin poked him in the shoulder and said, "Henchman."

"I'm not your bloody henchman."

"You are now."

John got an arm round his neck. Sheridan and Harry ducked out of the way of the brawl. Philip demanded, "Who the devil wrote it?"

"It just says By A Lady."

"I've a pal who can probably find out if you want," John offered, slightly breathlessly, since he'd more or less got Corvin's face into the back of the couch.

"Let me go, you oaf. Ouch. If it's a success I expect we can wait for the rumours," Corvin said, straightening and rubbing his neck. "Nobody ever keeps these things quiet for long. God, I hope it's a success. Let's make it one."

Philip rolled his eyes. "You've been waiting your whole life for someone to write a Gothic novel about you, haven't you?"

"It's a small tribute to my genius," Corvin said modestly. "But Sir Peter the strange scientist is good too. He probably intends complicated villainies which I trust and pray will involve root vegetables. Can I have it when you've finished, Sherry?"

"Not a chance," John said. "I asked first."

"I'll send for more copies," Philip put in. "One each. Go on, read me the bit about Corvin."

Philip pinned Frisby down after luncheon, as the man came into the hall. He'd had a feeling that Frisby had been lying low, and the man's blush suggested he was right. "Good afternoon," he said breezily. "How is Miss Frisby today?"

"Uh, better, thank you. She had a bowl of beef broth this morning, which Dr. Martelo says will be restorative. Your cook is wonderful."

"Not mine; Corvin supplies the household."

"Oh. Of course," Frisby mumbled.

"Excellent news, though. I rather wondered—if you feel it appropriate—if you would care to introduce me to the lady. When she is well enough to receive visitors, naturally."

"Oh. Yes. Yes, I am sure she will want to thank you."

"Please tell her not to," Philip said. "My contribution is simply that I own the property, which is accidental anyway, so hardly praiseworthy. Have you been for a walk?"

"Dr. Martelo ordered me out, yes. He's very keen on fresh air."

"Oh, I know, it's so tiresome. I wish I had done the same, since I shall be obliged to spend the latter part of the afternoon sitting perfectly still."

"Why will you need to sit perfectly still?" Frisby asked.

"For my portrait. John is working on a commission for Corvin. Do you know that he is an artist?"

"Mr. Raven? I had no idea."

"He does engravings mostly, satirical ones. Highly satirical. Usually about two inches to the left of a prosecution, in fact, which is one reason we're here now and he has leisure to work in oils. The word *horsewhip* came up in conversation with one of his recent victims in London, and discretion is the better part of valour in these cases."

"Oh!" Philip had meant only to entertain, or possibly shock, but Frisby seemed to have found something to chew on. "Oh. So…"

"So?" Philip prompted.

"Well, that is, many people would take great offence at seeing themselves depicted satirically or—or unfairly," Frisby said in something of a rush. "You don't mind that Mr. Raven does it?"

"He picks deserving targets. Then again, 'use every man after his deserts and who should 'scape whipping'? I am of the opinion that one must be the sole judge of one's own value. There is no point listening to the opinions of others: the world always has its thumb on the scales."

Frisby's mouth rounded. It really was a very expressive mouth. "Can you do that? Ignore people?"

"Given practice, it becomes second nature."

Frisby gave an abrupt little gasp, as though he'd intended to say something and stopped himself. He shook his head instead. "Perhaps. If you can afford to ignore them, if you don't need them, or you have enough friends to be shocking with. If you didn't grow up with people always talking about—about you, or your family—"

"But I did," Philip pointed out. "And 'talking about' understates the matter considerably, as I'm sure you can imagine."

"You mean your brother? Yes, I suppose that must have been a great scandal for you too."

"I don't mean my brother. You are aware of my family situation, yes?" Frisby shook his head. "Good Lord. I would have assumed it was known to every man, woman, and dog in the locality." He examined Frisby's face. "Oh dear."

"What?"

"You're visibly teetering between the urgent need to ask and the awareness of how very rude it might be. Curiosity at war with courtesy. It's like watching a morality play on your face."

The colour washed into Frisby's cheeks. "I beg your pardon," he said stiffly. "I had no intention of prying."

"Good God, man, unbutton yourself."

Philip hadn't actually meant it as a double entendre, let alone a command, but there was no question of how Frisby heard the words. He went from pink to scarlet in a second, eyes widening visibly.

"Which is to say, please don't feel constrained by civility," Philip went on as calmly as though the man hadn't reacted at all, because he had a sudden vision of Frisby running out of the house screaming for help. "You must have gathered the nature of our society by now." Christ, he was making it worse. "The pursuit of knowledge, I mean. We like to discuss things as we please and we tend to speak frankly. If I wanted to keep my family scandal a dark secret I shouldn't have raised the subject. I would have to burn quite a few portraits to achieve that, though."

Frisby blinked, though at least his colour was returning to normal. "I don't at all know what you mean by that. But if you'd like to explain then yes, I am curious."

"I wouldn't precisely say 'like to' but it really seems only fair," Philip said. "Have you seen the family gallery?"

Frisby shook his head. Philip gestured him upstairs, along to the corridor where the pictures hung, just near the pleasant little parlour where he and Corvin had enjoyed each other yesterday. Frisby lagged noticeably behind, steps slowing as though expecting attack, for reasons Philip couldn't guess at and decided to ignore.

"Here," he said, indicating a painting. "Sir George Rookwood, who held the title before James."

Frisby frowned. "You mean, your father?"

"Well, no, I don't. That's rather the point."

Frisby looked at him, and then at the dark-haired, red-faced, stocky man with the jutting chin, and up the line of portraits at two more dark-haired, red-faced, stocky men with jutting chins. "Uh. Do you take after your mother?" he tried, a desperate last stab at decency.

"No. I take after my father."

"Oh."

"His name is Sir Donald Hamlyn," Philip said. "I'm his living spit. My mother's connection with him was a matter of notoriety, but the birth of a child quite so marked with his looks—"

"Oh."

"My supposed father had never troubled to keep his own vows; nevertheless he did not appreciate the cuckoo in his nest. Nor did my mother, actually. After some years of very public estrangement they reconciled, and I was left as an unwanted reminder of her error. I lived in the Corvin household from the age of ten, which was best for all concerned, since the Rookwoods are cousins of the family."

"So you and Lord Corvin are related?" Frisby asked, and then, "No."

"No indeed."

"But you still inherited?"

Philip shrugged. "I was born to the wife of Sir George Rookwood. In law I'm his son. I dare say he might have attempted to disinherit me if he'd dreamed James would die without issue, but he was a stupid and unimaginative man. And James was evidently not thinking about posterity, given his passion for a woman he couldn't marry. So the Rookwood estate is mine, greatly to the distress of my—or rather James's—cousin, who is next in line. He attempted to get up a lawsuit, with no success. He can have the place when I'm dead."

"I'm so sorry, Sir Philip," Frisby said. "It must have been dreadful for you, all of it."

Philip was sure he hadn't sounded distressed enough to evoke such a response. His illegitimacy had been a lifelong insult, but he had long ago vowed not to feel it as an injury. His parents' failings were not his fault. That was not the popular view, and people mostly reacted with embarrassment when he mentioned it, or shock. Frisby's quick, open sympathy was unexpected.

"I dare say that I might have had some of the same experiences," Frisby went on. "People talking about one's mother, and making remarks. It's vile."

"It is rather," Philip said. "And then I decided I didn't give a damn for such people or their opinions. I had no hand in my own conception, any more than you played a part in your mother's decision to follow her heart. I am, myself, of the opinion that if anyone deserves condemnation for the acts of Mrs. Frisby and Lady Rookwood other than the ladies themselves, it would be—"

"This Sir Donald and your brother," Frisby completed. "Yes."

"Actually, I was going to say the ladies' husbands. Perhaps your father was blameless, though my one encounter with him was not at all pleasant, but I knew my mother's husband well enough, and I wouldn't have wanted to be yoked to him."

"You said they reconciled?"

"My mother became an adherent of an extremely religious sect," Philip said. "She felt it her duty to return to the marital home, where she bemoaned her sin on a frequent basis. The Bible does tell us that the sins of the parent are to be visited upon the child."

"The New Testament tells us that children belong to the kingdom of God," Frisby said. "And that the erring woman was forgiven, and that only he who is without sin is entitled to cast a stone at her. I'd rather hold to that."

He spoke with a slight hesitation, but he said it all the same, and Philip felt a mild satisfaction at having elicited a bit of spine from the man. Standing for his beliefs suited him a great deal better than the scurrying.

"You're quite right." He enjoyed the look of confusion that brought. "That is how it should be. I don't believe in divinity, but I hope I can appreciate a solid moral precept when I hear one. If only more Christians were guided by Christ."

"Well. That's true." Frisby's shoulders dropped a little.

"I don't mean to compare our situations," Philip added. "I know what it is to have one's family talked about, especially when one's mother commits the cardinal sin of behaving in a way that is only acceptable for fathers, but it must have been far worse for you."

"No: it was worse for Amanda," Frisby said. "Not for me. I had boys calling my mother names and—well, that sort of thing. But Amanda... She went to London for a Season and people assumed— they thought, because of what our mother had done more than a decade before—"

"Ah."

"How dare they," Frisby said low. "How dare people make assumptions about her character because of what someone else did when she was five? But they did. And *I don't care what other people say* is all very well when you're a man with an independent income, but it isn't all very well for women, because what other people say is all that counts. If enough people repeat that Eleanor Frisby's daughter is just like her mother, it becomes true. And you may think Dr. Bewdley a fussy old fool, but I know why he was concerned, because he saw it all happen before. He knows perfectly well that if there's the slightest breath of scandal, it will taint Amanda forever because nobody will ever give her a fair hearing thanks to Mother, and it's not right!"

He was standing tall now, chin up and back straight, self-consciousness burned away by anger. Frisby was roused for his sister, and those green-flecked eyes were wildly expressive when they were lit with passion. This was what he ought to look like, Philip thought: not shuffling back into the shadows because to be noticed was a misery. He *ought* to be noticed, and Philip was bloody well noticing him now.

Frisby shifted slightly, hackles settling. "I beg your pardon. But that's what I think."

"Will you do me a service, Frisby?"

"Of course," he said at once, and then his expressive eyes widened as though he was wondering what he'd let himself in for.

Philip tried not to smile. "Will you please never again beg pardon of me for having an opinion? Under my roof, you are welcome to think and speak as you please, and I hope you will. It suits you."

And there it went again, the betraying flush of colour in his cheeks. Philip had once heard a naturalist lecture at the Royal Society on animals that changed colour as a means of communication to their kind; Frisby was evidently of that species. He looked pink and startled and pleased, and Philip wondered—

"Oi! Phil! Get your baronet arse along here!"

Frisby blinked at John's bellow from a nearby room. Philip sighed. "The artistic temperament. Apparently my presence is required for the sitting. Would you care to watch?"

Chapter Five

The painting was taking place in the upstairs parlour. *That* upstairs parlour.

Guy had frozen in place when Rookwood had led the way, then followed with numb trepidation fearing heaven knew what; he couldn't have said himself what could happen, or why he followed if he thought it might. But there was no orgy of any kind in here. The criminal couch was pushed to one side; there was an easel by the window bearing a large canvas, and sketches pinned up to the walls. Guy didn't know if they had been there before. He hadn't looked.

John Raven was sitting at the easel. He lifted a hand in greeting to Guy, then motioned Rookwood over to take his place on a chair. Guy came cautiously up to see.

The picture was half done, with the background sketched in light brush strokes, the figures most detailed in face and hands. At the centre of the composition was Raven himself, seated at an easel, in the middle of painting a picture. He was looking round at the viewer with a decidedly sardonic expression. Lord Corvin was right behind him, leaning on the back of his chair, pointing at something on the canvas with that terrible, delightful smile. Rookwood was shown seated on a chair next to Raven, also looking at the canvas. He leaned forward, elbows on thighs, wearing the look of intense, absorbed interest that had twisted in Guy's chest the previous night. Perhaps that expression spoke to Raven as strongly as it had to Guy.

Raven dabbed his brush on his palette. "If you want to watch, pull up a chair. If you chatter I'll shout at you."

"He tells no lie," Rookwood said.

"Shut up and lean forward."

Guy did as bid, watching with fascination as Raven's brush dipped and dabbed, building the image. He'd never seen painting in oils, only Amanda's unenthusiastic watercolours, and it was compelling. Raven would use a dab of green or blue on Rookwood's skin, so glaring that Guy wanted to point out he'd picked the wrong pigment, and then a few more strokes made the colour part of a shadow or a vein, obviously right all along. He wondered if Raven saw the world as blobs of different colours where Guy saw pink or brown.

And he wondered about the picture. Lord Corvin had commissioned it, Rookwood had said. It was extraordinary to think a lord would commission a portrait of himself with his male lover, but if one was going to do such a reckless thing, why include a third party? And while Raven was clearly on the most friendly terms with the two titled men, to put himself rather than Corvin in the middle of the picture was extraordinary. Everyone knew the lord ought to be at the centre. The viscount came first, then the baronet, with the jobbing artist well off to one side. That was how things were.

But it seemed Raven didn't agree, and, since they were posing for the picture, Guy had to assume that Corvin and Rookwood didn't either.

Under my roof, think and speak as you will. Rookwood had said that. Suppose he'd meant it.

Perhaps he did. He'd told Guy about his illegitimacy with staggering unconcern. Guy couldn't imagine saying *My mother abandoned her husband and children to run away with her lover* out loud; the misery of people knowing at all or, even worse, commenting, had dogged every day of his life since he was eight. Rookwood's situation was on the face of it far more shameful, yet he spoke of it openly. As if he didn't care, or as if he preferred to take the shame by the scruff of the neck and thrust it in people's faces. *This is the skeleton in my family's closet; come and shake its bony hand.*

What would it be like to do that? Could one really say, *That is my mother's disgrace, not mine, and I am not tainted by it?*

"Philip!" Raven snapped. "Stop gawping."

"I'm sitting here thinking seriously, which is what you asked me to do."

"While looking in the wrong direction. All right, hold on. Frisby, would you mind?" He waved at Guy to stand, moved his chair a foot or so, changed its angle, and gave a nod. "Right, you can sit."

Guy sat, somewhat baffled as to how moving him would help anything. He glanced to the canvas for answers, saw none, looked up, and realised the alteration had put him directly in Rookwood's line of sight. And Rookwood was indeed looking at him, fingers steepled, eyes so direct that Guy felt his face heating.

"He needs something to focus on," Raven said. "Hope you don't mind. It's that or have Harry and Sheridan bring out the stone horrors."

"That's not *entirely* flattering to my guest," Rookwood said.

"Shut up."

"I don't mind," Guy said. He rather thought he minded a great deal, but Raven had helped set Amanda's leg. Dr. Martelo had praised his cool head in a crisis as making all the difference, and said he believed the bone was mending straight. If Raven wanted Guy to sit and be looked at, sit he would. Under the intent gaze of the man who'd been in here yesterday with Corvin.

That was the wrong thing to think about. Guy knew it instantly, but couldn't stop the picture filling his mind: Rookwood, looking down into Corvin's eyes so tenderly, with his hand on his—his parts. Guy hadn't seen any more than that but his mind was filling in the swelling of firm flesh, the stroke of fingers, Rookwood's full undivided attention.

He was going red, and it wasn't his body's only reaction, because he realised with abrupt horror that he was roused.

This was hell. He wanted to shift position to hide the evidence, but that might draw attention to it, which would be infinitely worse, and especially under Rookwood's intent eye. Guy didn't even know why the man was looking at him so. He ought to be thinking about Corvin—well, no, he ought to be thinking about a young lady, or nobody, but if he *had* to think about men it ought to be Corvin. It was one thing, and very wrong, to be committing unnatural acts with an illicit lover; it was quite another to do that and then smile into another man's eyes and tell him that speaking his mind suited him. If Rookwood was Corvin's, or anyone's sweetheart, he had no right to pay other people compliments. He had no right to be looking at Guy, and Guy had to stop looking back.

He forced himself to contemplate the canvas. It was no improvement. All he saw was Corvin's wicked smile, which seemed to suggest acts that Guy would never know, and Rookwood's intent look that saw far too much. Did Raven know they were lovers? How could Rookwood sit so calmly in the room where he'd said and done such things, with the very couch on which he and Corvin had done them right there against the wall, possibly even *stained*—

Guy glanced round. It was an involuntary action, and a nonsensical one, as though the upholstery would bear evidence visible from a distance. But still he felt compelled to look at the couch behind him, seeing nothing but a piece of furniture, and when he turned back Rookwood's expression had changed. His eyes narrowed, his mouth opened very slightly, and he breathed, "Ah."

He knows. The thought was like a drenching in ice water which, had it come for any other reason, Guy would have welcomed. He feared he'd betrayed his guilty knowledge over and over again, with his blurting out of accusations and his ridiculous flinches at remarks in which others would have seen no sinister meaning. Now Rookwood had unquestionably realised, and Guy was in more trouble than even he could possibly imagine.

Except that Rookwood didn't seem furious, or afraid. He was still looking at Guy, still intent, and as Guy fearfully met that grey-blue gaze, he smiled. It was just a tiny, conspiratorial twitch for Guy alone; not apologetic, not hopeful. It was a smile of recognition.

Guy sat gripping the seat of his chair, and panicked.

The sitting lasted an hour, and felt like a decade. Guy leapt up from his chair as Raven was still saying, "Well, that's enough for today", babbled insincere thanks for the interesting experience but he needed to visit Amanda, and fled. He more or less ran down the stairs to the sickroom, and thought he heard laughter from the room he had left.

Amanda was propped up on pillows, talking animatedly to Dr. Martelo. She looked over as Guy entered and her face lit. "Oh, hello. I wondered where you'd got to."

"I've been watching Mr. Raven paint Sir Philip." He wasn't going to think about anything else, not in here.

"He's very good," Dr. Martelo said. "He could make a fine living as a portraitist, I think, if he didn't waste his time on those satirical prints that infuriate everyone."

"Sir Philip said someone had threatened to horsewhip him for a picture," Guy remarked, mostly for Amanda's delectation.

Her expression repaid him. "*Oh.* Really? What was it of? Do you know, Doctor?"

"Some Society scandal, I believe. Or was it a politician? It happens all the time; you'd have to ask him. He won't mind," the doctor added. "He enjoys provoking people. It's why he does the prints instead of portraits. He says, why should I flatter the rich when I can insult them?"

Amanda gave a delighted gasp of shock. Dr. Martelo smiled down at her. "Now, I shall leave you with your brother. No wriggling, mind."

"Yes, Doctor," she said, adopting a dutiful expression. He laughed and departed; Jane requested permission to take some time also.

"Well," Guy said once they were alone. "You look better."

"I feel *so* much better. I've had buckets of soup, and I don't feel feverish in the slightest. You know how that happens, when one feels so ghastly and then quite suddenly you realise you aren't sick any more and you aren't even sure when it stopped. It's marvellous. Except for my leg, which is aching dreadfully, but that's different. Guy! We're in Rookwood Hall!"

"I know," Guy said, with some restraint. "It's been several days for those of us who weren't busy frightening everyone."

"Yes, but, the Murder!"

"I know. And—" He checked the door was shut. "What on earth were you thinking? You lent Mr. Street your book!"

"I did, didn't I?" Amanda grimaced. "I wasn't quite sure where I was. I probably shouldn't have. Do you think he'll notice anything?"

"I expect so, yes. They're not a stupid set. In fact— I have such a lot to tell you, Manda. But for heaven's sake if anyone mentions the book, don't say anything, will you?"

"Of course I won't. But what are they like? Have you met Lord Corvin? Is he awfully wicked?"

"He, uh." Guy's mind juddered on that. "He's not at all the thing. Not respectable in the slightest and quite outrageous. But he laughs a great deal, and he likes it when his friends laugh at him."

"Oh." Amanda considered. "Well, he can't be all bad, then, surely."

"That's what I thought, though you still shouldn't associate with him. Then, two of them are musicians, awfully good and very pleasant but not terribly talkative. Mr. Raven is a painter, and rather plain-spoken," Guy said, understating the matter considerably. "And Mr. Street and Mr. Salcombe study—oh."

"What?"

"I'm not sure…" He trailed off, rather than finishing the intended *I'm not sure I ought to tell you.* He really ought not. It was one thing to be inadvertently exposed to casually atheist claims about monsters of the past frozen in millions of years of stone, quite another to repeat them to one's overimaginative and occasionally irreligious sister. And yet he couldn't but think of the dinner, and Rookwood telling Corvin that he treated knowledge as entertainment for drawing rooms. Rookwood, who told the truth without shame, and was free.

"They study the past," he said. "The distant past. The origins of rocks and things. They have some rather shocking ideas."

"Shocking ideas about rocks?"

"Yes."

"Goodness," Amanda said dubiously.

"It's rather odd. Street has a sort of stone monster that— Well, I can't explain it, and I'm not saying I agree with any of it. But it was awfully interesting."

"I'm so jealous. You are remembering for me, aren't you? And you will tell me everything?"

"Of course," Guy said, permitting himself a considerable area of exception.

"And what about Sir Philip? What's he like?"

"He, uh. He wants to meet you."

"Me?"

"Well, we are his guests," Guy said. "He asked for an introduction when you're well enough. Just for politeness' sake, I'm sure. Shall I—"

"*Yes.* Yes, do. I suppose I look a fright," she added regretfully.

"You look wonderful."

"Don't talk nonsense."

"You look wonderful," Guy repeated. "Because you aren't feverish and you aren't lying there barely breathing and I'm not afraid of—of— Don't do that again, Manda, please."

She reached for his hand and gripped it. "I'm sorry, dearest. I didn't mean to fall."

"I know."

They held each other in silence for a little while, then Amanda settled her shoulders. "Well. Perhaps I could ask Jane for my good shawl, and to dress my hair a little better. I don't like sitting here like an invalid. And yes, I know I can't move my leg and I won't try. Dr. Martelo said. He's awfully nice, isn't he?"

"He's mostly shouted at people in my hearing," Guy said, and gave her a highly coloured account of the early stages of her treatment. Amanda gasped and shrieked and interjected in a way that put any lingering fears of her health to rest, and was vocally supportive of the decision not to bleed.

"I hate it. Dr. Bewdley always does it, the old vampire."

"He's only trying to help."

"But it doesn't help. It just makes me feel worse, and I've always said so. Dr. Martelo is dreadfully clever, I think."

"Yes, so do I. They all are. Well, I'm not sure about Lord Corvin, but Sir Philip is far more thoughtful than I'd have imagined, and extremely considerate, too." Amanda was giving him a narrow look. "What is it?"

"I don't know. You're thinking about something."

"No, I'm not," Guy said, an automatic denial.

"You are. I think they've got you wondering. You're not going to join the Murder, are you?"

"I'm sure they wouldn't invite me to." It was true, such an obvious, banal truth it didn't need saying, and it made no sense at all that Guy heard his own words with a painful shock of disappointment, as though he'd been denied something he desperately wanted.

"Guy?" Amanda was frowning.

"Nothing. It's nothing. They're all very good friends, and I just… It's been awfully lonely without you to talk to. Everyone's been kind but I missed you."

"You ought to have more society," Amanda said. "And I know it's my fault we can't—"

"It is not your fault."

"It is. You stay in with me every night."

"I'd far rather do that than go to a political club or some drinking society," Guy said. "You know I don't like new people."

"You seem to like these new people well enough."

Guy opened his mouth and found nothing immediate to say. "Well, yes. That is— I shouldn't have chosen to come here. It's only that we were forced by circumstance."

"And you never speak to anyone unless you're forced by circumstance, or by me." Amanda sighed. "I know. I wish you would. Otherwise we're both going to stultify, sitting here in the countryside until we turn into turnips."

"Manda," Guy said reprovingly, but it was true. They had been confined to a very limited life for some time, squirrelled away from any but the most limited Yarlcote society by Amanda's situation, their aunt's iron rule, and Guy's own fears. It had been a great relief at first, and then become a habit. Amanda had been chafing for a while. Guy wouldn't previously have said the same was true of himself.

They talked a while longer. Guy could have sat in here for hours, both to enjoy the pleasure of his sister's company and because in here, behind this closed door, he could avoid thinking about all the things that might await outside. Too soon, though, there was a knock and Dr. Martelo entered, with Jane. Amanda had to be moved to avoid bedsores, her leg examined, massaged, and measured.

"I want to apply a weighted splint," Martelo announced, at the end of this. "It's the best technique I know to avoid shortening of the limb."

"Well, I'd prefer that. Will it hurt?" Amanda asked.

"It will certainly be uncomfortable," Martelo said. He had no bedside manner at all; Dr. Bewdley always reassured his patients that his treatments would be entirely painless, even when they proved agonising. "We will, in effect, attach a weight to the end of your leg, perhaps two bricks, so as to pull the two halves of the break apart."

"I thought we wanted the two ends to come together."

"They will. The bone wants to knit, but this way we make it work a little harder and grow a little longer before the parts are reunited. It will be all the stronger for the treatment."

"I should certainly rather have my legs the same length," Amanda said. "Since I have to lie here anyway." She gave a martyred sigh.

Martelo looked down at her with a glinting smile, and Guy revised his opinion of the man's bedside manner. "I diagnose the natural boredom of the invalid, Miss Frisby, and I prescribe good books and company. You may have as many visitors as you want. A lively, cheerful state of mind is the best aid to healing I know."

"That's what I think!" Amanda exclaimed. "I should never get better sitting in a room on my own wishing I was outside. And I should love more company, instead of poor Guy having to sit for hours. Do you suppose Mr. Street would tell me about his shocking rocks?"

"Try to stop him," Martelo said, over Guy's muted yelp. "And send for any friends you wish. Sir Philip will want you to consider your house his own."

"I think we should ask him," Guy said. "Since he hasn't precisely invited society himself. And, uh, people might not come."

Martelo made one of his impressive scornful noises. "English propriety. Well, ask. And in the meantime, you must have entertainment. Do you like music?"

Guy left Amanda a little later. It was half past six; they kept fashionable hours here, dining at eight. It would take no more than twenty minutes to ready himself physically for dinner, even if he dawdled. He wasn't sure he could ready himself mentally given a week.

He'd seen Rookwood with Corvin, and Rookwood knew it. He'd watched Rookwood when he shouldn't have, and Rookwood knew that too. And he couldn't push aside the little sneaking, nagging thought that if he asked questions, Rookwood might even perhaps answer them.

Which was all very well for Sir Philip of the Murder who lived in London and was independently wealthy. He could talk and think as he chose. Guy Frisby of Yarlcote could and should not. And if that stolen glimpse of a kiss, and the way Rookwood had looked at him, and the stealthily-thumbed pages of classical poems Guy would never have admitted to reading or dared translate had all started adding up to something too large to ignore any more—well, he'd just *have* to ignore it, that was all, because the alternative was beyond his imagining.

He went outside rather than upstairs, for the evening light and a chance to walk. Exercise usually helped to clear his mind, or at least to let him sort through his worries, and perhaps it might have done now except that as he headed towards the garden, he encountered Corvin and Rookwood strolling the other way.

He couldn't pretend he hadn't seen them or turn away, so he raised his hand in greeting as they approached, and tried not to read anything into Corvin's frankly examining look. "Good evening."

"Good evening to you," Corvin said. "I hear you've been helping Phil maintain his pose of fascinated concentration. I'm sure John appreciated that assistance. And talking of John, I must find him, so take this one off my hands, will you?" He clapped Guy on the arm and strolled off, leaving him speechless if not breathless. He risked a look at Rookwood, and saw an expression of mingled amusement, annoyance, and affection.

"Uh," he managed. "I won't trouble you."

"No, walk with me," Rookwood said. "You and I need a conversation."

"I really *don't* want to trouble you," Guy said desperately.

"Too late." Rookwood crooked a finger. Guy found himself following, legs numb, as the man led the way past the orchard, where the apples were just starting to swell, and into an area of lawn. "Right. Not to put too fine a point upon it, Frisby, I take it you saw something you didn't intend to. That's not a complaint," he added. "Entirely my fault; I'm not used to bothering with discretion here. But since you did, I feel we should both know where we stand."

"I don't know anything of the sort," Guy said. "I— You— What you do in your house is not my business and you've been immensely kind to Amanda, and I shouldn't dream of making trouble for my host. I really don't think anything else need be said."

"Don't you?" Rookwood said, with a lift of his eyebrow.

Guy's stomach clenched. "I don't know what you mean."

"Oh, I'm sure you do. Frisby—may I call you Guy? We don't stand on ceremony here. And it's Philip. I don't know why all my friends insist in shortening me to Phil; it's so inelegant."

"Of course," Guy said, because he couldn't think of a polite way to say no.

"Guy, then. You'll have gathered we don't pay a great deal of homage to, let's say, conventional morality here. I hope you understand that does not make us monsters. Gossip notwithstanding, it is possible to be an atheist without being a villain, or a democrat without bringing out the guillotine. And that goes for intimate relations as well."

"There are laws," Guy said.

"Laws are made by man, and plenty of them are absurd."

"Well then, there's right and wrong!"

"Yes, there is. In my view, what's right is that one's partner should be willing. If people freely choose to take their pleasure together, where is the wrong?"

"I don't know how you can say that to me," Guy said. "With our mothers? Really?"

"If my mother had been permitted to part from Sir George when the sight of him sickened her, everyone would have been spared the obnoxious consequences of my bastardy. Suppose that we stopped the pretence that the sordid financial business of matrimony is a holy sacrament, and permitted people to make their own arrangements?"

"Society would fall apart!"

"Instead of being mortared with misery, adultery, and hypocrisy. People already act precisely as they please, Guy. The only question is whether we all have to keep up the pretence they don't."

Guy attempted to formulate an argument, and found himself struggling. "Then maybe people should do better," he tried. "To *be* better, instead of simply indulging themselves."

"We have three score years and ten on this earth, if we're lucky. Is it so bad to devote some of that time to enjoyment? What do you achieve by restricting yourself from pleasures that hurt nobody?"

"But they do hurt people," Guy said. "Because, supposes aside, what my mother did hurt me and Amanda very much."

"That is quite true. And I don't argue for unbridled selfishness. Nevertheless, it is possible to live outside convention yet not hurt others."

"Like Lord Corvin?" Guy flashed, and instantly wished he hadn't. It wasn't up to him if Rookwood betrayed his lover with flirting.

"Corvin doesn't hurt people," Philip said, evidently not grasping Guy's meaning. "He's never forced himself on anyone in his life."

"He's ruined innocent women's reputations!"

"One. Just one. And, between us, that was by request. The lady in question was desirous of being ruined in order to escape an engagement that was repugnant to her, but on which her family insisted. Corvin made it impossible for any self-respecting suitor to approach her, and she remains blissfully unmarried and in sole possession of her fortune to this day. She's a very good friend."

Guy realised his mouth was hanging open. "Nobody would ask for that!"

"Believe me, if you were faced with the fiancé her swine of a father had arranged, you'd beg for it."

"I would never wish to be ruined," Guy said stiffly.

"That's a pity. You might enjoy it."

Guy felt like he'd swallowed his tongue. "I—what—"

"I beg your pardon." Philip was smiling in a way that was doing unnerving things to Guy's stomach. "Feel free to ignore that remark. Or, feel free to act on it. This is Liberty Hall."

"Libertine Hall, more like!"

Philip gave a crack of laughter. "Oh, very good. But we are not villains, despite popular opinion. I would like you to believe that."

"Then why are you called the Murder?" Guy asked, feeling that was a winning blow. "Lord Corvin killed a man, didn't he?"

The amusement dropped away from Philip's face. "That is not my story to tell. He had no choice, and it is not something of which he is proud, but—well. It was necessary; if he hadn't done it I should have, and that is all I shall say on the subject. As to our name, though, have you really not seen it?"

"Seen what?"

"Guy, Guy. Surely, to a countryman and a classicist, it should be obvious. Corvin, Rookwood, and Raven? We've been the Murder to ourselves since the three of us were boys."

Guy looked at him blankly, wondering what classics had to do with anything, then understanding stirred. "Corvin," he said. "From *corvus*, crow. And rooks and ravens are of the same family— For heaven's sake, you're a murder of crows. That's appalling."

"I thought you'd get it," Philip said with satisfaction. "May I say that Corvin has been landing us in trouble with this sort of joke for *years*."

"That is outrageous. Why on earth would you lead people to believe the worst possible things of you for a pun?"

"You've met him."

"You do it too."

"It's a peculiar thing," Philip said, "but when one is taunted for years as a notorious bastard, say, or grows up to parents who struggle to remember one's name, or is treated as a tradeable commodity rather than a human being, one can easily decide that society may go to the devil. I spent eighteen years as the object of society's contempt because of my birth, and am ever liable to find myself at the wrong end of its arbitrary laws. Why would I seek its praise, or accept an approval that was finally offered simply because my brother died?"

They had reached the thin treeline that separated the grounds from the fields beyond, and were walking in the dappled-gold green shade. Guy's mind was too full to think. Too full, he dimly realised, even to worry. He'd thought this conversation might be embarrassing or dreadful; it had gone infinitely beyond that, into vast uncharted waters, as though he'd nervously taken his boat onto the river and found himself on the Pacific Ocean.

"You were lucky," he said at random. "With the names, I mean. Three crows."

"John's name is deliberate. The old viscount named him Raven as a jest when they bought him."

"Bought," Guy repeated.

"Naturally; how else would he have grown up with us? He was meant to be a pageboy, but the fashion changed and Lady Corvin forgot about his existence. Corvin has no siblings, and liked having someone to play with, so John remained."

"He isn't still a, uh, a slave." Guy felt uncomfortable even saying it. He knew people brought slaves to England, of course, but he'd nevertheless always thought of human bondage as a remote thing, a horror that happened on hot islands a long way away. To think of someone he knew being enslaved—not a crowd of faceless victims, or an image on a china plate, but John Raven, a man who smoked cheroots and got paint-smears on his cuffs and argued with his friends—was as jarring and unnatural as to consider himself subjected to the same thing.

"Good God, no. Corvin had him emancipated at fourteen, once he was old enough to make his will law."

"So you all grew up together?"

"Almost exclusively. Corvin and I were sent to school for a year at eleven, but that left John alone, and I didn't enjoy being the butt of schoolboy humour, so he decreed that we would have tutors at his home instead, all three of us."

"How did he decree that? Guy asked. "That is, surely his parents would have decided?"

"They rarely remembered we were there," Philip said. "Lord Corvin was—to say *uninterested* barely scrapes the surface. His lady was pleasant but almost continually drunk."

"Good heavens!" Guy said, as shocked by Philip's casual tone as his words. "Really?"

"Oh, indeed. When I was twelve, I encountered his lordship, the then viscount, on the stairs. It was the first time I had met him since my arrival in the house. He looked at me, puzzled, and said, 'Are you Octavian?' I said no, I was Philip Rookwood. He looked blank. I said, 'I live with you,' and he nodded vaguely and went on his way. I believe I saw him twice more in the six years before his death."

"Oh," Guy said, and then, "Octavian?"

"Corvin's first name. Do not, if you value your life or mine, let him know I told you. We called him V before he inherited, as a compromise."

Guy could understand that. "So that's how you're the Murder." Three parentless boys holding together, standing for one another and helping one another stand. Guy imagined what it might have been like to lean on someone, to have a friend, when he'd been entirely alone. "You were awfully lucky, all of you," he said without thinking, and caught himself. "I beg your pardon. I didn't mean that."

Philip shrugged. "You probably should. I came to the household when not a soul on earth cared if I lived or died, and found the friends of a lifetime. Corvin is dripping with wealth and unencumbered by expectation or obligation, which most people would consider the height of fortune. As to John—well, that's harder to say. If the elder Lord Corvin hadn't ordered a present for his wife, perhaps John would have had a free life on his native soil in the bosom of his family. Or perhaps he'd have endured years in some filthy hell of a plantation. We'll never know."

"He doesn't know where he's from?"

"He can't remember anything. He was only four when he came here. We tried to find something out when we were old enough, but the records had been lost or thrown away; we couldn't even discover which ship brought him to these shores, far less where it had come from."

Guy couldn't imagine not knowing one's family. He lived in a house that had belonged to his great-grandparents; he had a family Bible with a list of thirty names in the flyleaf; he had Amanda, and a life deeply rooted in the earth of his native shire, and the remnants of an extended family even if he and Amanda were in disgrace with it. What would it be like to live without those foundations? "That's dreadful."

"He'd tell you that others have a great deal more to repine about. I'm not sure how I came onto this subject."

Nor was Guy. He had thought this would be some dreadfully embarrassing exchange, to be kept as brief as possible, and instead they were strolling, chatting together like intimate friends. He needed to drag the conversation back to where it ought to be. "Well, you've explained your, uh, friendships. And I see that you must be very fond of one another."

"Deeply."

"Then that's all very well, and none of my business," Guy said firmly. "And I've nothing more to add except that—well, in our acquaintance you've said several times that one can have, uh, unconventional morals yet not be selfish and still tell right from wrong, and be true to people who deserve your loyalty. I hope that's the case, and I also hope I will always live up to my own morals, which *are* conventional. Thank you for clearing the air and I'm sure we need to change for dinner now."

Philip's brows slanted. "I feel I have been rebuked. May I ask—"

"It really isn't any of my business, and I must go in," Guy said, and set off at a slapping pace, not waiting to see whether he was followed.

Chapter Six

"Not to state the obvious," Corvin remarked, "but I can't help noticing you haven't got the little Frisby into bed yet."

"Thank you for your restraint. I should hate it if you stated the obvious," Philip said, somewhat testily. "It would be so dull."

"Temper, temper," John said, puffing out smoke.

They were upstairs. Guy had retreated to his sister's side after dinner, accompanied by David, Sheridan, and Harry, who were to give the woman nightmares by telling her all about historical horrors. George and Ned were absorbed in the new piece; the sound of piano and violin drifted up from below. Philip, John, and Corvin had gathered in the parlour-cum-studio upstairs, feeling—on Philip's part at least—rather snubbed.

"I did my best," Corvin added. "All but pushed you into his arms."

"Have you considered he might not want Phil in his arms?" John enquired.

"Of course he does. Look at him, the poor boy is smitten."

"Smitten, yes. Game for a tupping is another matter. We're in the country."

John loathed the countryside. He resented being stared at as though he were a raree-show, and had been known to respond uncharitably when people asked Philip or Corvin, "Does he speak English?" It was yet one more reason they brought their own staff and

admitted no visitors. Philip had heard David out on the topic of
Amanda Frisby's need for entertainment but put his foot down about
Yarlcote guests. She could have as much company from the assembled
Murder as she wished and Guy allowed; he was not filling the house
with gawpers at his friends' cost.

"Country folk fuck," Corvin said. "Well, they must; it's not as if
other entertainments present themselves. Plant things, dig things, knit
things, fuck things. Make cheese."

"Cheese?"

"They may do in general," John said, before Philip could be
dragged down this particular byway. "Fuck, I mean. But I bet you the
plank doesn't."

"He's not a plank," Philip said. "There's more to him than meets
the eye."

"I thought the whole point of this conversation was that anything
more *hasn't* met your eye."

"Not yet, perhaps," Corvin said. "Put some effort in, Phil, it's a
matter of time."

"Achieving what?" John asked. "Serious, now. For one thing he's
a Frisby, for another he's a neighbour and we talked about fouling
your own nest. You don't want to come back here and learn your
labourers have downed tools because he's spread word all over the
county."

"I don't think he'd do that. And, since he walked in on me and
Corvin in flagrante, that cat is well out of the bag anyway."

"And for a third," John went on without remorse, "what about
him? Bloke's a bag of nerves, doesn't look like he knows what to do
with his own prick, let alone yours. What are you going to do, give him
a few lessons and then get in the carriage and drive away for another
six months?"

"A few lessons might be what he needs," Corvin said. "You
normally argue for knowledge, rather than ignorance, John."

"Yes, well, some people are quick learners, and some people spend the rest of their life blue-devilled and fearing damnation because they decide they committed a terrible sin and there's nobody to tell them otherwise."

Philip sighed. "I have thought of that, you know."

"Then why not just leave him be?" John demanded. "Are you that bored?"

"Oh, don't be silly," Corvin said. "Phil's not bored, the very opposite. He's *interested*."

John twisted round to examine Philip. "Really? Nah."

"He is."

"No he isn't. He's never interested."

"I am here, in this room," Philip said. "Sitting next to you."

Corvin ignored that. "Interested. What's interesting about the plank, Phil?"

"He is not a plank. I don't know. I think he has a good mind under the swaddling blankets of convention, and a depth of feeling. A delightful mouth, you must have noticed. And a great deal of courage."

"Courage?" John said. "Bloke looks like a scared rabbit nine-tenths of the time."

"But stands up for his sister despite being afraid," Philip said. "And, I suspect, doesn't have many friends around here, if any. As one would not, if his schooldays were anything like mine, and they were probably worse. The sins of the mothers visited upon the children. Is there something against Amanda Frisby's name, Corvin?"

"Good Lord, how should I know? Why do you ask?"

"Something he said. I wonder— Well, anyway. Let's say I have fellow feeling for him."

"That doesn't have to lead to feeling the fellow, though," John said, making Corvin yelp with laughter.

Philip glared at them both. "You are no help. Either of you."

"What assistance do you want, oh light of my life?" Corvin asked. "I did try to lead your horse to water."

"That didn't help in the slightest, and don't do it again. John is right; I'm not going to cause trouble for someone who has quite enough on his plate as it is."

"Not even if he wants you to?" Corvin gave him a sideways look. "You might be his only opportunity, you know."

"I'm not a charitable institution for the relief of frustration," Philip said. "And some people consider their moral principles more important than the call of their pricks, *Corvin*."

"Moral principles," John muttered. "Moral cowardice, more like."

"For God's sake, let him alone," Philip snapped. "It's all very well for us, isn't it? It was certainly very well for me, with you two to show me the ropes and a title falling into my hands. I grew up armoured against all the things he fears, the stones the world throws at one, and he didn't, so I'm not going to call him a coward for flinching. And nor, my friend, are you."

John had his hands and his eyebrows raised high. "Fine. I hear you. I take it back."

Corvin didn't comment. He did, however, interlace his fingers behind his head and begin whistling. His musical skills did not match his appreciation of the art, and it took a moment for Philip to identify the tune as "Love Will Find Out the Way."

He told Corvin to sod off. It didn't relieve his feelings at all.

Guy was hiding with his sister again the next morning. Philip found things to do in the study—this was not at all the same as lying in wait, despite John's sarcastic comments on the subject—and caught his guest as he emerged into the corridor.

"Guy. Marvellous. I wondered if you might introduce me to your sister today. I feel entirely remiss in my duties as a host."

That was, as intended, impossible to refuse. Guy begged a half-hour's grace, manfully meeting Philip's gaze as he did it, and alerted Miss Frisby to an impending visitor, and very soon Philip was once again in the sickroom with Amanda and Guy Frisby.

Miss Frisby awake proved to be a very vibrant individual. Like her brother, her features were by themselves no more than moderately pleasing to the eye; it was animation that made her attractive, and she was very animated indeed. She had darkish brown hair, simply dressed, sparkling brown eyes to Guy's hazel, and a generously plump form of the sort that both John and Corvin liked, and she was scanning Philip with fascinated examination. He had a vague feeling she might take notes at any moment.

Guy made the introductions with an understandable stiffness. Philip bowed over her hand. "Miss Frisby. A belated welcome to Rookwood Hall, and please accept my sympathy for the circumstances of your visit."

"Thank you. And I am terribly sorry for trespassing on your land, and now invading your house so. I dare say you may think I had my just deserts."

She had her splinted leg attached to a block, which was in turn attached to two bricks hanging off the end of the bed. It looked excruciating. "On the contrary," Philip said. "I can only apologise for whatever it was that caused your horse to throw you. I shall order the rabbit holes filled at once."

"It was a squirrel. Bluebell was startled."

"In that case, I shall have them all shot."

Miss Frisby gurgled with laughter, to his satisfaction. "Please don't. The poor squirrels, and poor Bluebell. I was so glad she wasn't harmed. Quite seriously, Sir Philip, Guy told me not to overwhelm you with thanks, but I am very sorry, and very grateful for your hospitality, to me and to my brother. Dr. Martelo tells me we will be imposing on you for an absurd length of time, and I feel terribly awkward to spoil your party."

"Parties can be repaired more easily than bones," Philip said. "Don't give it another thought. Speaking of the doctor, he has advised me at length, as is his wont, about the need to keep your spirits up in the face of whatever Gothic tortures he's inflicting on you." Amanda gave a startled yelp of laughter that sounded almost alarmed. Guy went instantly red. Philip scanned the sentence for indecency, couldn't detect anything that would bring a blush to a reasonable cheek, and gave a mental shrug. "Is there anything I can provide—?"

"Oh, not at all!" Amanda said earnestly. "Mr. Street and Mr. Salcombe have been telling me the most wonderful things about rocks and—what's the word?—fossilised things. Animals in stone, you know. It's given me the most marvellous ideas for— That is, it's wonderfully interesting. And Mr. Caulfield played the violin for me and explained how it works, and Dr. Martelo is telling me all about medicine, and Lisbon, and his travels, and really, breaking my leg has been the most fascinating time I've had in *years*."

Philip threw back his head and laughed. "Miss Frisby, you may have hit on the answer for reluctant scholars."

"If you're suggesting we should break schoolboys' legs to make them attend…" Guy said, then paused with a comical look of consideration that sent Amanda into a fit of gurgling and made Philip laugh again.

He stayed for half an hour, thoroughly enjoying himself, although aware of the maid's disapproving presence in the corner. Amanda Frisby was a joy in herself, but it was her effect on Guy that Philip liked most. After his initial wary guard-dog hackles had flattened, he'd relaxed in her presence, joking and laughing, his changeable eyes bright with pleasure. That was delightful to watch, and Philip knew an urge to see if he could elicit the same unselfconscious enjoyment, but there was something else too, something that underlay every interaction of the pair.

Guy loved his sister. It was as simple and complex as that. Guy loved his sister overwhelmingly, and Amanda Frisby was bright and confident and happy in the way people were when they had never doubted in their hearts that they were loved. In the way, in fact, her older brother was not.

Guy had given her that certainty. Philip was sure of it, and the knowledge felt like a clenched fist in his chest.

He bowed out reluctantly after that half-hour, promising to visit again and to order her a selection of novels and periodicals. Guy stayed with her, but emerged for luncheon, and Philip caught him in the hallway after they'd eaten, and when he didn't feel irritatingly aware of Corvin and John's carefully neutral expressions.

"I am quite sure it's time for your mandated fresh air," he said. "David will have your hide otherwise."

"I thought I'd go for a proper tramp," Guy said. "Up to the Gallows Oak, perhaps."

Philip had no idea what that was. "Perfect. I feel like stretching my legs myself. I shall join you."

"It will probably be very stony." Guy shot a look down at Philip's Hessians, which were well polished and had rather pleasing tassels. "And thorny. And it's a good four miles each way."

"I detect a challenge," Philip said. "Wait for me while I change."

"Uh—"

"Even better, there's John. Introduce him to Miss Frisby, would you? David has insisted she be kept amused and entertained." He gave John an assessing look, then shrugged. "Needs must. I suppose you could talk about drawing."

John responded in equally uncomplimentary fashion, but took Guy off to make the introductions. Philip changed, reflecting he'd managed that rather neatly, and set off with Guy in his second-best boots, feeling as close to a countryman as ever he did, which was not greatly.

It was a lovely day for a walk. The early summer sunshine was warm but not oppressive, there was a breeze, and the shady lanes of Yarlcote were shot with green and gold light.

"What is this Gallows Tree to which we head?" Philip asked after a few moments of nothing but birdsong and the scuff of feet. "It sounds rather gloomy for such a pleasant afternoon."

"It's just a tree on a hill. Very good for climbing, for children, and you get a wonderful view."

"And the name?"

"We used to hang people from it, or so they say, but that was stopped years ago."

"I am relieved. Any particular reason?"

"Well, it's hardly proper legal procedure. Oh, you mean, what were they hanged for? Terrible bloody murders and highway robbery, that sort of thing. Or at least, that's what I think, but you know how children invent things to scare one another. I told Amanda any number of ghastly tales. We used to sit in the branches with apples and a hunk of bread and I'd make up stories for her, until she was old enough to make up stories for me. Hers were far worse. She gave me nightmares once. I woke up screaming and babbling about Rawhead and Bloody Bones, and Nurse wanted to know where I'd heard such a thing, and I was too embarrassed to say my eight-year-old sister had scared the daylights out of me. She has always had the most lurid imagination." His lips were curved in a smile that Philip would bet he didn't realise he was wearing.

"Miss Frisby is a remarkable young lady," Philip observed. "She's better company with a broken leg than most people in full health."

"Thank you," Guy said. "She is, isn't she? I—well, she's the best sister a man could ask for. I'm awfully proud of her."

"I can see why. She has a lively mind, intellectual curiosity, a great deal of charm, and courage on top of all. She reminds me very much of you."

Guy's mouth dropped open. "What?"

"I said—"

"I heard. I mean— Why does she remind me of you? I mean, you of me?"

Philip counted on his fingers. "Lively mind, intellect, charm, courage. I think that was all."

Guy shook his head. "That's not like me."

"It's very like you. The difference is, I suspect, that Miss Frisby grew up with an older brother to cherish and protect her from the world's blows, and you did not. It makes a great difference when one is shielded from these things, as I know; it made all the difference in the world when I came to live with Corvin. I don't know how it is to be the one doing the shielding: I never had to do that. But I do know that it wears one down when one's life is at the mercy of people who ignore their responsibilities."

He was guessing; Guy's long silence told him he'd guessed right. Philip glanced over, saw the man had his face averted, and looked away. If they were really going to walk eight miles in total to see a tree, he had time.

"It does rather," Guy said at last, sounding stifled. "I don't know why we're talking about me. There are surely more interesting subjects."

"You interest me."

"It's kind of you to say so. I didn't really expect a Rookwood to be kind—uh—"

"Quite. No, don't apologise, there's really no need."

"I am sorry, though," Guy said. "The accidental remarks are almost as bad as the deliberate ones. I had a friend at school who would say things like, 'Does your mother know you're out?'—just jokes, you know, but he'd look at me and apologise every time, and it rubs rather."

"We were in a gambling hell of the worst sort once," Philip said reminiscently. "A filthy hole, full of sharps. There was a fellow there with a gentleman's birth and upbringing, if not manners. He swore continually, and every time he called someone a bastard he looked over at me, winked, and said, 'No offence.' He did it perhaps four times. On the fifth occasion, Corvin leaned forward, said, 'No offence to you either,' and threw a full glass of gin in his face."

Guy gaped. "Was that when—you know?"

"Good God, no, it wasn't a killing matter. He leapt up to take Corvin by the throat, reasonably enough, so John punched him in the head, which brought the conversation to an end, and the doormen dragged him out by the heels."

"Oh. That's, uh…"

Philip grinned. "I can't have shocked you. We are the Murder, after all."

"Yes, but I'd rather got used to the idea that you and your friends *aren't* the disreputable set everyone says."

"Oh, I think we're disreputable by most standards. I don't think we're wicked, but public opinion doesn't pay much attention to that."

"It's unfair."

"Not in our case. We've cultivated public perception like a rare orchid."

"I don't understand why," Guy said. "That is, I suppose I understand that you don't care to win good opinions, but why would you deliberately court bad ones?"

"Well, Corvin enjoys the attention, and it's been of immense professional help to John. It's something of a dogfight for anyone to succeed in his line of work. His dubious aristocratic connections and the whiff of brimstone gave him an edge, which his talent for excoriating humour turned into a blade. As for me, I find Society's cold shoulder saves a great deal of time. It keeps matchmakers at a distance, and I prefer to socialise with people who are either like-minded or open-minded."

"I'm not sure I'm either of those things."

"You saw me with Corvin, and didn't run to the nearest magistrate to demand the full force of the law."

"I might have done, though. Shouldn't you be more careful?"

"I am," Philip said. "I don't let judgemental, narrow-souled, ignorant people over my threshold. And if I had found myself afflicted with one in your person, I assure you I'd have…" He considered. "Probably locked the door."

Guy made a strangled noise. "You could be arrested! Does that not bother you?"

"In terms of the risk and inconvenience, yes. As a point of moral principle, no. I see no crime in doing as I please with my own body. If it was good enough for the Greeks, the Romans, and the Spartans, it's good enough for me."

Guy opened his mouth, stopped, and held up a finger, asking for thinking time. Philip let him think, strolling on down the lane. They'd emerged from the shade and the sun was bright, the gentle rise of the landscape around them very green. Philip had travelled the far more dramatic landscapes of Europe: mountains, valleys, forests, and foaming rivers, operatic in their beauty. England felt more like a long, slow breath.

"I see what you mean," Guy said at last. "That is—I suppose you don't want to argue about how the New Testament has replaced the teachings of the ancients."

"I'm game if you are," Philip lied. "But I don't believe anything is good or bad because I am told so by authority. We find ourselves on this earth with a capacity for reason and a wealth of history from which to learn. I believe we are obliged to think for ourselves, and reach our own conclusions about what is right and wrong, which may not be the conclusions foisted on us by church or law."

"We still have to obey the law."

"If a man with a pistol tells us what to do, we will probably obey him too. That doesn't make it right, only convenient."

"Yes, but... All right, say I agree. Just for the sake of argument. Suppose we say there is no harm in—in intimacy of that sort, between men, outside marriage. Do the other precepts of morality not apply?"

"Which precepts? I would say that if all parties have a free choice—"

"Yes, but what about—about fidelity? If there is no marriage, I mean?"

"I don't think either of us is in a position to argue that marriage is a guarantee of fidelity."

"Perhaps not." Guy was decidedly red in the face, and not just because the road was winding notably upward. "But it should be, shouldn't it? I mean, if one has made a promise?"

"A forced promise is no promise," Philip said. "Every day women are required to love, honour, and obey men of poor character, whom they frequently barely know. If they don't love and there's nothing to honour, they can hardly be expected to obey with grace. Or to stay faithful to men who show no inclination to reciprocate, come to that."

"No, no, no," Guy said. "I won't have that argument. 'It's all right if everybody else does it'? That way lies every sort of wrong. If you're going to discard conventional morality, you have to offer better."

"Define 'better'." Philip was enjoying this enormously. Guy had forgotten his nerves in the urge to talk, and was evidently thrashing out ideas in his own head as well as arguing. "Who is to say that fidelity is a good in itself, rather than a means to secure the inheritance of property to the paternal line? Why should we confine ourselves to one person only?"

"Because it's right!" Guy cried out, stopping and swinging round. He looked actually distressed. "Because if someone loves you, truly loves and—and adores you and gives you their heart, and you disregard that gift, that affection to—to approach others for your own pleasure, that's not right. Not for man or woman or anyone. It's betraying someone who loves you, and that's cruel, and I wouldn't expect it of—" He snapped his mouth shut, colour flaming treacherously over his cheeks.

"Expect it of whom?" Philip asked, and realised with a tingle across his skin that he might be able to guess. "Someone who you think has been kind?"

Guy turned his face away. Philip cast his mind back, felt a brief urge to kick himself, and sent the absent Corvin a heartfelt curse.

"Guy." He waited for the man to turn back, which he did with visible reluctance. "I think we may have been speaking at cross purposes. Are you under the impression, at all, that Corvin and I are lovers in more than the physical sense? That I have his heart?"

"I didn't mean to overhear," Guy said stiffly. "It's none of my business."

Philip had no idea what part he'd witnessed, but he knew Corvin's lovemaking well enough. "If anything you overheard led you to imagine that Corvin and I have any sort of quasi-matrimonial relationship, you couldn't be more wrong. He's very prone to endearments." *Beloved, my sweet, my angel.* "John says he does it because it's easier than remembering all the names. That's a gross slur," he added hastily, lest Guy have an apoplexy. "But not entirely inaccurate in principle. He is very dear to me, but I assure you that there is no question of fidelity, or wish for it, on his part or mine."

"Then why were you—" Guy blurted out.

"Amusement. It's a pleasant way to spend one's time."

"Is that all? We're men, not beasts. Shouldn't we strive for more than *amusement?*"

"Undeniably we should, but I don't see why that should rule amusement out entirely. 'To everything there is a season; a time to embrace and a time to refrain from embracing.' Ecclesiastes."

"'The devil can cite Scripture for his purpose'," Guy said. "Shakespeare."

"Oh, very good. But, quite seriously, I don't believe that any reasonable deity would create humankind with the sexual urge and then damn us for using it. Using it poorly, or unkindly, yes. But not at all."

"That's what marriage is for. Or should be, at least."

"And for those of us, men and women, not made for marriage?"

"I don't know why you say 'those of us'." That didn't sound challenging or aggressive. It sounded very like a question.

"For the moment, consider it wishful thinking," Philip said. "Let me be frank. I find you intriguing, and extremely appealing, and delightful company, and very much a man who deserves more pleasure in his life. If you'd like to take that pleasure with me, I'd be honoured. If you aren't so minded, don't take offence at the offer, and I shan't at the refusal. And if you decide you'd prefer Corvin, for example, I shall bow out like a gentleman, although I shall probably kick him in the shins at some point from pure envy."

Guy's eyes were huge, catching the green of the lush lands around them. Philip smiled into them. "You are entirely lovely and I'd like to prove that to you, but only if you wish. And now we are going to walk on, and you can tell me what you think when you've found out what it is."

He set off. Guy was stock still, but hurried to catch up in a scrape of stones and dust.

"Is that the tree in question?" Philip asked, pointing at a huge, bare-branched tree some way away, on top of a hill.

"What? Yes."

"It looks less leafy than I'd expected."

"It was struck by lightning, several times. I really don't want to talk about trees now. How on earth am I supposed to reply to what you just said?"

"Exactly as you prefer. You could say no, and I shan't approach the subject again. Or you could say you'd like to think about it, and do so for as long as you need. Or you could say yes, and allow me to expand your knowledge beyond the pages of Suetonius and Catullus.

May I add, though, that 'yes' now is not 'yes' forever. You have the prerogative of changing your mind."

They walked on a few more steps. "I'm sorry," Guy said at last. "I've never had a conversation like this in my life and I've no idea how one ought to conduct it and I don't really have any idea what you're offering me, or asking of me. I've only ever read about, uh, amours in novels, and this is not like the novels."

"Not the generally available ones, certainly," Philip said. "It really is quite simple, you know. I'm entirely charmed by you, and I've been wondering for some time how you might react if I kissed you. Any thoughts?"

"I don't know," Guy whispered.

"Between us, and feel free to tell me to mind my own business, have you ever been kissed?"

Guy shook his head, looking away in obvious embarrassment. Philip sighed. "People are so obtuse. I shouldn't let it worry you. We all have to start somewhere, if we start at all, which is not compulsory."

Guy made a stifled noise. "Is it not hard, just—just making all your own rules to live by?"

"Near impossible I should think, if you're alone. I don't have the courage or the intellect of the philosophers who change the world, although I dare say each of them stood on the shoulders of giants themselves. Had I been alone, I should probably have made some miserable, resentful attempt to fit into the preordained rules and restrictions. One must when there is no alternative, and I suppose a life of stifled endurance is better than none. But I wasn't alone."

Guy turned his face away. They walked on in silence, amid the sound of birdsong and the chatter of jays, the low hum of insect life busily working around them, Guy's harsh breaths as he struggled for control. Philip would have pulled one of his friends into a hug without a second thought. He'd learned physical affection from Corvin, albeit late in his childhood and with horrible awkwardness, and he was far more aware than the others of the impact of a loving or kindly touch, and how long some people might go without feeling such a thing.

They walked up the hill to the great tree, the silence stretching out between them but not, Philip thought, uncomfortably. He was content to be silent when someone needed to think, and Guy was very clearly thinking.

The Gallows Oak was an impressive skeleton of a tree. A long blackened gash jagged down the top of the trunk, but even so a few green leaves sprouted from odd branches. Evidently the oak wasn't quite prepared to give up.

Philip stood with the tree behind him and took in the view. The Yarlcote countryside stretched ahead of him, rising and falling in gentle curves of green edged with darker hedges or stone walls. They had gained enough height over the walk that one could see it as a landscape, and also that Philip's thighs were aware of the unusual effort.

"I should bring John here," he remarked. "I don't know if he'd change his mind about the countryside, but he'd like this."

There was an answering scrabble behind him. Philip turned and saw that Guy had seated himself on a thick branch, swinging his legs like a schoolboy.

"Good God. What are you doing up there?"

"We always used to sit here," Guy said. "You get a better view and it's peaceful. I can come down if you need."

Philip gave him a narrow look. "You appear to be suggesting I can't climb a tree."

"Can you?"

"I don't know. I haven't tried. All right, where does one put one's hand?"

Guy pointed out a helpful knot and a stub of a branch. Philip followed instructions, slipped twice, cursed, put some effort into it, and found himself, after a brief, undignified scramble, more or less up at the branch. Guy extended a hand. Philip grabbed it—

I haven't touched him before.

—hung on for dear life, and managed to twist round and plant his arse next to Guy's. Regrettably, he had to let the man's hand go to do it.

And there they sat, in a *tree* for God's sake, legs dangling, looking out at England. Philip was conscious that the climb and the lichen on the old dry bark had probably played hob with his breeches, that he would appear ridiculous to any passer-by who recognised him as Rookwood of Rookwood Hall, and that he wouldn't want to admit to John or Corvin what he'd been doing. *How fortunate that I don't care*, he told himself, the old saying that one could repeat until it was true.

Except that Guy was looking serene here in a place he loved, and he'd been on the back foot since Amanda's accident. This was good. It would probably be even better if Philip underscored his own ineptitude by falling out of the tree or some such, but he felt they had enough broken legs to be getting on with, so he shuffled a bit to seat himself more securely.

"You're very well there. The branch won't break."

"I'm glad to hear you say so. I suppose you could climb to the top if you wanted."

Guy twisted to give the branches above them an assessing look. "I have done, though not for years. You can see for miles if you reach the top, and the tree sways under you like a cradle in the wind. We'd sit here for hours, Amanda and I, watching the clouds and listening to the birds. We once sat here in a summer storm, getting soaked to the skin, because she wanted to know what it would be like. Nurse was furious— the clothes, but also the danger of lightning—but it was worth it. It's a wonderful place to think."

"I must own dozens of trees," Philip said. "And Corvin has vast tracts of the things, and yet it's never occurred to me to climb them. That feels like a serious omission."

"You were probably too busy doing disreputable things."

"Nameless crimes and Godless orgies and all the other evils people think I come here to pursue."

"What did you come here to pursue?"

"My original quarry was Silesian white beet," Philip said. "Although it does now seem to be you."

"You don't give up easily, do you?"

"You haven't asked me to. If you'd rather I dropped the subject for good—"

"No," Guy said, very quietly. "Don't do that."

Philip had two stalwart, handsome, experienced friends game for more or less any activity he might suggest and, in Corvin's case, some he'd never think of unaided. It was ridiculous that something as trivial as that soft permission should constrict his chest with anticipation. "That would be preferable for me. I'd rather like to expand at some length on what I find irresistible about you. Are you aware how much your eyes change colour in different lights? And the way you blush—yes, exactly like that. The colour sweeps across your face so readily and it makes me wonder how responsive the rest of you might be. Your mouth, regarding which I think the less of John as an artist because he hasn't abandoned his canvas to paint it. And the fact, above all, that you're listening to me rhapsodise on your charms and you're smiling. I did say you were like your sister. Your beauty hides itself away, invisible until you decide someone is worthy of seeing it. And then you smile, and it shines."

Guy's expression was living proof of that. He was blushing fiercely, and his eyes were bright, and Philip cursed every single impulse that had led them to the bare branches of the most visible landmark in the county, with a special malediction for the four-mile walk back to privacy and safety.

"Do you always talk like this?" Guy managed.

"Almost never."

"You needn't pretend. I do know you've plenty of, uh, experience."

"I do. It just hasn't been of the type that involves excruciatingly lengthy walks and climbing trees in order to win a hearing."

"I suppose that would be difficult in London."

"And time-consuming, though doubtless terribly healthy."

"What would you normally say?" Guy pressed.

The answer to that was, *Care for a fuck?* Philip doubted that would help his cause, and in any case, it wasn't actually true. It was what he'd say to John or Corvin, but this situation was in its way as foreign to his experience as it was to Guy's.

He took a breath. "To be quite honest, I haven't found myself in this precise situation before."

"Up a tree?"

"With an innocent. I've never seduced anyone until now. That's generally Corvin's job."

"Is that what you're doing? Seducing me?"

"I think I must be. Is it working?"

"It…might be." Guy shot him a look from under his lashes, glanced away almost at once. Philip had seen it done a hundred times, and far more skilfully, by paid boys and wondered why they bothered. Now he understood.

"You're very charming," Guy went on. "I'm sure you know that. And I'm quite sure you know precisely what you're doing when it comes to—to seduction. But I'd rather you didn't say things you didn't mean."

"I haven't," Philip said, somewhat indignantly. "I am, if anything, notorious for my refusal to utter polite lies. If I tell you you're lovely, you may believe I think it."

"My experience—well, not mine—that is, I believe that people, men, tend to say a great deal to get what they want. I would really prefer honesty. I don't know if I could tell if someone was lying to me, and I don't think that would be kind."

"No. If I recall correctly, the only promise I have ever made you on this matter is that I will take no for an answer. You have my word as a gentleman on that. Otherwise, what honesty do you want?"

"I'd like to know why you're, uh, seducing me," Guy said. "Because you've said lot of nice things but I'm not, well, Lord Corvin, and I'm not really sure what you want, or why me. And I would rather know. I don't much want to be made a fool of. I'm not saying you would do that," he added hastily. "We wouldn't be having this conversation if I thought so. But I would like to understand."

Philip exhaled. "Well. For one, I know you're not Corvin, but I fail to see how that is a point against you. I'm not Corvin either. I believe I just told you in some detail at least some of the reasons why I am going to these extreme and arboreal lengths; I might add that I very much liked the way you looked at me at dinner the other night, and during that uniquely interesting hour sitting for John, and I'd like to see that look again. No, I'd like to see that look satisfied, and if you would care to be relieved of your innocence, I want to be the man to do it. I think I could please you, Guy, and I should love to see you take pleasure from me." Guy shivered, a visible motion. "And if you ask why to *that*, well, any competent lover finds as much joy in giving pleasure as taking it, and I do hope I'm competent."

"I'm sure you are." Guy's voice sounded rather high.

"It isn't complicated, in the end," Philip said. "We eat, drink, and are merry, for tomorrow we die. Be merry with me?"

Guy nodded. It was silent, but it was heartfelt for all that, and Philip wanted nothing more than to get down from this damned obvious spot and find somewhere more discreet. Or, even just to be sure that no passing peasant could see them or was looking. He wanted to kiss Guy in the arms of this absurd tree, where he felt safe. He might have dared with Corvin, and be damned to anyone who might see; he wouldn't put Guy at risk in that way.

And, he realised, with the sun on his face and the land stretching out in front of him, he was enjoying this moment of awareness, and agreement, and quiet companionship. Everything happened as quick as you like in London: everything was available for the asking except time, which was always at a premium. He usually found the slower

117

rhythms and season-long deliberations of the country intolerable, and had spoken more than once about his desire not to die of old age waiting. Still, for now, he could take his time. There was no need to rush.

Chapter Seven

If Guy had been asked at any point in his entire adult life prior to this week how he might envisage himself speaking to Sir Philip Rookwood, "planning illicit amours" would have been the least likely answer imaginable, matched only in its implausibility by "up a tree". Yet here they were, unless Guy had taken ill and this was a detailed fever dream. Considering how heated he felt, it wasn't impossible.

He wasn't an idiot, even if he was inexperienced. He knew very well that rich London gentlemen toyed with country innocents for their entertainment; he'd heard enough ballads on the subject, and he was well aware that the erratic baronet with his unthinkable life wouldn't be staying in Yarlcote long, whereas Guy was here forever. Philip's words had made his skin tingle and his blood thump, but they were only words and, as he'd pointed out, held no promises.

But Guy wasn't a young lady who required promises. Far from it. He had carefully refused ever to think about the sort of feelings Philip evoked in him, let alone act on them, because the consequences were too terrifying, and because he wouldn't have had the faintest idea how to begin. And now he was staying in what might as well be an isolated castle for a period outside time, with its sinister master proving as unexpectedly hospitable as any fairytale beast. He was being offered something that might finally be an answer to the questions he couldn't ask and the longings he couldn't stem, and he was damn well going to do it. Whatever 'it' proved to be. Guy wasn't quite sure of that, practically speaking, but whatever it was, he would trust Philip, and snatch this chance because there wouldn't be another. He would not recoil in fear and spend the rest of his life wishing he'd been bolder. He'd done that too often.

It might prove calamitous; he could imagine a thousand ways in which it would. His mother had thrown her cap over the windmill and destroyed them all; it would be a bitter irony indeed if Guy too let himself be ruined at a Rookwood's hands. But he'd sat and listened to the Murder speak as they chose for hours, and it had felt as though he'd been in a box without even knowing it, and someone had taken a crowbar and pried off the top. Guy had blinked at first, and shied away from the light as too painful. Now he felt the urge to stretch.

Philip was apparently perfectly happy on the branch, contemplating the landscape. His well-cut and decidedly fashionable clothes were utterly incongruous in a blasted oak tree, but the sunlight haloed his fair hair and put sapphire into those cool eyes. Guy watched his profile, lost in wanting, and when Philip turned his head and smiled, Guy didn't look away.

"Shall we go back?" Philip suggested. "If you're ready. And if you can advise me on removing my person from this tree, because this is going to be inelegant."

It was indeed inelegant, and Philip swore impressively when he discovered a long scratch on his boot, but it didn't seem to impair his mood. He wasn't a precisely cheerful man so far as Guy could tell, his humour tending to the flippant or the sarcastic, but he seemed content to walk in silence, almost as though they hadn't agreed to…well. Nothing new to him, Guy supposed. No wonder he didn't look as though his every nerve ending was afire.

Guy cleared his throat as they walked down the hill. "Did you say beetroot?"

Philip shot him an amused glance. "I don't think I said anything, but if I had, it wouldn't have been that. I was thinking of an entirely different subject."

"I mean earlier," Guy ploughed on. "The reason you came here. Is that the white beet you're growing?"

"Indeed. With the right manufactory, one can extract sugar from it. The French are building their own domestic sugar industry as we speak."

"Actual sugar? Out of beets?"

"I assure you."

"But does it not taste of, well, beetroot?"

"It can be absolutely vile, yes," Philip said. "The strains, and indeed the manufacturing processes, are being refined yearly on the Continent. Domestic sugar production in the near future is a possibility, or should be. The French government is both mandating and funding their industry with a far-sighted approach to national sufficiency; you may guess for yourself if our own government is doing the same. Sugar production at home might mean less profits from the plantations, you see, and since the plantation owners sit in Parliament, we need not expect them to vote against their own interests. If we want to create an English sugar industry, we'll have to do it ourselves."

"So do you own a manufactory?"

"Corvin does, and we've a friend—an occasional guest of the Murder, not with us—who is an enthusiast of agricultural innovation and has studied the Silesian model. It can be done, I am certain of it: sugar not flavoured with human blood, as they say, but grown by free men, and sold at a price that more people can afford to pay. This may yet prove a white elephant, but we're giving it a try. Despite the lack of enthusiasm on the part of my steward, who is unconvinced."

"I don't think anyone quite understands why you're growing a worthless crop," Guy suggested.

"I know. He made that very point to me in explaining why I'm not getting a satisfactory yield."

"You could explain. Hold a demonstration, show them the process if you can do it there and then, let them see sugar come from beet. Taste it, even, if it isn't too beetrooty. I wouldn't have understood anything of what Mr. Street said about fossils if I hadn't had the stone creature in my hand. I think you could make people understand what it's for and believe in it if you took the time. You're awfully persuasive when you set out to be."

"So I hope," Philip said, with a smile that put all thoughts of root vegetables out of Guy's head.

The walk back home felt like part of the fever dream. One simply didn't agree to commit nameless and unlawful acts and then go for a pleasant country stroll with one's co-conspirator. But he had, and they were, and as they approached Rookwood Hall, Guy felt the nerves rising. What might be expected of him? What had he agreed to? What if he had, after all, made a mistake, if he found himself horrified, or incapable, or ashamed of his weakness, or ridiculed by the man who had exploited it?

The panic came on him with sudden, breath-stopping force as they walked up the drive, so dizzying that Guy grabbed at Philip's arm. He couldn't walk another step towards his doom, he had to say something—

And Philip's hand was on his, warm and gentle. "Guy? What's wrong? My dear, breathe, please. Just breathe. Do I detect second thoughts?"

Guy couldn't say no to that, and didn't want to say yes. He stared at his own fingers gripping Philip's sleeve, and the long slim fingers over his.

"Never anything against your will, your liking, or even your whim," Philip said. "I did give you my word, you recall. You are not bound to anything at all."

"Sorry," Guy muttered. "I just…"

"Nerves."

"Nerves," he agreed miserably.

"I wish I could say I know how you feel," Philip said, tugging him gently on, but veering off the drive and toward the gardens. "Or rather

I don't, because you look as though you feel rotten. I, by contrast, had Corvin showing me the ropes when I was sixteen or so, which made it a great deal easier. One can't panic with Corvin involved, he's too absurd and too warm-hearted. The only problem is that everyone falls in love with him, even when specifically and clearly warned that he won't reciprocate. I certainly did."

That cut through the gibbering in Guy's brain. "I thought you said—"

"I got better," Philip said. "I fell so hard that I feared I might die from what I couldn't have, and made an absolute copper-bottomed fool of myself for six months in which I tried even Corvin's patience to the limit—John has none to start with, so he was fairly trenchant about my idiocy—and then I got better. Because that's how life tends to work in all its aspects. We try things out, and make mistakes, and recover, and learn from our experiences. We live, we learn. There are no lifelong, life-ruining consequences to fear from a little private dalliance in my house, or under my aegis, and you cannot possibly be more absurd about matters than I've been in my time. Consider yourself shielded."

Guy nodded. "I suppose I'm being ridiculous."

"You aren't. You are, however, making a mountain out of—no, I'm not going to describe myself as a molehill. Let me rephrase that. Can you say 'stop'?"

"Stop?"

Philip stepped away, letting Guy's arm go. "And there you are."

"What do you mean?"

"Just that. You say stop, I stop. It is no more complicated than that."

He didn't sound impatient, or wheedling. He was simply explaining, in much the same way as he explained sugar beet, and it felt like a soothing salve to jangled nerves. Guy took a breath. "Thank you."

"Not at all," Philip said. "Well. Shall we sit out here a while, or would you care to accompany me inside?"

Guy dredged up his courage. "Let's go in."

They walked in silence, a few brisk strides. Guy could hear music from the sickroom, and assured himself, with a twinge of guilt, that Amanda didn't need him. He followed Philip up the stairs and around, not, to his relief, into the parlour where he'd seen Philip with Corvin, but up the little side stair. A door stood open at the top; Philip knocked anyway, then gestured Guy in to a very pleasant little sitting-room.

"If you'd care to lock the door, do," Philip said. "If you'd rather not, don't."

Guy did, leaving the key in the lock. His hands were rather shaky.

He turned. Philip was standing, waiting, watching him. Guy made himself meet those grey-blue eyes. "I'm, uh, not sure what I should do."

"Well, let's see. You might ask if you can kiss me."

"If I—?"

"You're doing this too, my dear. And you need my permission as much as I need yours."

"What do I say?"

"I think 'Can I kiss you?' would do very well."

Guy swallowed. "Can—can I kiss you?" It came out as a whisper.

"You can," Philip said. "Come here."

Guy closed the two paces between them, and found himself staring at a cravat, which was somewhat dishevelled after the walk and the tree. A gentle finger nudged his chin up.

"You've my permission," Philip said softly.

He'd assumed Philip would take the lead. Guy stood on the balls of his feet to make up the extra height, awkwardly tried to move his mouth to the right place and angle, and wobbled. Philip's hands came up, one steadying Guy's arm, one applying the gentlest possible pressure to the back of his head, and their lips met.

Met, and touched, pressing chastely together, and Guy had just enough time to wonder if this was what the fuss was about when he felt Philip's lips part against his. Guy's mouth opened in surprise rather than imitation, and then Philip was kissing him, mouth open, not hard but thoroughly. His mouth was moving, and the extraordinary thing was, so was Guy's, as if he knew how to do this all along. He felt the strong wet stroke of what had to be tongue, Philip's tongue in his mouth, and the idea sent a shudder directly to his belly. He tried to reciprocate, so strongly aware of his own tongue that it felt three times its normal size, and felt it touch Philip's. He pushed, tentatively, and felt Philip's tongue curl against his.

Guy wasn't sure how he could be doing this. He'd never kissed, he'd never so much as held hands with a girl, and now here he was with his mouth open to Philip's, and each slow stroke of lips and tongue felt like Philip reaching into his most intimate, private self. It might have felt like an invasion, except Guy had thrown the gates wide and welcomed him in.

His mouth opened on the thought, without his conscious intent, and Philip made a pleased noise that hummed in Guy's lips. He pressed harder, too, his mouth a little firmer, kisses a little hungrier, still slow, but now with an intent behind them that sent a shiver of anticipatory nerves and desire down Guy's spine. He couldn't help a little inadvertent sound of alarm. Philip stilled instantly, starting to move his mouth away, and that could not possibly happen now, so Guy grabbed his shoulders and pulled him in.

There was just a fraction of a second where Philip was completely still and Guy became aware that he might have been somewhat forward, and then Philip's hand tightened on the back of his head, not gentle at all, and Guy found himself hanging on to Philip's shoulders for dear life, because Philip was bending him backwards, other arm around his waist, his mouth ravaging and demanding and glorious. Guy was kissing and being kissed as wildly as anything he'd ever imagined, and oh God he was roused. He became aware of it very abruptly indeed, because Philip's thigh was pressed hard between his legs, and surely he would notice any second. Guy attempted to ease his hips back a little, to reduce the pressure of body contact, and failed.

Philip slowed, gave Guy one very deliberate open-mouthed kiss more, then lifted his head, not letting go his grip, but looking down with a smile. "Enjoying yourself?"

Guy didn't think he'd ever blushed harder. "I, uh, I'm—that is—"

Philip lowered his head, pressing his mouth to Guy's neck, sending exquisite shivers across his nerves. "You're meant to enjoy it," he murmured, moving his mouth up but not away, so the words vibrated against the skin. "You're meant to respond." A deliberate press of his thigh. Guy gave a sharp gasp, and another as Philip's tongue traced curves and lines on his neck. "You're meant to want me, and ache for me, and long for more, as I am quite, quite desperate for you. Am I pleasing you, Guy?"

"Yes. Oh, yes."

Philip's thigh shifted, rubbing against his trapped stand. "Do you want more?"

Guy had no idea what *more* would entail and wanted it anyway. "Yes. Please."

Philip smiled. "So polite. Let me know when you're desperate." He kissed up Guy's jawline, and then his teeth closed gently on the earlobe and Guy almost cried out with the shock of pleasure.

"Oh! *Oh.*" Philip's mouth was doing extraordinary things, and Guy's skin was more than tingling, the excitement almost overwhelming. He squirmed against Philip's thigh, setting off another wave of sensation, and heard himself whimper aloud.

"Christ, yes." Philip sounded ragged. "Oh, you beauty. I thought you were ripe for picking. My God."

"Please," Guy whispered.

"Anything. What?"

126

"I want—" He wanted Philip to keep doing what he was doing, and he wanted him to do the unnamed *more*, because his body was straining for it, and he wanted very much not to spend in his drawers, and that was an urgent concern. "I, uh..."

"I'm going to teach you to speak," Philip assured him. "It will make life a lot easier. I've my tongue in your ear and your cockstand against my leg. You can share your thoughts too. How may I serve you?" That wicked smile again. "Are you desperate yet?"

"I'm afraid I might spend," Guy blurted out, because that was slightly less humiliating than doing it. "Sorry. I don't want to stop, but—"

"We're not going to stop, dear heart. I'm going to please you till you can't stand up, starting here. May I touch you?"

Guy nodded. Philip moved his hands down, and then they were at the buttons of his breeches. He screwed his eyes shut.

"You don't have to watch," Philip said softly. "But I'm planning to commit the sight of you in my hand to memory. Let's get you out. Oh, good heavens. Lovely."

Guy half-looked, through half-shut eyes. He'd always found the sight of his member aesthetically displeasing: puny when flaccid, ungainly and undignified when roused. The Greeks had considered a large member a sign of low character and limited intelligence, and he could see why.

But Philip—cultured, sophisticated Philip—was looking down with a hunter's smile and no sign of distaste, and as Guy watched, he wrapped his manicured fingers around the straining shaft, sliding them up and down as though Guy's part was his own. Philip was touching him, *there*, and his other hand came around Guy's waist before he'd even realised his knees were like to give way. "You lovely thing. Hot in my hand. Ripe and ready and aching for pleasure, and waiting all this time for me to give it to you." His fingers were moving faster now, commanding Guy's pleasure, owning it. "Are you desperate now?"

"Yes! Philip, *please*—"

"Spend for me, beloved. I need to watch you spend."

Guy couldn't have stopped himself. The glorious sensation of Philip's sure fingers on his quivering piece, the outrageousness of those murmured words, the wetness still on his ear, which caught the faintest air current and tingled under it, most of all Philip's certainty that this was good and right, which was so overpowering that Guy simply let himself be told: all of that came together in an overwhelming rise of need that burst out of him, jerking and shuddering in pulse after pulse, until he collapsed, gasping, against Philip's strong shoulders.

All over the carpet. He'd self-polluted, or had Philip self-pollute him—no, that wasn't right—well, whatever you called it, he'd done it all over what looked like an old and fine carpet.

Which belonged to Philip, and he surely wouldn't have asked Guy to do it if he hadn't meant it. Although Guy wasn't quite sure why he'd wanted to watch that. Would he want to watch Philip spend, and hold him as he did it, even stroke that helpless response out of him?

Christ, yes, he would. He truly would.

"Thank you, Guy. That was beautiful." He felt Philip's lips brush his hair. "And thank you for trusting me with your pleasure. Could I persuade you to trust me a little more?"

Guy almost laughed. "I think you could persuade me to do anything."

"Oh, don't say that," Philip said. "Keep a critical mind at all times, that's my advice. Could we get this coat off?"

Guy found himself bare to the waist in short order, coat and waistcoat and linen all discarded, breeches still hanging open, sprawled on a couch as Philip stripped off his own shirt. He was pale, chest sprinkled with sparse golden-brown hair, much leaner than Guy's own compact build and thick muscles that betrayed his domestic work. Philip was all refinement, except for the way he spoke, and behaved, and thought.

He dropped to a knee by the couch, gently running a finger over Guy's chest, curving around the swell of muscle, then tapping lightly up to the nipple. "You may touch, if you like, or you can lie back and let me touch you. Do you think you could speak?"

"What should I say?"

"What pleases you. What you think you might like. What you're hoping I'll do, if you care to say it: you won't shock me, and I'll let you know if it's impractical. You could start with how this feels." He leaned forward, and licked Guy's nipple.

"God!" Guy yelped, the blasphemy coming to his tongue without volition.

"I'll take that as a yes." Philip's lips closed over the nub, which hardened almost painfully, tense with sensation. His head was bowed over Guy's chest; Guy dared to put his hand on the fair hair, running his fingers through it, felt Philip's purr of pleasure against his skin, even as fingers went to the other nipple, rolling it gently to hardness. He could feel his piece stirring again, which seemed implausible. Philip's hands and mouth were roaming and Guy let himself explore in return, wanting to touch more. "Philip?"

Philip raised his head. He was flushed, lips reddened. "Mmm?"

"Could—could I kiss you?"

"Yes," Philip said, with emphasis, rising to get a knee on the couch, which was of the sort without a back for most of its length. He more or less crawled over Guy, bracing himself with an arm, so they lay against one another, bare chest to chest, lips gently closing together, Philip's arousal a hard presence against Guy's thigh. He'd never been so close to another person in his life, and it seemed only natural to rock his hips forward.

Philip grunted into his mouth. "Christ."

"Was that wrong?"

"The opposite. If you squirm under me like that, you'll have me begging."

The very idea of squirming under Philip's weight went straight to all the over-sensitised areas of his body. Guy wriggled experimentally, heard Philip's deep groan, and could have shouted for triumph.

"I want to debauch you as thoroughly as any virgin has ever been debauched," Philip whispered. "I want to lick every last shred of innocence off you, piece by piece. Will you touch my prick?"

Guy nodded. Philip fumbled at his breeches; Guy reached down with tentative fingers, and found Philip's—prick, he supposed he should learn to call it, a rigid length encased in oddly soft skin, and stickily wet to the touch already. He moved his fingers as Philip had, and felt a thrill of power as his lover's face convulsed. "Is that good?"

"Very. Up and down. A little harder. Christ, yes."

"But mightn't you spend on me?" Guy blurted. There would be nowhere else for Philip's seed to go but between them, on his skin. His chest tingled at the thought.

"I might indeed, my sweet, and joyfully too. Or would you rather I didn't?"

Guy had no idea at all. Furtive nocturnal stickiness had always been a regrettable necessity, to be hastily concealed. To have Philip do that, deliberately— "I don't know. Um, do you want to?"

"Oh, I want to, very much indeed. I don't have to if you'd rather not."

"It's all right." Guy had no idea if it was anything of the kind, but he could hear the urgent desire in Philip's voice and the thought of pleasing him outweighed all else. "If you want, then do. Please do. I'd like it."

"Jesus Christ." Philip's voice was rather high. "Say that again. Ask me."

Guy couldn't previously have imagined himself asking that of anyone, but then, he hadn't imagined this business would involve nearly so much talking. He'd always heard coupling described as men *having their way* with their partners. The idea that one sought permission to do things, that one asked other people to do things to one...

It meant this was up to him, in his control. It meant that he could give pleasure to Philip, rather than Philip taking pleasure from him. He could say the words and let, *make* this thing happen.

"Spend on me," Guy whispered, moving his hand faster. "Please spend on me. I want you to."

"Christ Jesus *God*," Philip said, face contorting, hips jerking, and Guy felt the splatter on his skin with a surge of pure triumph. Philip grunted with something like pain and came down hard, hitting Guy's mouth with glorious clumsiness. They rocked together, sticky and sweaty, and kissed and stroked and mumbled incoherencies until Guy found he was thrusting up against Philip once more, his stand rising inexorably to attention.

Philip propped himself up on an elbow, hips heavy over Guy's with delicious pressure. "How's the debauching?"

"I think it's coming along quite well."

Philip snorted with laughter. "God, you're marvellous. You have no idea. My uncertain virgin, begging for my spend. I'm going to be thinking about that every solitary night for *years*."

Guy couldn't help a whimper at the picture that conjured up. Philip grinned down at him. "Do you like the idea? Me, bringing myself off, thinking about you with my hand on my prick?"

"Oh God."

"As I thought. And in the meantime, what are we going to do about this?" He moved his hips indicatively, thrusting against Guy's stand. Guy gasped; Philip all but purred. "Ah, the joy of youth. You've got a lot of time to make up, don't you? Two possibilities leap to mind. You could see how you feel on top of me. Put your cock between my legs, and get a sense of how it is to fuck a man. Or, alternatively, you could recline like the prince you are, and let me get my mouth to your prick."

"Your *mouth*?"

"You don't think I'm good with my mouth?" Philip leaned down, tongue flickering over Guy's ear with much the effect of before, mercilessly tormenting. "You wouldn't like that on your prick?"

"Do you really want to do that?"

"I'd love to do it, and I'd put a substantial sum on the probability that so will you, and on no very distant day. Why don't you think how it might feel to take me in your mouth while I show you how delicious you are?"

"I don't know how you say things like this." Guy felt almost envious as Philip slid down to the floor. To be so shamelessly free, so confident in saying such outrageous things, as though there was nothing embarrassing in doing *that*—

Then Philip's tongue curled around the head of his piece and Guy stopped thinking altogether. He stared down at Sir Philip Rookwood, baronet, performing an act for which he only knew the Latin name and even that was omitted from most dictionaries, mouth wet, with that look of intense absorption that Guy had wanted so much, and it was truly all for him. Philip kneeling, one hand on Guy's thigh, the other exploring between his legs with tantalisingly light strokes to untouchable places. Philip's lips closing over his member, and his head moving, so that Guy's piece slid into his mouth in a movement so obscene and animal and glorious he couldn't look away. He thrust up without meaning to, and felt Philip chuckle around his stand.

And dear God, yes, he wanted to do it. He wanted to kneel and let Philip do that to his mouth—no, he wanted to do that *to Philip*, take him in his mouth and make him feel this rising, burning need, the banked fire building and building as Philip tormented him until it erupted in a surge of heat that remade the world.

He lay back, chest heaving, Philip's mouth still on him, barely touching. He could feel Philip's throat work, and realised with a disturbed thrill that he was swallowing.

"That was wonderful," he said. "At least, for me it was."

"Oh, the same, believe me. I've been thinking of doing that for some time." Philip manoeuvred himself back onto the couch to lie by, or over, Guy. "It was a privilege. May I make an observation?"

"Um…yes?"

"You're probably going to start worrying that you made an almighty fool of yourself, said or did terrible things, and looked ridiculous. Accept my assurance now that you didn't." Philip brushed a kiss across his lips. He tasted odd, slightly astringent, and Guy realised with a shock that must be the taste of his own seed. "You have been generous and open-hearted and truly lovely, and please remember that I said so. I would like to stay in here with you doing nothing else for several days. Or weeks. I'm not suggesting your sister break another leg, but if she *wanted* to—"

"Philip!"

"But you hear me, yes?"

"Yes. Thank you."

Philip rested his head on Guy's shoulder. They lay in silence a moment, skin to skin, the rise and fall of chests coming into time. Lying with a man as with a woman, the Bible called it, and said it was an abomination. Guy had never lain with a woman, but he couldn't really see how the experience could be like at all, except in the closeness, and if it was wrong to lie close to someone and feel beloved—

Philip had called him that. *Beloved.* It was just a word, just the way he spoke, as he had spoken to Corvin, and doubtless others. Still, he'd said it, and Guy had felt it, and he was damned if he was going to let his habit of worrying spoil this charmed, forbidden interlude.

That resolution lasted until he was back in his room tidying himself up for dinner. Philip had helped him adjust his clothing, assuring him that he looked very well and it didn't matter if he didn't. Guy had accepted that blithely, gone back—thankfully without meeting anyone—looked at himself in the mirror, and almost had a conniption. His hair was a tangle, his face marked with the tracks of tears and saliva and the dust of the road, he was feverishly flushed, and his eyes bright. He looked different, he was sure. He looked as though he'd eaten the fruit of the Tree of Knowledge, and everyone would be able to tell it on sight.

Oh dear heaven, they'd know. What if Lord Corvin jested in the coarse way some men did? What if Philip was wrong and his other lover took offence? Why had he even done those things with a man who had another lover staying in the same house?

Guy grabbed the mantel. Philip had told him he'd feel like this, and given him words to remember, and Philip knew what he was about. He'd said, *Consider yourself shielded.* He wouldn't let Guy twist in the wind, having got what he wanted. Surely he wouldn't. Would he?

He managed to restore himself to decency and be down in Amanda's sickroom before the dinner gong was struck. She was sitting alone, absorbed in a book, but looked up with a smile that made him feel a swine for having all but forgotten her. "Guy! I thought you'd disappeared from the face of the earth."

"I'm sorry. I went for a walk."

"With Sir Philip, I know. David—Dr. Martelo told me. And I'm only teasing, it's marvellous you're making friends. Wouldn't it be lovely if we stayed on terms whenever he came down? You may take some time to yourself, Jane," she added at the maid's audible snort.

"Such nonsense," Jane said, rising. "This is a wicked house, and the sooner you're home and away from these people the better."

"It is *not* a wicked house and you're being very rude about our host and his friends," Amanda said.

"I've heard how they talk, miss. It's not right and it's not Christian."

"You don't sound very Christian yourself, talking that way about people who've been nothing but kind. Go and take some air." Amanda regarded the departing woman with a darkling eye. "Ugh, Jane is trying my patience. I've had one or another of the Murder in here most of the day, just to keep me entertained—Mr. Raven was here for an hour or more and he says I could draw perfectly well if I tried and he'll bring me some pencils—and she just sits in the corner and sniffs. I'm so *tired* of judgemental people. I don't think I realised how much until we came here. One feels as if one could say almost anything to Sir Philip's friends and they shouldn't disapprove. They might argue or say one was an idiot, but they wouldn't shake their heads gravely and sigh about one's character. It's such a relief. Guy? Are you all right?"

"Yes, of course, why?"

"You're quite pink."

"It was hot. We went up to the Gallows Tree."

"Oh, lovely. Oh, I *wish* I could walk. Is that all? You look rather— I don't know. Unsettled."

"Well, it's unsettling," Guy said. "I've had more to think about here than I've had in my entire life till now."

"That's true. What did you talk about with Sir Philip?"

Do not blush. Do not blush. "Oh, this and that. Beetroot."

"Was that unsettling?" Amanda asked doubtfully.

"No, but it was very interesting," Guy said, thankful for the escape, and launched into Philip's grand plans for a domestic sugar industry. Amanda listened with surprising attentiveness, asking for more detail, and that took up the time until the gong struck for dinner, and there was no avoiding it any more. He would have to face the Murder, and dine with Philip, with his guilty knowledge upon him.

Consider yourself shielded, he told himself, and did his best to walk in with his head high.

"Frisby," Raven said, lifting a glass of wine in salute as he entered. "I hope you had a good walk? I spent the time teaching your sister to draw, and I'm telling you now, you had the better of that bargain. I don't know who she had as a drawing-master but I'd like ten minutes with him and a sharp pencil."

"Oh, she loathed him. She wanted to draw knights and castles and he only let her paint watercolours of flowers. Not even any flowers; they had to be things like daisies or blossoms. Low and gentle, he used to say, without thorns or long stems. He thought those were unladylike."

Raven choked on his wine. "Are you serious? No thrusting stems— Oh my God. Corvin! Come and hear this!"

Guy didn't understand for a second more, and then he did. Well, that was a childhood mystery solved, albeit not in a way he could share with Amanda. It was perhaps the last subject he'd have wanted to raise in the entire world, but Raven was repeating the drawing-master's edict to the others now, and the room erupted in laughter.

"Glorious," Philip said, shoulders shaking. "It takes a truly special gift to find indecency in flowers."

"Not at all," Street said. "They're disgraceful things. Notoriously promiscuous with bees *and* butterflies."

"I quite agree with the drawing master," Corvin said. "One only has to look at a daffodil to be consumed with inappropriate thoughts. And don't soil my ears with talk of goldenrod."

"Nobody needs to know about your goldenrod," Raven said.

"I recommend mercury treatments for that," Dr. Martelo offered, and that had them all howling again, even Guy. It was unseemly, perhaps, but—well, they were all gentlemen, and it was more silly than anything else. The coarse jests one heard in inn-yards tended to carry so much contempt for their object, but it was hard to be offended by people talking nonsense about flowers to make each other laugh. And he had a glass of wine in his hand, congenial company around him, people laughing at his comments but not at him, and it was, in fact, possible that he might be enjoying himself.

"Where did you walk to?" Corvin enquired once they were seated. "I heard rumours of some great exploration." He gestured at Guy to fill his glass again.

"About eight miles roundabout here." Philip graciously acknowledged the cries of disbelief. "Yes, thank you, my feet are very well apart from just a *few* blisters. I also climbed a tree."

"You did not," Street said. "You never climbed a tree in your life."

"He did it very well," Guy put in. "Considering."

"I suspect 'considering' hides a multitude of sins," Corvin said.

"And rents, and scratches," Philip added. "I dare any of you idle swine to do the same. In fact, there are some rather marvellous views around here, in their way. It's not Italy, or even Wrayton Harcourt, but it has its charms."

"Who knew that Philip would find the English countryside so full of beauty," Corvin said. Guy felt a pulse of instinctive alarm, but the Devil's Lord sounded teasing rather than mocking, and there was a distinct laugh in his eyes.

"What's Wrayton Harcourt?" he asked, hoping to change the subject anyway.

"My estate in Derbyshire," Corvin said. "There's a certain amount of jagged mountainous…ness to the view—"

"Not a word," Raven told him.

"—and the weather is only tolerable three months of the year. We'll be going up there soon enough. John is remodelling my gardens."

"I'm not taking any responsibility for this," Raven said firmly. "I'm drawing damn fool things for you only because if you draw the damn fool things, they'll fall down as soon as built."

"It's going to be a garden of pagan follies," Philip said, grinning. "Which should conclude Corvin's programme of distressing the neighbours with an impressive flourish. Are you doing an Indian temple?"

"No, he is not," Raven said on Corvin's behalf. "If he's doing this bloody stupid thing at all, it's going to be follies that look right for the landscape in materials that'll survive the weather. Northern Europe and Ancient Briton. Roman if we must. Not Hindu ones."

"A stone circle," Corvin said. "Druidic. I might purchase a robe."

"*No.*"

"With a sacrificial altar?" Street clasped his hands. "*Please* have a sacrificial altar."

"Just like the book. I wonder if copies have yet reached the circulating library."

It was like a slap, a blow from nowhere just when he was relaxing. "Which book?" Guy asked, every muscle in his body tense.

"*The Secret of Darkdown.* Have you read it? I believe we had it from your sister."

"It's a Gothic romance, the usual nonsense, but it's set in a hellfire club," Street put in. "A hellfire club led by a red-headed rake—"

"*Russet,*" Corvin said.

"With his best friend, Sir Peter Falconwood, who happens to look exactly like Phil. They go around with their sinister band sacrificing people to Satan and in the end Corvin, sorry, Darkdown murders Phil by accident and throws himself off a roof in remorse."

"The entire thing is a slander beyond all bearing. Do we know the author yet, John?" Corvin's smile curled as wickedly as any Amanda had ever imagined on Darkdown's face. Guy stared at his plate of perfectly cooked veal and wondered if he was going to be sick.

"I've sent to a friend who writes these things himself. He's got an entry with most of the publishing lot. Shouldn't take him long to winkle it out."

"What are you going to do?" Guy asked. His voice didn't sound quite right in his own ears, and he saw from the corner of his eye that Philip's head turned, but he couldn't meet the eye of the man he'd betrayed. "When you find out who wrote it, what will you do?"

"In the name of God, don't bring a lawsuit," Salcombe said. "You'll end up telling the court you are a devil-worshipper after all, just to annoy them, and find yourself gaoled, if not burned at the stake."

"You could horsewhip the author. It's all the rage," Raven suggested, somewhat sourly.

"I'll write you an opera based on the book," Penn said. "*Don Corvino.*"

This met with general hilarity and various suggestions of how to refine the plot. Guy had to stop himself from shouting at them all to be quiet. "But will you go to law?" he asked again, as the riot died down. "Or—or ask for the book to be withdrawn?"

"That's not a bad idea," Corvin said. "Actually, I think I'll send a threatening letter to the publisher. John, can you write me a threatening letter?"

Raven shook his head despairingly. "A viscount, and you can't write a letter for yourself."

"But you're so much better at it," Corvin coaxed. "Excoriating rage, denunciation, and vows of revenge. With copies to all the newspapers, and you could have a satirical print ready."

The conversation moved on. Guy couldn't make himself rejoin it; he couldn't swallow another bite of food. He sat and pretended the world, which had been so briefly bright, wasn't collapsing around him, and as soon as the meal was finished he mumbled an excuse, pretending not to hear Philip speak his name, and hurried to see if Amanda was awake.

She wasn't. The old woman who would sit the night in the room looked up with a smile and put her finger to her lips as though Amanda were a baby, not to be disturbed. Guy backed out obediently, and bumped into Philip, who was waiting with a frown.

"Is everything all right?"

"Yes. Of course. I just…I want to go to bed."

"Guy." Philip's hand closed on his elbow. "Whatever alarmed you, whatever distressed you, will you please speak to me? If it was one of my friends, I'll deal with it. And if you've had second thoughts—"

"It's not that," Guy said wretchedly. "Honestly. Please, I just need to go."

Philip released him. Guy more or less ran, feeling the gaze on his back like a touch.

He collapsed face down on his bed, wishing he hadn't had the second glass of wine. This was a calamity. He'd persuaded himself that it didn't matter, that the Murder would simply laugh off the absurd nonsense as they seemed to do everything else. He hadn't thought that Corvin might find himself in serious trouble if he allowed such implications to pass unremarked. He hadn't thought that they'd take the absurd plot, rather than the characters, as an affront.

But Corvin and Philip had been lovers for years. Philip had been *in love* with his friend, and Corvin adored him, and that thrice-damned book had Corvin killing him, and how would they not want revenge for that?

The guilt and self-reproach hammered in his gut. Philip had taken them in and paid for Dr. Martelo and the attendants, let them upend his party, directed his friends to entertain Amanda, and made love to Guy so kindly that he hadn't even thought to fret. And all the while Amanda's book had slandered him, and Guy had deliberately hidden his knowledge. Why had he not admitted the truth earlier, before Philip had lavished him with so much care? How had he persuaded himself that the accursed book would go away?

And now there would be consequences, and they would have to be faced. He couldn't hide behind the hope Amanda's authorship would go undiscovered. It wouldn't be fair on the publisher, to be exposed to whatever terrible things John Raven might write; it was utterly unjust that Philip should unknowingly host his slanderer. He would have to admit the truth, and that he'd been too much of a coward to tell it earlier, and pray that he and Corvin would be merciful.

What if they weren't? What if Philip ordered them gone from his home, with Amanda's leg still mending? What if Lord Corvin took his revenge? He could destroy any hope Amanda had left of ever making a decent marriage with a few cruel words. All he'd need to do was say that he'd stayed in a private home with an unmarried, unchaperoned woman to destroy her. If he added that it was Miss Frisby, staying with Sir Philip Rookwood...

Bile rose in Guy's throat. He wanted to tell himself that surely they wouldn't, surely they'd permit Amanda to withdraw the book, but he was too overwrought to believe it, and in any case, could she do that? Would the publisher expect her to bear all the costs? They couldn't possibly afford to pay for that—but if they didn't even offer—

"Oh God," Guy said aloud. "Oh, Amanda."

He could take the blame.

The thought came to him, horribly plausible, sickening in its implications, impossible to deny. If he said he'd written the book himself, not just known of it but spun its slanders without Amanda's knowledge, Philip would be furious and betrayed, but he surely wouldn't punish Amanda. Guy could do that for her, and if it ended his new friendships, well, that would have happened anyway, when they left for Corvin's estate, or Philip's London home, and Guy was left here, with Amanda, on their own.

He stared at the ceiling long after his candle had burned out, listening to the faint hum of voices from downstairs. It sounded like the Murder were enjoying themselves.

Chapter Eight

Philip woke early. He wasn't a slugabed, but neither did he have any communion with the lark as a general rule, and he lay irritably awake, wondering what to do.

He'd missed the point where something had happened to disturb Guy. Everything had been going so well. He'd felt a flush of real pride to see the pallid, nervous plank of a few days back joking with his friends over that absurd conversation. Guy had found his feet, and that wasn't the only part of himself he'd found.

Christ, he'd been lovely in Philip's arms. Philip had never seen the point of seducing virgins; he liked people to know what they were about, and it had always seemed to him that those who prized virginity were actually seeking ignorance, or chalking up points in a game where their win was someone else's loss. Whereas helping Guy to discover what he wanted, and teaching him to ask for it…oh, he could see the point of that.

Debauching, indeed. Philip was uncaging Guy, tearing down the bars that held him stiff and trapped, setting him free from the misery of a life that could barely be lived because so much of it was denied.

Or, he'd thought that was what he was doing, and then Guy had gone a truly bad shade of green and fled the evening.

Maybe he was sick. Except he wouldn't have gone to his recuperating sister then for fear of contagion. No; something had happened, someone had said something, and Philip was going to find out what the devil it was, because he wasn't going to watch that vibrant, open, responsive loveliness retreat back into a shell of conventional opinion.

He dressed himself rather than ring for Sinclair early and suffer the inevitable consequences when Corvin's Cornelius voiced his objections. Some might consider that refusing to disturb one's valet because he was in bed with someone else's valet was taking considerate employment too far; Philip preferred to tell himself it was an investment for his future comfort.

He went downstairs. Breakfast would not be served for another hour, but there was bustle in the kitchen, and he stuck his head in to request a cup of tea. It occurred to him he might drop in on Miss Frisby. He felt an urge to talk about Guy with someone who wasn't John or Corvin, someone who might actually understand, even if she didn't understand what it was she was discussing.

He strolled along the corridor, therefore, cup and saucer in hand, approached the door, and heard muffled shouting. It was Amanda Frisby. Her voice was high and shrill and tearful, and if someone was bothering her, Guy's sister, in Philip's house—

He reached for the doorhandle, ready to dispense brimstone, and only just stopped himself as another voice rose in angry, distressed protest and he recognised it as Guy's.

Philip stepped back, unsure of what to do. He had heard that siblings argued fiercely as a matter of routine, but even if that were the case, Guy was not an argumentative man, and Amanda hadn't struck him as either hectoring or lachrymose. Something was badly wrong if the Frisbys were going at each other this way.

And it was not his business and if he stood here any longer, it would indubitably qualify as eavesdropping. Philip made himself step away, into his study, where he drank his tea in a worried frame of mind. He felt restless and unnerved. He did not at all like the idea that, having deflowered the man, he'd left him in a state of nervous tension, shouting at his sister. He hadn't meant to do harm.

There had once been a picture of Sir James, his half brother, on the wall. Philip glared at the empty space from which he'd removed it. "Christ, have we not done enough damage to that family?" he muttered aloud. "Did I have to do more?"

No: he wasn't tolerating this. He was going to—actually, he was going to do some work until breakfast, let the Frisbys calm down, and then he would have it out with Guy, find out what had distressed him, and deal with it. Preferably by taking him back upstairs and giving him something else to think about, starting with those gloriously sensitive earlobes.

But Guy wasn't used to soothing his nerves with pleasure, and Philip couldn't root the convention out of his soul overnight. If he had to apologise and promise their dalliance would go unmentioned and unrepeated, he'd bloody do it. He told himself that firmly, and wondered why he should feel so bleak at the idea that Guy would cut himself off from joy.

"Do some work, Rookwood," he said aloud.

There were papers about the beet crops on his desk. That made him think about Guy again, so certain Philip could persuade his men to believe in this sugar-beet castle in the air.

Philip had never talked to his labourers. The fact was, they weren't his. They doubtless all knew him to be a bastard, and even if they didn't, he was always conscious of it. The house was not his, the lands were illicitly borrowed. If he'd been a gentleman he would have resigned the property, and the title if he could, to the cousin who would inherit both on his death. That would have left him without a penny, and he was disinclined to embrace poverty for a point of principle. So he held the house, and reminded himself that the only difference between the Rookwoods and half England's other families was that his illegitimacy was famed rather than concealed or only suspected.

Still, he could never quite rid himself of the fraudulent feeling when it came to men whose fathers had worked this land, and whose sweat had tilled it. Or whatever the word might be; he wasn't a countryman. His true father was a cold-hearted swine with exquisite lace ruffles pinned to dirty sleeves: a man who never paid his tailor, lied to women he wanted, and had probably never left London in his life. Philip had encountered him a few times in the sort of hells no decent man would visit. He'd bowed the first time, and received a chilly stare and the amused curl of a lip; they had ignored each other ever since. Even so, it was probably better than a father like Guy's, who knew one intimately yet still didn't care.

And his thoughts were on Guy again. Philip picked up some papers, purely so he could throw them down in disgust, shoved his chair back, and went for an irritable and solitary walk.

He returned to the house for breakfast. Guy was at the table. He'd taken a single bite from a piece of toast, and was making monosyllabic responses to John's efforts at conversation. John shot Philip a look composed of concern and accusation. Philip glowered at him.

Guy lingered at the table like Banquo's ghost until Philip had cleared his plate, then said, with determination, "Sir Philip. May I have a moment of your time?"

Sir Philip? "Of course," Philip said, with equal courtesy, and a sense of impending doom. "Please come to my study."

He led the way, ushered Guy in, shut the door, turned, and said, "What the bloody hell?"

Guy looked sick as a dog. "I need to make you an apology."

"Guy, for God's sake. There is absolutely no need for this distress. If you're concerned about yesterday—"

"Can you just listen?" Guy's fists were clenched, knuckles white. "I need to tell you, I have lied to you and—and betrayed your hospitality, and you will have every right to be furious with me. I want you to know it's all my fault, nobody else's, and I hope that—"

"Wait, wait, *stop*." This was sounding bad. If Guy had complained to a magistrate or some such in a fit of prudery, they could be in deep trouble. "What exactly have you done?"

Guy licked his lips. "I wrote the book."

Philip stared at him blankly. His mind was so entirely turned to the possibility of denunciation for unnatural offences that he couldn't make any sense of a book. A letter, yes, but— "What book?"

"*The Secret of Darkdown.*"

"You did *what?*" Philip yelped.

Guy flinched, and opened his mouth, but at that point there was a thunderous hammering on the door, which was unceremoniously flung open, and David Martelo strode in. "You. Both in the sickroom, now. Amanda is saying she will get up if you don't come in, I've her woman holding her down, and if she damages that leg I'll throttle the pair of you. Move!"

"Oh no," Guy said. "No, she can't—"

David grabbed him by the collar and physically dragged him out. Philip shouted an enraged, "Hoi!", sprinting after, and the three of them crashed through the sickroom door, where Amanda Frisby sat up very straight, face red, all flags flying.

"Well, I never!" the attendant woman yelped.

"Please leave us, Jane," Amanda said, and waited for the door to shut. "Guy Frisby, I will murder you. I *told* you—"

"Manda!" Guy shouted.

"No! Don't you *dare*— I wrote it, Sir Philip. Not Guy. I wrote the book, and I'm very sorry, but he is not going to take the blame, and I dare say it was very foolish of me and you're furious, but it's me you should be furious with and I can prove it because the manuscript is in my hand and—"

Guy was trying to talk over her, voice anguished. Philip lifted his hands. "Stop. Stop," he begged. "In the name of sanity. Miss Frisby, are you saying you wrote *Darkdown*? Not Guy?"

"Yes. Me. He always tries to take the blame for me, even though I'm twenty-three, and I won't have it." Amanda spoke emphatically. David hovered behind her, with a distinctly protective look. "And if you do choose to throw me out I shall understand, and I'll write a letter of apology if you like, but *please* don't blame Guy. I didn't even let him read it till a few weeks ago."

"Guy didn't write it and it's not his fault. I grasp that. Why are you both so appalled at making this admission? What on earth is this panic about?"

"Lord Corvin said he'd pursue the publisher," Guy said. His lips were pale. "And we can't afford it if they sue or ask us to bear the cost of withdrawing the book, or any of the other things that might happen. I realise he's deeply offended, but truly, we never intended it to seem an insult."

"I. Not you," Amanda snapped.

"But who the devil says he's offended?" Philip almost shouted. "Nobody's offended!"

"That is absolutely true," David said. "We've all been laughing over the book for days. Not, uh, disrespectfully," he added quickly. "It's a marvellous read. Everyone's fighting over who'll have it next, and Phil's ordered copies for us all."

Guy gaped. "But Corvin *kills* you, Philip. In the book. He said it was a gross slander!"

"No, he— Oh God, he did. All right, yes, but he didn't mean his portrayal as a villain. He will have been speaking about the description of his hair. Or perhaps the part where Darkdown feels remorse about shoving me off a roof instead of saying, 'Whoops,' and trotting on with his day," Philip said, brutally sacrificing his best friend on Guy's altar.

"It was just Corvin being Corvin," David added. "You mustn't listen to him. Nobody does."

"He and Mr. Raven were talking about horsewhipping the author or pursuing the publisher!"

"Oh, hell and the devil. Guy, I promise you, none of that was out of a desire for revenge. It was—"

"A desire to be further talked about," David said over him. "To turn a minor scandal into a major one by whatever means necessary, to provoke a month's chatter over teacups from the pages of a book. The Three Birdwits can't see a fire without throwing fuel on it."

Amanda gave a squeak of laughter and clapped her hand to her mouth at once. David smiled down at her. She looked up, eyes bright.

"Harsh. But not unjust. We didn't consider the feelings of the author in the matter, but no harm has been done, or will be. I will speak to Corvin," Philip said. "He will tell you himself that you have nothing to fear, and nothing for which to apologise other than describing his hair as red instead of russet, for which you will never be forgiven, but I shouldn't worry because we all know he's deluding himself. For heaven's sake, don't give it another thought."

Guy's mouth worked. He looked utterly sick, and Philip didn't even think. He strode over and put his hands to Guy's shoulders. "It's all right. I promise you. It is *all right.*"

Guy was rigid under his hands for a second more, then Philip felt him shudder. He pulled the man close, just about remembering to make it a comforting embrace rather than anything more, and glanced over at Amanda Frisby with what he hoped was a suitable expression of wry amusement. She was regarding him with something uncomfortably like assessment, but that expression fled on the instant, replaced by a smile of relief.

"Thank you, Sir Philip. I did try to say to Guy you wouldn't throw us out. And I truly am sorry. I wouldn't have done it if I'd known you."

"That would have been a great pity, because I'm impatiently waiting my turn to read it. There is nothing for which to apologise, and my friends will be delighted beyond words by this development, particularly Sherry. He adores Gothic novels." Philip realised he was rubbing Guy's shoulder in a soothing manner, and stopped.

"He's right," David said. "And I'm sure John will want to discuss the finer points of caricature with you, expert to expert."

"And with that, if you'll excuse me, Miss Frisby, I think I might take your brother to recover himself," Philip said. "He's a little overwrought."

"That's a good idea," Amanda agreed. "I'll speak to you later, Guy Frisby."

Philip dragged Guy up the stairs, through the house. Guy didn't resist, but Philip felt his arm tense as they approached the little room where they'd made love yesterday.

"We're not going there," he said shortly. "Come on."

He led the way up into the attics and out onto the roof. The sun was blindingly bright now. Guy put his free hand over his eyes. "Why are we on the roof?"

"It's the best I can do for a view without a four-mile walk. Sit."

There was a convenient sitting-place he'd found on previous expeditions, a flat rectangle raised sufficiently high that one could see over the parapet and across the fields and trees. Gazing out over the landscape had worked very well yesterday. He sat next to Guy, stone warm through his breeches, not touching. "Right. Now, will you please tell me what that was about? Not the book, be damned to the book. But what on earth did you think I was going to do, and why did you think telling me you'd written the thing would help?"

Guy's shoulders were heaving. "I— I'm sorry. I panicked. I thought— You've been so kind, and I've lied to you since I got here."

"Trivially."

"It's not trivial! The damned book slanders you in the worst way. It insults Lord Corvin and has him killing you—"

"It's a Gothic novel," Philip said. "A particularly ridiculous one. Anyone who looks at Sir Peter Hawkwood and sees me is a bloody fool."

"Falconwood."

"Whatever bird you like. I don't care."

"I do," Guy said. "I know what it feels like to be talked about, and you probably know it worse than me."

"Being talked about because one is a notorious bastard is a very different thing to being talked about because one is painted in ludicrous colours for popular entertainment. If I found that an unacceptable way to go on, I should hardly be friends with John. Very well, I understand that you were afraid you'd caused me harm."

"And lied about it," Guy said, stifled. "I let you—let you say things, yesterday—"

"Your eyes are no less lovely because your sister wrote a book," Philip said. "I grant that you should have told me earlier, though I can entirely see that there may never have seemed a good opportunity, and you have had a lot on your mind. What I actually want to know is why you were so afraid of telling me the truth that you named yourself the author, evidently against your sister's will, to protect her. What did you think I was going to do to her, Guy?"

Guy made a choking noise. There was a long silence. Philip didn't break it.

"It wasn't just you," he said finally. "I was afraid— You know all Corvin would have to do is mention her name—"

"He doesn't ruin women except by request," Philip said. "I told you that. Did you think I should have thrown her out of her sickroom bed to get my vengeance? Were you truly afraid that I would respond to ridicule with cruelty? Can I possibly, at all, make you see that I don't give two fucks for being caricatured in some literary farrago, but to realise you believe me so callous and malicious and selfish—"

His voice had risen. He bit the words off, distantly surprised to realise he was shaking.

"Yes," Guy said. "I see why you're angry. I, uh. I didn't really think you would do something cruel—"

"You seemed to think exactly that."

"Not you. Not the man I know but—but in my head, it seemed— I couldn't stop fearing it anyway. I'm sorry, I know it doesn't make sense. It's as if the more I don't want something to happen, the more it seems like it will. Because it always does. People do dreadful things, and they don't care, and they lie, and I can't have anything else happen to Amanda. That's all."

Philip breathed in and out. "It's a beginning. If that. Would you perhaps tell me what you are actually afraid of? Not some nonsense about this accursed book, but what has made you so suspicious? Because I'm finding it a little hard to understand you when you don't ever speak to me!"

He didn't think he'd get an answer, and the silence stretched out for long enough that he began to question whether he had the right to demand one, but after what felt like some hours, Guy leaned forward, forearms on knees, back hunched, staring straight ahead. "I don't know where to start. I suppose when Mother ran away with your brother, except I remember my parents shouting a great deal, from long before. They weren't happy. I don't remember an evening where there wasn't something said. Whenever I was brought down and we were together as a family, I'd wait for one or the other of them to begin, and they'd shout, and I or we would be sent away, or just run. I used to make up games with Amanda to be out of the house, or ones where we had to keep our hands over our ears or put a blanket round her head so she wouldn't hear. And then, finally, Mother left. And Father raged, and swore, and went away after her for months on end, and he, uh, he forgot to send money quite often. Nurse wasn't paid. And she wrote to Aunt Beatrice after a while but it was difficult. Amanda was only five or six. She didn't really understand where our parents had gone or why we didn't have anything nice to eat. And Nurse used to say to me every day, 'You have to look after Amanda, Master Guy. It's your job now.'"

"How old were you?"

"Nine, by then. Then, well, Father started gambling. And he spent all the money, you see. We weren't rich, but we were comfortable, before, but quite soon we had nothing left at all except the house, and he mortgaged that to the hilt. He couldn't pay the interest, and that was when he went to Aunt Beatrice—my mother's sister, Lady Paul Cavendish. She had been utterly ashamed of my mother, and my father's career made it all worse, so she bought the mortgages. She held them, so he couldn't borrow against the house any more, and she paid for my schooling, and Amanda's tutors. She wouldn't give us any money directly in case Father spent it, which was quite right. I think he tried to put her name to debts, and she was forced to put a notice in the papers. She is awfully proper and the whole thing was unspeakable for her. And then he had the stroke. He collapsed and never really recovered, though he lived for another six months."

"It sounds as though that was not before time."

"It wasn't. One isn't supposed to say one was glad that one's father died, but it was like living under the Sword of Damocles, never knowing when he'd find a way to bring disaster on us. It was so wonderfully *quiet* when he'd gone. Aunt Beatrice certainly thought so, she was most relieved, and in due course she very kindly offered to give Amanda a Season."

He didn't say it in the tones of a man recalling a wonderful gift. His eyes were still on the horizon. Philip glanced down to his hands and saw the fingers were knotted.

"It *was* kind," Guy said again, insisting although Philip hadn't argued. "We didn't expect a great deal; Amanda had no marriage portion any more. But she's wonderful. I think she might have found a man who didn't need money—it wouldn't have had to be in London, she didn't have great ambitions of snaring a title or any nonsense. She would have been very well if she'd stayed here, probably. But Aunt Beatrice gave her the Season, and—and she met Mr. Peyton."

Philip riffled mentally through men of that name and pulled out a joker. "Please tell me you don't mean Hugh Peyton."

"Do you know him?"

"We're acquainted, in that I once kicked him in the balls."

Guy looked round at that. "Really?"

"Not hard enough, I suspect. I take it this will not be a story with a happy ending."

"No. He persuaded Amanda— She was only seventeen. She said he made wonderful promises, that he was charming and handsome."

"Not any more. Someone paid several men with cudgels to see to that last year. He'll never walk again without a cane, either."

"Good," Guy said. "Well. So Amanda was in London, and Aunt Beatrice had been quite sure that her credit would carry Amanda off, because she's very respectable and her brother-in-law is a marquess, but she was wrong. There were a lot of people who said sneering things, young ladies who didn't choose to associate with her, and a lot of men who spoke in a disrespectful way because they assumed she would be like Mother. A *lot* of them. She was lonely, and very unhappy and angry. She said that was why she liked Peyton, because he was always respectful. Until he had her alone, and then it was too late."

"The shit. Do I understand he needs his other leg broken?"

Guy grimaced. "He, uh, he didn't attempt anything to which she objected. She's impulsive, especially when she's upset, and she was very upset, and he was kind to her, and—well."

"We're all fools at seventeen."

"Yes, perhaps. In any case they were at a ball and they were caught together and—and she obviously wasn't protesting, and then it was all over. Aunt Beatrice was so angry. She ordered Peyton to offer Amanda his hand at once and he laughed in her face and said he didn't buy soiled goods."

"Whatever ending this story has, it could have been worse," Philip said. "If your aunt seriously considered tying her to that creeping thing—"

"She just wanted Amanda to go away," Guy said. "She has three daughters of her own, younger ones, who—who Amanda might have tainted, you see, with her reputation."

"Christ."

"So Amanda was sent back here in disgrace. We were rather afraid Aunt Beatrice would wash her hands of us, but she didn't. She still gives us an allowance, which is very generous of her, on the condition that we stay in Yarlcote."

"What? But—"

"Our family have been nothing but a humiliation to her and she wants the world to forget that we exist." Guy tried a smile. "It's not unreasonable."

"Perhaps not, but she can't forbid you to leave a village."

"Well, yes, she can," Guy said. "Or at least she can make it practically impossible for us to do so. She can keep us here because we don't have anything to live on except what she gives us. Father pawned everything of value in the house, and she holds the mortgages. That's why she wouldn't help me to a profession, afterwards, to keep me here. And she isn't obliged to support us at all so she's entirely within her rights to put conditions on the help she offers us, but—but it leaves us without any choice, you see. I'm not qualified to do anything except teach Classics, and I have tried but there aren't many people around here who want their sons to have that sort of education at home, and if I went away to become a tutor or a schoolmaster I'd have to leave Amanda, and Aunt Beatrice would be angry. And Amanda would never be employed as an upper servant, and she really couldn't be a governess. She can't draw, and she isn't good at being an uncomplaining drudge, and if anyone found out about her past—"

"No." Philip knew very well what he meant, and he knew the precarious position of impoverished gentrywomen in particular, too well-bred to earn, too poor to live.

"No. So we're stuck, you see, she and I. Because Amanda has never, not once, had a single person who cared for her but me, and I'm not very good at looking after her but I have to do my best. So I realise I wasn't fair to you, earlier, and I'm sorry, but to be honest, I wasn't thinking about you at all."

Naturally he hadn't been. Amanda would always come first in Guy's life, and she would have to. She was a vibrant, fierce, determined woman, but that didn't make her any the less vulnerable, or improve her chances of safe employment one jot, and Philip was a swine to take that *I wasn't thinking about you* as a little jab to the heart. "Thank you for explaining. Of course I see. Of course you worry for her. I should have thought harder."

"No. You were right to be angry. I'm sorry."

Philip slid his hand over Guy's, interlacing their fingers. "So you've said. Do you know what I'd rather have than another apology?"

Guy's eyes widened wonderfully. Philip smiled into them. "I wanted quite desperately to kiss you in that tree. This seems to me a very practical alternative."

"Out here?"

"Nobody can see us but the birds, and nobody in the house knows the way to the roof or has any reason to come up,. And if they did, none of them would care."

"I think some of them might!"

"No, none," Philip said. "Trust me."

"Consider myself shielded?"

"Precisely. So if you would like to be kissed on a rooftop—"

Guy nodded frantically. Philip twisted round, leaning in, and met his mouth with a deep sense of something wrong coming right.

They kissed long and gently. Guy felt tremulous under his hands, and Philip took it slowly, soothing his own ruffled feathers, relaxing into the touch as they explored one another. He wrapped an arm around Guy just to ensure he knew he was held, and they ended up some uncertain time later lying on their sides, entangled on the roof, with Guy looking dizzily into Philip's eyes, and Philip's trapped arm slowly losing all sensation. He would probably have to have it amputated, he thought, and decided that would be a small sacrifice.

"Better?" he asked.

"Much." Guy snuggled into his side. "I think I let myself get so overwrought, not just because I was afraid of what might happen, but because I felt so guilty about lying to you. You've been——"

"Please don't say kind," Philip said.

"But you have."

"I have not. I wanted you, beloved. I have not sacrificed my comfort in any way, except for my arm which does feel just a little as though I will never use it again."

Guy moved hastily. Philip winced at the fiery rush of returning blood. "Ouch. Come over here, the other one still works. What was I saying?"

"That you haven't been kind, which is nonsense. Look at Amanda. I'm not trying to burden you with thanks. Only, you say so many lovely things to me, and... Well, I'm not going to tell you how handsome you are because I'm sure everybody does, but you should know that you're—you're the best person I've ever met."

"I can't be," Philip said. "That's patently untrue. I'm nothing of the sort."

"Of course it's true. And—well, you said we live and learn, and I've lived and learned more in the past week or so than in my whole life, thanks to you. So it doesn't really matter what happens, does it?"

Philip felt he'd missed something. "What doesn't matter? What's going to happen?"

"Well, nothing really. That's the point, isn't it? I spend so long worrying about what might happen because I'm afraid of the worst, but fearing one will be unhappy later shouldn't stop one being happy now, should it? You're right about that: a time to weep and a time to laugh. And, as you said, I'll get better. Sorry. I'm just rambling."

"You are a little." Philip was trying to place that phrase. Guy was definitely referring to something he'd said, and he couldn't for the life of him think what it might be. Get better from what?

You talk too damned much, Rookwood, he told himself with annoyance, but then Guy tugged him closer, and he forgot all about it for the moment.

One couldn't stay on a roof forever, unfortunately. All too soon the sound of church bells drifted through the clear air, and Guy sat up. "Blast. I must go."

"Where?"

"To church. It's Sunday."

"Ah. Well, enjoy yourself."

Guy gave him an examining look. "You really are an atheist? It isn't just a pose to shock people?"

"I really am. So are most of us. George is"—Philip bit back *conventional*—"a man of faith, so you might let him know if you're attending. Take horses, or the carriage if you like."

"Thanks. I must tidy myself up. How do we get down?"

Philip led the way, and watched Guy hurry off, cursing the day. He hoped the vicar wasn't one of the hellfire and brimstone type; the last thing he needed was an attack of conscience, not when Guy was becoming so delightfully comfortable with himself in Philip's arms.

He went along to the improvised artist's studio. John and Corvin were there, sitting close, because John was concentrating on painting Corvin's hands, the one extended, the other holding the back of a chair.

"Everyone will think you got that wrong, you know," Philip told him, after observing for a few moments. "In a century's time people will come to see this picture and point and laugh."

"I'm going to put it in the title," John said, without looking round. "On a plaque on the frame. 'Portrait of a Six-Fingered Art Critic.'"

Corvin did indeed have six fingers on his left hand. All of them were equally spaced and of similar proportions, so people didn't immediately notice: Guy hadn't yet, and Amanda clearly hadn't known or that detail would surely have made it into the book. Philip was glad it hadn't; Corvin was impervious to slights on his character or intellect, but jeers about his physical peculiarity were resented, and avenged.

Other artists would have adjusted the pose to conceal the problem altogether. John had composed his picture with Corvin's left hand at the very centre, fingers entirely countable. Philip was only surprised he didn't have two of them raised in an obscene gesture.

"'Still Life with Three Birdwits and Six Fingers'," he suggested.

"It's not a still life, you crackbrain. What was all the slamming and shouting about?"

"Ah, yes," Philip said. "Well. You know *The Secret of Darkdown*? You'll never guess who wrote it."

Corvin turned. John put down his brush. "Go on."

Philip gave it a dramatic pause. "Amanda Frisby."

The reaction was precisely as he'd predicted. Corvin was crying with laughter by the end of his account; John had doubled over and was making urgent gestures with his hands that indicated he couldn't breathe. Philip, who had had to sit down himself, felt slightly disloyal to find the business so funny given Guy's earlier distress, but his friends' hilarity was always irresistible.

"Marvellous," John said at last. "Bloody hell, Phil. So that's why she was on your land?"

"Seeking ideas for her next book, yes."

"That's a devil of a woman. Well, they kept that titbit quiet."

"You might find it awkward to be immobile in the house of one of your victims."

"Just a little."

"I absolutely insist on meeting her," Corvin said. "I really cannot be denied further."

"With Guy there, and Sheridan," Philip said. "At a minimum. And her woman. And a bishop of the church of England, preferably, you know how people talk. And you are not to flirt with her."

"I thought you were pursuing the brother," Corvin said. "You can't have both. Or can you?"

It was obvious bait, and Philip rose to it anyway. "Leave her alone, Corvin. She doesn't need your maledictory influence on her reputation."

"My what?"

"Anyway, David will have your hide if you try."

Corvin's brows shot up. "The wind's in that quarter, is it?"

"Let's say, I don't think she needs nearly as much medical attention as she's getting."

John grimaced. "I hope he knows what he's about."

"I doubt he's about anything. I just think it would be ill advised to flirt."

Corvin sighed. "Well, I shall restrain my natural charm."

"Restrain the jokes too," Philip told him. "Absurd it may be, but Guy was deeply distressed at the thought of having caused offence."

"You told him it was the best thing that's ever happened to Corvin, right?"

Corvin raised a brow. "I'm not sure why he cared about causing me offence. Fear of retaliation I understand."

"He felt it as a betrayal of hospitality, I think, or friendship, although it was nothing of the sort given we'd never met when the blasted thing was written. And he worried he ought to have admitted the truth earlier, though I entirely sympathise with the difficulty of doing that."

"I'm sure you do. And he was afraid this business would upset you," Corvin said. "May we conclude from this and your notable disappearances that matters are progressing?"

"If you must."

John picked up his brush. "Hands where I can see them, V. Fingers wider—no, a bit more. Right, Phil. You were going to tell us about how and why you've talked a strait-laced bundle of rustic nerves into bed."

Corvin's brows shot up. "A little harsh?"

"Not really," John said. "We talked about this. When was the last time Phil had an amour that involved crying and slamming doors?"

"That was about the book," Philip objected.

"You just told us what it was about. That's a boy who takes things seriously, Phil."

"He's not a boy, and I know him rather better than you do. I don't see why there's anything to criticise in taking things seriously."

"Because the last time you took an affair seriously, it was him." John pointed his brush at Corvin. "Which I don't remember you much enjoying, and you weren't a countryside innocent with nobody to talk to, either. You don't want to do that to someone else."

Philip found himself speechless for a moment. "I am not 'doing that', whatever you mean by 'that'. I've no intention of lying to him—"

"I never lied to you," Corvin said gently.

"No, I know that, but John seems to think I'm playing the London rake with the country boy and that's not fair."

"Lots of things aren't fair," John said. "All I'm saying is, you don't normally do slamming doors, or seducing innocents, or amours. When was the last time you fucked anyone who wasn't us?"

"Yesterday," Philip snapped.

"Before that."

"It was— I don't know, why does it matter? A few months, I suppose. A year, at most."

"Oh yes? Who?"

"God, I don't know. Obviously I know, I've just misplaced the name. His father was a Cit, cotton manufacturer." John was looking at him sardonically. Philip cudgelled his brain, and came up with, "Maudsley, that's it. Happy now?"

"If you mean Mabersley, and you do, it was more like two years," Corvin said. "I remember, even if you don't. He cried on my shoulder about you."

If Philip had ever known that, he'd entirely forgotten. He felt a mild twinge of guilt. "Over me? Why?"

"Don't worry about it. I cheered him up."

Philip glared. "I bet you did. Would you mind—"

"The point *is*," John said loudly, "it's two years since you fucked anyone else, and longer since you fucked anyone you cared to remember the name of. But now you have to have the country boy who doesn't know what he's doing and has nowhere to go with it. That's not seeming fair to me either."

Nowhere to go.

That was truer than John knew. Guy was tied to Yarlcote and to Amanda, and that was a problem. Philip had no desire to spend more time than necessary here in this house whose every room reminded him of his ill-starred birth. He far preferred London's excitements and comforts, and even if he had harboured an urge for rural simplicity, he'd burned his bridges very thoroughly indeed with the neighbours. He could probably increase the frequency of his visits to a few times a year, but he could never set foot in the Frisbys' house for fear of endangering Amanda's reputation, and of course every visit Guy made to him without the excuse of her convalescence would be spoken about with shock and disapproval because of the Frisbys' runaway mother and Philip's sodding prick of a half-brother.

"Shit," he said.

"If I may make a contrary point?" Corvin suggested. "I agree our beloved bastard baronet is not known for heartfelt affairs. Or even for putting in more than the very minimum of effort, come to that. Yet you're bothering now. Is he special, Phil?"

Philip thought about Guy's sunlit eyes, his steadfast heart, his stammering, unfurling desires. "Yes. Yes, he is. Which doesn't make John wrong."

"Yes and no," Corvin said. "Love is no less because it doesn't last forever, or even for long. You may be the only man who ever makes him feel wanted, after all. I trust you to do a good job of it, and to leave him with pleasant memories in the end."

"You always say things like that, and I've never known it help at all," John said. "'Heart broken, crying your eyes out? Don't worry about it. This will just seem like an amusing diversion when you're fifty.'"

"I don't see any advantage in reaching the age of fifty without pain if you've also reached it without pleasure," Corvin said. "And really, a broken heart is a great deal less than a broken leg. 'Men have died from time to time, and worms have eaten them, but not for love.' We get better. Phil? What is it?"

"We get better," Philip repeated. "Oh God. Oh *shit*."

"What on earth—" Corvin began, but Philip was already heading out of the room. He needed to think.

Chapter Nine

Guy did not find the eleven o'clock service at St. Mary's to be a particularly spiritual experience. For one thing, he was attending with a member of the Murder, albeit the respectable-looking George Penn, who proved to be a pleasant, thoughtful companion. For another, he was vividly conscious of his own less than virtuous goings-on and felt a peculiar lack of remorse over them. He didn't in truth believe he'd done anything wrong, and the sermon, which was on the topic of Exodus 28, The Manufacture of the Breastplate of Aaron, did nothing to prick his conscience. Several people fell asleep and Penn began to hum, almost but not quite imperceptibly, clearly working on a tricky phrase.

Guy didn't daydream, because he knew what he'd daydream of and that was definitely not appropriate in church, and because he was being looked at. It was a familiar and unwelcome sensation, and he wasn't surprised to be accosted once they were allowed out into the sunlight once more.

Mr. Welland made his way over, and Guy turned to him rather than the several others heading in his direction. Penn slipped away to examine the old carvings. That was a relief. Guy could see people looking at him and murmuring to one another and felt himself shrink on Penn's behalf. It must be bad enough to have people gathering around one because of one's colour; he didn't want to imagine how things might go if Penn were identified as a member of the Murder.

"Mr. Frisby. I'm glad to see you. How is Miss Frisby?"

"Recovering, I'm glad to say. It was an extremely bad break, you may have heard? We were afraid for her life and she suffered a terrible fever for days, but she's very much on the mend."

"And…she is still at Rookwood Hall?" Mr. Welland lowered his voice in a conspiratorial manner that just drew attention.

"Yes, Sir Philip has been extremely generous," Guy said, willing himself to seem calm. "We've entirely disrupted his household, but the doctor feels she can't be moved at all for another week at the very earliest, and probably longer. The bone has to mend straight, you see."

"But Rookwood Hall," Mrs. Arnold said. She was the churchwarden's wife, and a moral pillar of the parish. "It cannot be right."

"Sir Philip has been extremely generous," Guy repeated, slightly louder. "Amanda has attendance day and night to keep her company, and I'm staying in the Hall as well. There is really no other choice."

"But does he not have that disreputable set of persons present?" Mr. Welland asked. "I've heard nothing but ill of his set."

"I haven't seen any disreputable behaviour," Guy said inaccurately. "Sir Philip's guests include a composer, a famous London violinist, and several men of science. And none of them have been anything but gentlemanly in my presence, still less Amanda's. Believe me, I was as concerned as you, but I have reached the conclusion that he doesn't entirely deserve his reputation."

"Mr. Frisby," Mrs. Arnold said, swelling. "I have never—not once!—seen Sir Philip at divine service, nor heard that he has a clergyman in his household, and I am not aware that he takes the slightest interest in parish affairs."

"No, well, I couldn't speak to his beliefs," Guy said. "I think that's a matter for his conscience."

"And is it not true that he associates with"—she lowered her voice—"Viscount Corvin?"

"Well, yes, but—"

Mrs. Welland shook her head. "There's such terrible things said of him, Mr. Frisby. My nephew is a tailor in London, he sends us all the latest on-dits."

"I'm not sure they're entirely—"

Mrs. Arnold put her hand to her bosom. "Is Lord Corvin present? In the Hall?"

"I've barely seen him," Guy said loudly. "And he has neither sought nor been permitted to converse with my sister. Mrs. Arnold, we have no choice but to keep Amanda at Rookwood Hall until her bone has healed. I don't think you understand that her life hung by a thread. To be moved might have killed her. Under the circumstances, I think Sir Philip and his guests have been extremely considerate. Sir Philip expressed the hope to me that we might bring the bad blood between the Rookwoods and Frisbys to an end. I think he has done as much as anyone could to ensure a situation of nobody's seeking went as well as could possibly be expected."

"I am astonished to hear you say so," Mrs. Arnold said. "I hope I am capable of Christian charity, but I should find it very difficult to extend a hand of forgiveness to Sir Philip, still less to allow a young lady to remain in his household, after the manner in which he has conducted himself. Very difficult indeed."

"I shouldn't worry; I don't suppose he'll ask you to do so," Guy said, causing Mr. Welland to turn away and cough. "Amanda would probably have died without his hospitality, and the help of his doctor; I certainly doubt she would have walked again. Her recovery is all that matters to me, and Sir Philip has been as attentive and concerned and kind to us as anyone could possibly be, and I shall always be grateful for his consideration. Now if you'll excuse me, I must get back to my sister."

"Something wrong?" George Penn asked, as Guy set a slapping pace down the lane.

"Just people. Gossip and spite. They all wanted me to say that Philip was a monster."

"I wouldn't worry. He and Corvin bring it on themselves."

"But it's not true. He's been marvellously kind. All of you have."

Penn shrugged. "No harm done. Philip won't care."

"I care," Guy said, before he could stop himself.

"I see you do. If you don't mind my saying so, I'd let him look after himself. He doesn't need defending and there's no need to get heated on his behalf."

It was a warning, Guy realised. Kindly meant, not a rebuke, but a warning all the same, and he still felt a little unnerved by the time they arrived home.

At Rookwood Hall, rather. Not home.

He had luncheon in the sickroom, feeling that he needed more time with Amanda, and spent much of it being told off.

"I'm sorry," he got in, after her lengthy exposition on why he was a snake and a weasel for claiming her responsibility as his. "I was just fretting so dreadfully, and I got terribly tangled up in my head."

"I don't understand why," Amanda said. "I know why you fret and why you constantly try to protect me even though I'm twenty-three and I haven't done anything stupid since—"

"—writing the book—"

"—my Season," she went on firmly, "but I don't see why you thought Sir Philip of all people would be unkind even if he was angry. Nobody talks about him having a bad temper or fighting duels or killing people."

Guy wondered whether he could decently tell Amanda that Philip had kicked the man who'd ruined her where it would do most good.

He decided he couldn't, with a small pang of regret. She'd have been pleased. "No. He isn't that sort."

"And you've told me a dozen times how kind he is."

"Have I?" Guy asked, with a pulse of alarm.

"Yes. I think it's marvellous, dearest. Neither of us has any real friends here, do we?"

"No." Since her disgrace, Amanda had not been invited to gatherings with other young ladies of her age and class, and Guy had declined invitations from those who cold-shouldered his sister until they dwindled to nothing.

"I can see you didn't want to lose his good opinion," Amanda went on. "But I don't think you're in danger of that. He seems perfectly lovely to me. David thinks awfully highly of him."

"Are you sure you ought to be on first-name terms with Dr. Martelo?" Guy asked.

Her eyes narrowed. "I don't see why I shouldn't be. He is my doctor."

"You're not on first-name terms with Dr. Bewdley." Amanda glowered. Guy held up his hands. "I'm just asking, Manda."

"Considering everything, I can't see it does any harm," Amanda said. "I'm enjoying having a friend as much as you are and there's nothing improper in it."

"I know there isn't," Guy said, all too aware which of them was up to impropriety. "Just as long as Jane doesn't gossip."

"It doesn't much matter if she does. It's been five years since my Season and people are still talking about me. I dare say people at church had opinions on me staying here."

"More about Philip than you, but…well, yes."

"Of course they did, and I'm quite sure they're gossiping now. I made a mistake and nobody will ever let me forget it, or think anything else about me. So I don't see what I gain by trying to be virtuous now if nobody will believe me anyway."

"It's about what you know," Guy said. "Not what other people think. For goodness' sake, people seem to believe that Philip is a monster of depravity, and that other people are sinners when they're just human and not doing any harm. If you know in your heart you're not doing wrong or hurting anyone including yourself, I think that's as much as we can ask of anyone. And I'm sick of living in fear of people who are so desperate to find fault they'll make it up where no harm exists."

"Goodness," Amanda said. "You sound fierce."

"Mrs. Arnold." Guy knew no further explanation was required.

Amanda rolled her eyes. "And she's thick as thieves with Dr. Bewdley. I suppose she thought you ought to drag me out of here with this horrid block and tackle still attached to my foot. Well, if people insist on having nasty minds, we can't stop them. I shan't let it spoil things now, and I hope you won't either."

"Agreed," Guy said, and tried not to worry about what things might be spoiled. "I was wondering, Manda. Do you think I ought to write to Aunt Beatrice?"

"Good heavens, no. Why would you do that? The last thing we need is for her to learn we're staying here."

"Except it would be even worse if she found out and we hadn't told her."

"Ugh. Yes. But she won't find out, surely? Nobody here is in her circle, and they've all been very careful about not compromising me, as if they could. I'm sure nobody will gossip."

"What if someone in Yarlcote writes to her?"

Amanda considered that. "Surely not. She's not on terms with anyone here, is she? Far too high and mighty. No, honestly, Guy, I think it's best not. Imagine if she came up to chaperone me in person."

That was a horrific thought. Guy let himself be persuaded, since he truly didn't want to write to Aunt Beatrice, and left Amanda with Martelo, trying not to look too interrogatively at the man. It was only first names.

Philip was neither in his study nor the drawing room. Guy knocked at the door of the parlour upstairs, in case, entered at Raven's shout, and found the artist in a chair contemplating his canvas and Lord Corvin sitting on the floor by him. He was resting his head against Raven's thigh; Raven was stroking his long reddish hair. Both looked up as Guy came in; neither changed position.

"Oh. Uh. Excuse me."

Corvin waved a languid hand, making no effort to move. "Not at all. Do I understand your sister is the authoress of that glorious book?"

"Uh. Yes. Yes, she is."

"How entirely marvellous. I must offer my apologies for my remarks last night; please do me the favour of forgetting I spoke. And please offer her my congratulations, also. You may decline without offence, but I should love to be introduced to Miss Frisby. She has a sprightly style that I found charming, and I would be delighted to be of service if she has future works in mind and needs inspiration."

"Sweet Jesus, no," Raven said.

"Why not? She needs colourful detail, and intimate social references to catch the readers' imagination. I can supply those aplenty."

"In two years' time, when St. James's is a smouldering heap of ashes, I'm going to remind you of this conversation and say I told you so."

"He's so gloomy," Corvin told Guy, in confiding manner. Raven tugged at his hair. "Ouch. Don't do that unless you mean it. Are you looking for Philip?"

"I was," Guy said. "Er, about my sister…"

"By all means observe the proprieties as you and she see fit," Corvin said. "But do tell her she's marvellous and I hope she writes more, and if you ever travel to London, you must ask John to introduce her to his friend in the same field. Professional connections are terribly useful. Talking of fields, that's where you'll find him."

"What? Who?"

"Philip, dear boy. I am told that, unfeasible as it may seem, he was looking for trees to climb. It seems you're having an *extraordinary* influence on him."

Raven pulled his hair again, harder this time, jerking Corvin's head back. He gave a sharp hiss, but his lips curved unmistakably. "Let him be, you prick," Raven said. "Don't mind this one, Frisby, he's an idiot. Phil's out somewhere past the back of the walled garden."

Guy stammered excuses and fled. He wasn't entirely sure what he'd just seen, but he was entirely sure that he'd been meant to see it. Raven and Corvin? Philip had never hinted at such a thing. Did he even know? Then again, he'd been adamant that his friends wouldn't care if they knew about himself and Guy. It was possible that there was more going on among the Murder than he'd realised.

He found Philip in the orchard, sitting on a bench in the dappled shade, reading *The Secret of Darkdown*.

"Good afternoon," Guy said. "I was told you were climbing trees."

"I would have been if any of them looked climbable." Philip put the book down and smiled. It was an extraordinary smile, oddly tentative, a little uncertain even, but so warm that Guy lost his breath. "Apparently someone cuts off the lowest branches, I assume for good, practical reasons. Or possibly I have the wrong sort of trees."

"Why did you want to climb a tree?"

"I thought you might join me in, or up, one. You could join me here instead."

Guy wondered as he approached how it would be to sit at Philip's feet, as Corvin had, and rest his head on those tight buckskins and the strong thigh they hid. He didn't dare try such a thing, so he sat on the bench instead and let himself exhale.

"Goodness, that was heartfelt. How was church?"

"Much as ever."

"And Miss Frisby?"

"Also that. Philip?"

"Mmm?"

"Would people usually pull other people's hair as a—a sign of affection?"

"Well, I'm told small boys do it to pigtailed girls," Philip said. "I hope the pigtailed girls kick them. Oh, no, I think I grasp your meaning. Have you by any chance encountered Corvin recently?"

"I wanted to know where you were, and he and Mr. Raven were in the upstairs parlour. I did knock."

"I'm very sure you did. Problem?"

"No. Only, Mr. Raven pulled his hair and…" Guy wasn't even sure what he wanted to ask.

"In front of you. Of course he did."

"I didn't know if you'd mind," Guy blurted. "That he, they—"

"Not remotely. Are you shocked?"

"Well, I am, rather. That is, I suppose if you're spending time with me there's no reason Lord Corvin shouldn't spend time with someone else."

"Dear heart, Corvin spends time with *everyone* else. He loves widely and generously, and the only lovers he disappoints are those who want sole possession. That's a polite way of calling him a shameless trollop," Philip added. "And John is not 'someone else'. Corvin loves him deeply. As do I."

"Oh," Guy said cautiously. "You mean… Oh."

"The three of us share tastes, and a long history, and each other's beds when we choose. I fell in love with Corvin, as I told you, and that ended poorly; John was once married, and that worked even less well. I'm not sure Corvin's ever been in love in his life, unless he's in love with everyone: it's hard to tell. In any case, fidelity and betrayal and such don't come into the matter. Think of it as a particular friendship with extra trappings. Or a love affair without the obligations."

"It seems complicated to me," Guy said. "And I still don't see why Mr. Raven would pull his hair."

"That's another matter entirely," Philip said, with the sort of gravity that Guy knew hid a laugh. "John reacts when provoked. Therefore Corvin provokes him."

"I don't think I understand."

"They have a complicated relationship. Suffice to say, there is a push and pull, and talking of such things, I can think of far better ways to spend the afternoon than discussing Corvin."

Guy's throat closed. Philip grinned at him. His fair, narrow features were entirely dissimilar to the Viscount's, but the smile made them look blood brothers. "Care to come upstairs?"

They went to Philip's bedroom. Guy hadn't been in there before. It had lead-paned windows, old paintings, and a four-poster, a lovely thing of carved wood with red hangings. Philip walked him backwards, and pushed him gently onto the bed, on his back.

Philip knelt beside him. His fingers skimmed down, between Guy's thighs, then slid upward. "Push..." He cupped Guy's balls in a deliberate grip, and stroked up over the length of his stand, which strained against his breeches in response. "...And pull."

"What are you going to do?"

Philip's palm was flat against the front of Guy's breeches, the pressure delicious. "What a good question. I would very much enjoy having you in my mouth. Would you like that?" His lips curved at whatever he saw in Guy's face. "You find that rather shocking, don't you?"

"Well. Yes."

"What is it, particularly? The act itself? The fact that I like to do it? Or just talking about it?"

Guy was ridiculously aroused already, to the point where it was difficult to think. "All of those."

"Odd," Philip said. "Because your mouth tells me you're shocked, and your face is a picture of maidenly blushes..." His hands were at Guy's waist, unbuttoning, easing the springing member free. He wiped his thumb over the silky wetness at its damp tip, spreading the moisture over the head. "But this pretty plaything can't restrain its enthusiasm. Mouthwatering." He ran his tongue deliberately over his lips. "I don't think you answered me, you know."

"Uh—what was the question?"

"Would you like me to suck you?"

"Please," Guy said hoarsely, and Philip dipped his head and took him in his mouth.

Guy thought he might spend on the spot. Philip was doing it differently this time, mouth tighter, the lightest scrape of teeth along his shaft. He had one hand between Guy's legs, palm pressing against his balls, fingers just nudging at the base and cleft of Guy's backside. That was frighteningly intimate, and Guy almost wanted to pull back, but only almost, because he was on the brink of climax already and he didn't want anything to stop at all.

Philip raised his head. Guy moaned protest.

"Eager?" Philip's mouth looked wet. He brought his free hand up, stroking Guy's lips with his dampened thumb, pushing them open. "Why don't you show me how you want to be sucked?"

Guy closed his lips on Philip's fingers. The feeling of intrusion in his mouth matched that between his legs, disturbing, delicious. He wondered if it might feel like that to take Philip's stand in his mouth, if he could learn to bring Philip to this state of glorious sensation, and then he didn't think about anything except the building, exquisite, tormenting need.

He spent, almost unexpectedly, feeling Philip's fingers curve in his mouth and over his balls, jerking and spasming helplessly, Philip sucking hard as if to drain him dry, until the sensation was too much, and he cried out. Philip loosened the suction but didn't move his mouth away at once, licking lightly, until Guy was a mass of shudders.

Philip crawled up the bed, bracing himself with an arm each side of Guy's head, looking down. "My God. You are glorious."

Guy tugged him down, wanting his weight and his kiss. Philip's mouth met his, wet and astringent, tongue stroking as commandingly as his fingers had. "Mmm. Was that good?"

"Wonderful. I don't know how you do it."

"I don't fear my pleasures," Philip said. "Once you know what you want, everything becomes a great deal easier. On which topic, you could tell me what you like too, and you don't have to wait to be asked. Name your desire, put it in words, claim it as your own."

"I—I don't think I can."

"I think you could. You don't have to, but I think you might find it educational. And—may I be honest?"

Guy almost laughed. "I think we're a bit beyond polite exchanges."

"Honesty's more than that," Philip said. "Honesty strips you bare. I want to hear you. That beautiful mouth of yours, which seemed at first so terribly prim, asking for my spend, or begging for despoiling— you have no idea what that does to me. If you speak your pleasures, beloved, you will undo me entirely."

Their faces were so close. Philip's eyes were intent, pupils huge. Guy had to swallow the constriction in his throat to speak. "I, uh, I'm not sure how. I don't know what to say. I'm sorry."

Philip ran his fingers over Guy's cheek. "Don't be sorry. Rome wasn't built in a day, as I'm sure you already knew."

"No, but if you want me to talk as you do—"

"I want you to enjoy yourself. I'm not asking for your discomfort."

"I could learn," Guy tried. "If you could just...well, tell me what to say."

"Dear boy, that's exactly what I can't do. You need to voice your own pleasures—which means that you need to feel safe doing so. Time

174

enough when you feel ready to do that, though I do give you my word to treat your trust as it deserves."

"I know you will," Guy said wretchedly. "It's not that I don't trust you, it's just, I've spent my whole life not saying anything to anyone, barely to myself in my own head, and now you want me to say it all out loud, and I *can't*."

Philip cocked his head. Guy had a sudden fear he would reveal irritation or impatience when he spoke, but he sounded as calm as ever. "Actually, dear heart, you just have. I asked you for something, and you've told me you don't want to do it. That's every bit as important as what you *do* want to do."

"But it's not that I don't want to, honestly." That wasn't exactly true, but he wished it were. "I'm just...not very brave. Not good at trying new things."

"I dispute both of those assertions," Philip said. "We've done a number of new things, my virgin, to which you've taken like a duck to water. You seem to me to be made for gamahuching, for a start."

"For what?"

Philip grinned. "Sucking pricks."

"Gamahuching?" Guy repeated incredulously. "Where on earth does that come from? Etymologically, I mean."

"Good God, I have no idea. The Greek, I expect."

"It does not."

"French, then, probably. I know it's not Latin because obscenity was the sole aspect of my classical studies to which I paid attention. I believe the word there is *irrumare*," Philip added, somewhat smugly.

"*Fellare*," Guy corrected without thinking.

"I'm sure Catullus has *irrumare*."

"He does, but it doesn't mean quite the same thing."

Philip's grin was an evil joy. "You really will have to explain the distinction."

Guy gulped. "In this context, *fellare* is to suck, but *irrumare* is to, um. You know."

"Clearly I don't."

"Well, to, uh to put your—in someone's mouth—to do it *to* someone. Forcefully."

"I am absolutely delighted by your Latin vocabulary, even if your English is sadly lacking. What is that line of Catullus again?"

Guy knew exactly which line Philip meant. "*Pedicabo ego vos et irrumabo.*"

"Translate for me, my sweet."

"Uh. He says—it's a threat, of a sort—he says, 'I will sodomise you and defile your mouth'," Guy managed, wondering vaguely how hard one could blush before passing out.

"I'm sure that's not *precisely* the spirit of the original."

"I dare say you could come up with a more colloquial translation. It's your area of expertise, after all."

Philip gave a crack of laughter. "Very true. How about 'I will ram your arse and fuck your face'?"

"Well, that certainly sounds right," Guy said. "Philip, will you teach me?"

Philip blinked. "Teach you what?"

"To, um. *Fellare.*" Guy plucked up his courage. He absolutely *was* going to say this. "I was thinking, before, about kneeling down and doing that. What you did." He couldn't use that ridiculous word. "Sucking your prick."

He was rewarded a hundredfold by Philip's expression. "Were you indeed. And that pleased you?"

Guy licked his lips. "I was thinking about it when I spent."

"Oh Jesus," Philip said. His voice sounded constricted. "I don't know what I did to deserve you, but I shall definitely do it again."

"Good, but, can I—?"

"Yes. God, yes. Do you want me standing?"

Guy nodded. Philip clambered off the bed with some awkwardness, and leaned against one of the posts. His lips were parted, he was watching Guy with an almost inebriated look, and the bulge in his buckskins was impossible to ignore. *I did that,* Guy thought. *I did that, to him. Oh heaven. Now what?*

He climbed off the bed, tucking himself away but not doing up the buttons of his breeches. Philip's breathing was the only sound in the room, harsh and a little fast.

I'm going to kneel down, actually kneel—

It felt deeply wrong and, even worse, right. He'd said he'd do it and Philip was waiting with that hungry look. Guy took a deep breath and lowered himself, one shaky hand on the bed.

Down to one knee. The other.

And now he was kneeling, but not where he needed to be, in front of Philip. Idiot. He shuffled awkwardly over, his face ablaze, and dared to look up.

Philip seemed extraordinarily tall from here, and his arousal seemed very prominent. He was looking down, and their eyes met.

"You're beautiful," Philip said. "You cannot imagine how beautiful. Shall I guide you, or would you rather find your path yourself?"

"I'd like to try. You'll tell me if I get it wrong?"

"You can't get it wrong. Unless you bite, or similar," Philip added hastily. "Watch your teeth. Otherwise, make yourself free of me as you choose. Take your time. And if you don't like it, stop."

That seemed fair. Guy sat back on his heels and reached for the fastenings of Philip's buckskins. His fingers felt thick and clumsy, but Philip didn't brush his hands out of the way or tut impatiently. He simply stood, and when Guy looked up, he saw Philip had his eyes closed, head back.

He managed the front fall, and gently eased Philip's stand free of his drawers. It was slimmer than his own, with a slight curve, and somehow it didn't look quite so much like an undignified animal thing. Physical, yes, the flesh and blood evidence of Philip's desire, with the faint smell of male body to it, and he'd said, he'd *asked* to put it in his mouth.

Right.

He knelt up again, leaned in, and licked. Philip twitched.

That was heartening. He licked again, accustoming himself to the taste, the feel of firm, ridged flesh, running his tongue over the head. Philip swore almost under his breath, and Guy felt a hand run through his hair, a gentle caress.

He could do this. He opened his mouth and tentatively closed his lips around Philip's shaft.

"Christ," Philip said. "Yes."

This wasn't hard at all. Guy moved his mouth, sliding up and down, a little further each time, taking his time as instructed, Philip's hand moving spasmodically on his scalp. And he'd thought he might feel helpless or humiliated on his knees, but this was the opposite of helplessness, with Philip whispering endearments, responding to everything Guy did, and the taste of his arousal strong in Guy's mouth. Philip wanted this, and Guy was giving it to him, and he felt as though he were clinging to the top of a tree, watching the world sway.

Philip had used his hand. Guy removed his own hand from where he was gripping Philip's hips, slid his fingers between the tense legs, just to see, and was rewarded with a rasp of breath.

"Christ Jesus. Beloved. I'm going to spend very soon. Move your head if you don't want it in your mouth. *Guy.*"

Guy held on, moving his mouth and hand faster, tingling with the thrill of power. Philip groaned deeply, fingers tightening in Guy's hair with just a little tug, and then there was a rush of thick, salty, bitter-sweetness in his mouth, and Guy's attention was all on trying not to gag as Philip spent, hips jerking forward. It was two thrusts, a couple of seconds where Guy's mouth was alarmingly full, and his position suddenly seemed terribly vulnerable, and then Philip sagged back gasping, leaving Guy with a dawning realisation of what *irrumare* might mean in practice, and a mouth full of a lot of viscous stuff that he wasn't sure what to do with. Philip had swallowed, but it had the consistency of an oyster, and Guy didn't like oysters.

"Spit," Philip said, holding out some probably valuable porcelain bowl. Guy spat and sat back; Philip slid down to the floor next to him. "Jesus wept, my lovely no-longer-innocent. Thank you."

"That was right?" Guy was fishing for compliments and didn't care. He felt he'd earned them.

"That was utterly magnificent. Debauchery suits you. Come here." Philip extended an arm. Guy shuffled over, and they ended up in an awkward, sprawled embrace against the bed. "Was that comfortable?"

"I wouldn't say that precisely. I liked doing it to you." Guy examined his face. "You're thinking about something. Is it very terrible?"

"Actually, I was thinking that I want to see you bring yourself off at the same time. Your mouth on me and your hand on yourself, pleasuring us both at once."

"Oh, good heavens. Um, yes. I could do that."

"I'm sure you could." Philip kissed his brow. "And you? What do you wish for that I can give you?"

That was the devil's own question. Guy looked at him, at Sir Philip Rookwood of the Murder, who would be returning to London and his modern, sophisticated, wealthy existence, and his lifelong lover, or lovers, while Guy stayed in Yarlcote and watched the seasons pass, and he wished for so much it hurt.

What I can give you. Philip could give him memories, and experiences that Guy believed in his bones would never be bad ones because Philip was shielding him, and the courage to speak, if only Guy seized those things.

He plucked up his courage. "Well, I don't know about 'wish for', exactly—I hadn't precisely thought of it before—but I was wondering what it would feel like if you—I mean, I'd like you to—" He couldn't say it. "*Me irruma?*"

Philip blinked. "You cannot possibly expect me to remember my Latin conjugations now. No, give me a moment, I can do this. *Irrumare, irruma...* damn it. Future conditional?"

"Second person singular, active imperative."

Philip visibly worked that out, lips moving slightly, then his eyes widened. "Is that 'Shove your prick in my mouth'?"

"I don't mean hard," Guy said hastily. "Just...to have you doing it like that."

"Emphatically?" Philip suggested. "As though I were quite sure you could take it, and that you liked it?"

"With, uh, with you setting the pace. Yes." The words came out a little high, but they were out. He'd said it. He hadn't choked, Philip hadn't laughed, the world hadn't ended.

Philip was nodding slowly. "I said your honesty would undo me. I may have understated the matter considerably. Thank you, Guy. I don't think I have ever been so trusted. I'll try to be worthy of it."

"You are," Guy told him, and pressed his face into Philip's warm shoulder because his eyes were wet.

Chapter Ten

The next week or so felt like holiday. It was a perfect English summer, with a few showers of rain keeping the warm ground watered, bees and birds and flowers bringing the green land into vibrant life. Amanda was transferred with great care to a bath chair, which allowed her to be wheeled outside, her splinted leg out straight. She and Sheridan struck up a strong friendship and chatted for hours; she insisted on being introduced to Corvin despite Guy's reservations, which resulted in quite a lot of delighted shrieking on both their parts, and no signs at all of her succumbing to his charm. A working party was promptly formed with the addition of John to discuss new and ever more outrageous ideas for Gothic novels that would attract the right kinds of attention while avoiding tiresome matters of libel. Philip rather thought that Isabella Crawford would like her, and that, if the Frisbys lived in London, he would invite them to meetings of the Murder.

If. They wouldn't and couldn't, but he had no intention of thinking about that before he had to. The sun was shining, and he and Guy were making hay.

And, indeed, making love. Guy had taken his lessons to heart, and was learning to speak his desires in a way that shook Philip to the bone. He'd only wanted to make the man understand that the best way to get what one wanted was to say what it was, and instead Guy was putting his soul on the table, with hesitant confessions of longings that he barely understood himself, yet offered to Philip like a gift. *Touch me there. Speak to me like that. This is how I thought of you.*

It was that damned innocence of his. He hadn't understood the difference between baring the truth of his body and that of his heart, and Philip was finding himself increasingly inclined to beg him to be less trusting, because he couldn't bear the thought of Guy putting himself in the hands of some ignorant oaf who might respond with scorn or jeers or blows. And it would be all Philip's fault if that happened because he'd taught Guy to assume his desires and refusals would be respected, when there was no guarantee of that at all.

Guard your heart, he wanted to say. *Not with me, never with me, but don't trust anyone else. They won't understand.*

He pushed that impulse down. Guy had let go of so much of his fear, at least when the two of them were alone, as though it had salved something at a deep level to speak his truth and have it embraced and returned. Philip couldn't bear to take that away, not yet.

And in the meantime, they were loving more gloriously than Philip could recall, because Guy's soft voice whispering desire, and the light in his eyes when he looked up, added more than Philip had known possible to any act he could come up with.

Guy had proved every inch the apt pupil, including when Philip had fucked his mouth as requested, declining the Latin verb in his head for distraction, then aloud for comic effect. And, tentatively but with endearing enthusiasm, Guy was attempting more active roles too. He'd taken to frotting like a duck to water and had fucked Philip that way just this morning, driving between his thighs with impressive strength, after they'd woken up together for the first time.

That simple thing, a shared bed, was something Philip wouldn't soon forget. Guy had been understandably nervous, but he'd taken Philip's word for his safety, and slept by him, breathing steady, warm chest rising and falling under Philip's arm. In the morning, he'd woken and smiled up at him, and Philip's lungs had constricted so that he could barely breathe for the loveliness of it. He'd woken with John, Corvin, or both often enough, but that was different. That was a lifetime's trust and friendship, people who would always be there with him because they had made themselves the family all of them had been denied. They'd had to be there for one another because there had been nobody else.

But Guy chose to be there. He'd chosen Philip, chosen to let himself be seduced, chosen to trust, and Philip was increasingly aware that he'd plunged into the depths of his lover's heart with absolutely no idea how far down it went.

He was sitting in the orchard, thinking about it, when Corvin strolled up.

"Phil. I am amazed to see you."

"In my house?"

"In your house without your Patroclus. Move up." Corvin dusted off the bench with his sleeve, sat, and blinked. "This could be more in the shade, you know. You'll get a sun-burn."

"I like the sun."

"'My mistress' eyes are nothing like the sun.' Where is your mistress?"

Philip shot him a look, which was ignored. "If you mean Guy, he and David are managing that bath chair arrangement."

"For the irresistible Amanda. She's a charmer, isn't she? I'm astonished she hasn't married."

"There was an unfortunate situation when she had her Season. Remember Hugh Peyton?"

"That prick? Ah. Oh dear."

"Mmm. Caught in flagrante at a ball."

Corvin raised a weary brow. "What a shit he is. I'm amazed I don't recall."

"It was while we were in Spain."

"Ah. That explains her spinsterhood, I suppose, though one might think there'd be a man with the common sense to look past a youthful misstep."

"They don't have any money either."

"Makes it more difficult, I grant you."

"Not for a rich man." A thought dawned on Philip. "Christ, you aren't interested, are you?"

"Oh, she would have none of me, Phil. I'm far too frivolous. That laughing young lady will choose a serious man."

Philip didn't argue. He had no idea how Corvin could be so definite on the subject of other people's desires, but he had never known him be wrong, and would not in any case have wanted to present him to Guy as a candidate for his sister's hand. "I hope she has the chance."

Corvin leaned back. "Indeed. Yes, she's delightful. The brother's charms are somewhat less evident to the untrained eye."

"Is there something you'd like to say to me that isn't sarcastically allusive?"

"No. Sarcastic allusion is my preferred mode of speech."

Philip turned to look at him. "Let me rephrase that. If there's something you'd like to say to me, spit it out. If not, shut up. I don't know what the devil you have against Guy—"

"Nothing. Well, there wouldn't be any space, would there, with you so close."

"Sorry?" Philip said. "Are you jealous?"

"Of course I bloody am," Corvin said testily. "Keep up."

"If I could just tot up the number of lovers you've had in the past year—"

"It would be entirely irrelevant arithmetic. This isn't about fucking. If it was about fucking I shouldn't care in the least. No, I should be *thrilled* if you'd finally found someone you wanted to fuck."

"I have."

"That isn't what you're doing and you know it. Are we losing you, Phil?"

"Of course not, you bloody idiot."

"Really? Want to fuck?"

"I wouldn't have the strength."

"And seriously?" Corvin asked. "Without the shield of flippancy? Now, or later, back in London, which is where you live, are you still with us?"

Philip stared ahead. He hadn't yet let himself give serious consideration to *afterwards*, when he left for a place he could live in, and Guy stayed here, and his normal life began again. He hadn't fully thought about a practical way that Guy, or the absence of Guy, could fit into his comfortable, established situation. "I don't entirely know. I—don't know."

"You don't know if you'll want to be with us? Or you don't know if your green-eyed innocent would like it if you were?"

"I haven't discussed any of this with him, still less made any promises." Not out loud, at least. "I don't know, V. Do you have to ask me now?"

"Yes," Corvin said. "This feels very like when John married, and that wasn't good."

"I'm not getting married."

"Would you be, given the choice?"

"For God's sake. I've known him a few weeks."

"You've known everyone else for the best part of twenty years, and you haven't fallen in love with any of them."

"That doesn't even make sense," Philip snapped. "And it's—"

"Don't say none of my business, Phil." There was a very gentle warning in Corvin's voice.

"I wasn't going to." He had been about to say exactly that, like a shit, and was deeply grateful he'd been prevented. "It's your and John's right to know what I'm about, yes, but anything between me and Guy is his right. I'm not making a declaration to you that ought to be to him. And I haven't spoken about this to him anyway. For all I know he'll be glad to see the back of me."

"I doubt that. I repeat, this feels like when John married, and you know how that changed things. Unbalanced them. We're not the same two as three."

Philip wanted to protest, but it was true. John's absence from their circle, or triangle, had been difficult for them all. Philip and Corvin had barely seen him in two years, and it had been a guilty relief when the marriage had reached its abrupt and catastrophic end. Philip truly hadn't wished it to fail, for John's sake, but when it had done so, he hadn't regretted the fact nearly as much as he should have.

"No," he said. "I grant you that. But John didn't tell his wife about us. And he made vows."

"To forsake all others. Will you be forsaking all others for your country boy, Phil? Will he want that, or need it? Will you resent it, or not miss us at all?"

"His name is Guy," Philip said. "It's neither long nor difficult. Use it. And I *don't know*. I've no idea what he thinks on the matter and I don't even know if I'll see him again after we leave."

"If you don't, you're a fucking fool," Corvin said. "I haven't seen you like this in your life. You can't seriously intend to wander away."

Philip blinked. "What? You've just spent five minutes arguing me out of it!"

"I have not. Philip, you stupid illegitimate sod, you're in love, and the—Guy has handed you his heart on a platter, with garnishes. That much is entirely obvious. And I am truly glad for you, deep down, although if you imagine for a second I won't be an arsehole about it, you're optimistic."

"How deep down?"

"So far we might have to send Harry to dig it up. But I want you to be happy slightly—*very* slightly—more than I fear losing you."

"You won't lose me, you fool," Philip said. "John felt he had to stay away from us altogether when he married, but I'm not remotely in his situation. I don't know what might change, or how Guy might feel about any one of a dozen aspects, but if my prick dropped off tomorrow—"

"Through overuse?"

"Shut up. —I shouldn't love you and John the less. There is more between us all than just fucking, as you are well aware."

"Yes, but I'm *good* at fucking," Corvin said plaintively.

"You might consider being good at something else one day. Is John worried too?"

"Yes. Although he told me to let you alone and not be a prick."

"I see you took his advice."

"As ever. Promise me something, Phil?"

"What?"

"Promise me you won't trap yourself between lives," Corvin said. "Promise me that you won't find yourself as John did, resenting what you lost to someone who might not, if consulted, have asked you to give it away in the first place. We won't ask you to choose, or insist on a damn thing, but if it comes to a choice— Oh, I don't know. Honestly, if you want to bring him in, I'll welcome him. He's pretty."

"Keep your excessively fingered hands to yourself. Are you seriously suggesting—"

Corvin held up a hand. "I am open to anything that doesn't divide us, in whatever form works. If that means you don't want to fuck any more—well, I like your prick, but I can do without it. I need your friendship."

"I need you too, V. You know that."

"I do. Please don't cut us off, my best bastard, I don't think any of us could bear it again. John and I want you happy, and we'll do what we need to that end. Whether that means being a four-sided triangle, or anything else."

"So will I, for us all. But I don't think— Did you just say a four-sided triangle?"

"Exactly that."

"That's a square. Triangles don't *have* four sides. The clue is in the name."

"Pyramids do, and they're triangular," Corvin said triumphantly.

"That is not how it works!" Philip said, and let himself be drawn into the subsequent argument with a profound sense of the world steadying itself once more.

Corvin's words weren't the only problem. The Murder had been at Rookwood Hall for weeks, and the planned visit was coming to an end. John and Corvin intended to return to London, in John's case extremely discreetly, before heading up to Wrayton Harcourt, accompanied by the Street-Salcombes, who were excavating on his land. The musicians had engagements to fulfil. David Martelo had a practice to which he needed to return, but that at least Philip could stave off.

"Can you leave your patients to survive without you another week?" he asked, having tracked David down that afternoon while Guy and Amanda were having a quiet hour. "At my cost, of course. I'd prefer it if you could see Amanda walking again."

"So should I. What's your intention, Phil?"

"Well, we can't evict the Frisbys until you've given your professional approval, and I can't leave my guests here. I thought you and I might stay until they can return home, whenever that may be."

David gave him a look. "Would you like it to be a little longer?"

"Given the choice, yes. Wouldn't you?"

David grimaced in lieu of answer. "You're very taken with Guy, yes?"

"Apparently that is obvious to everyone."

"Including Amanda."

"*Shit.* Are you sure?"

"As sure as I can be without having a direct conversation on the subject. She's mentioned how clearly he adores you; I don't know if she realises you've taken him to bed, or what she understands to be possible. I wouldn't swear she's unaware."

"Jesus Christ," Philip muttered. How much damage could he possibly do Guy? "Shit."

"She loves him very much. But still."

"Yes. What the devil am I going to do?"

"I had assumed you intended simply to go back to London, having had your fun," David said. "I see I was wrong. How wrong?"

"Entirely wrong."

"Then you should speak to him. See if you can discover how he might feel about his sister marrying a Jew while you're at it."

Philip blinked. "It's that serious?"

"On my part, I'd propose tomorrow and take my chances," David said. "I've no idea about her part, because I can't damned well *say* anything to her while I'm constantly poring over her thigh. *Femur.* And for heaven's sake don't say anything to him, that was a joke. This is trying my nerves, Phil."

"I don't see what you have to worry about. Her leg will mend."

"And she'll still be a Christian."

"Granted, but would that stop you?"

"It might well stop her. I couldn't convert, not to save my own life. My family... It *matters.* I don't make any claim to devotion, I'm not particularly observant of my faith but—no. I could not do it. I'd resent it, resent the need for it. And I have to assume she would feel much the same, and why should she bow to a compromise I'm not prepared to make myself? What do I have to offer? 'Please accept my hand in marriage, offered with the condition you convert to a despised religion, and resign yourself to an existence scraping pennies as a doctor's wife'? It's scarcely the stuff of dreams, is it?"

"That's unusually humble of you. Have you spoken to her on the subject?"

"Of course not," David snapped. "I'm her doctor. I can't make a declaration—one which she might well decline—and then go back to examining her person. It would be grossly wrong of me and deprive her of the treatment she needs. If she had a doctor here I could trust, I could withdraw, but damned if I'm abandoning her care to that old fool who turned up to bleed her dry. Could they not come to London?"

"It's not likely," Philip said. "Financial issues. I…might ask."

"Do that. And in the meantime, you would do me a service if you found a decent doctor to replace me and then I could at least speak."

Philip went. He wasn't sure if Yarlcote could provide such a doctor, but he wrote a note to his steward, cursing that David hadn't spelled out his need before. He'd assumed the man wanted the excuse to be close to Amanda and hadn't really considered the ethical or professional issues it might create. He hadn't considered much, in fact, except that he wanted Guy, and he'd let that wanting blind him to the mounting problems it would cause to the people he loved best.

No, that wasn't right either. He'd deliberately chosen not to consider the consequences. He'd spent a lifetime not considering consequences because he didn't care about them, picking the most desirable or entertaining option because he could. He hadn't hurt anyone, much, until now, but it seemed he was about to make up for lost time in a spectacular way.

He didn't think he wanted to encounter Guy under Amanda's too-sharp eye, which meant waiting until past five in the afternoon, till Guy emerged from the sickroom, rolling his shoulders. He saw Philip in the corridor, and smiled, and Philip wanted to bang his own head against the wall.

"Come with me?" he said instead and led the way to the roof. It was private, and he could always jump if the conversation went badly.

Guy followed obediently and settled where they'd sat before with a pleased sigh. "This is lovely. It's such a beautiful house."

"It's a beautiful view. The house is ghastly, but at least from this vantage point one can't see it."

"It is not ghastly, though I'm sure it's cold in winter. I don't know why you dislike it so much."

"Because it's not mine," Philip said. "Because every square inch of Rookwood Hall, ancestral home of the Rookwoods, filled with Rookwood portraits and possessions, reminds me I am not one, and that my nominal father would have cut off his hand to prevent it coming to me. I didn't set foot here till after James died, did I tell you that? I wasn't permitted to soil the land with my presence, even as a small child. I wasn't wanted here, and I'm bloody not now. In the neighbourhood, I mean."

"That was your choice."

"Was it? I'm a notorious bastard, which might be overlooked if I was also an eligible bachelor, but I've never inclined to a woman in my life. I'm not like John and Corvin, I omit that entire side from my composition. I would be a swine to marry under false pretences, even if I felt it right to hand on the Rookwood inheritance to a child of mine. And yes, granted, I have made no effort to establish myself here as anything other than a gambling, drinking, probably devil-worshipping atheistical rake of the first water and with the worst friends, so I can hardly complain about the results, but I regret them now."

"But you don't want to mix in Yarlcote society. Do you?"

"Not at all, no. And where does that leave us after your sister has recovered the use of her leg, when you no longer have the excuse of her injury to stay in my house, when the world will see you enjoying the company of the man whose brother ruined your mother—or, worse, assume it's Amanda that I'm enjoying." Guy sucked in a breath. "Quite. Tell me if I'm wrong, please do, but I cannot see that it's possible for me to remain here, or visit you in the future, without causing you more damage than I am prepared to do."

Guy swallowed. "Very well. I see what you're saying."

Philip grabbed his hand. "No, you do not, if you think this is a polite dismissal. It's the very opposite. I don't want to go away and leave you behind. I am looking for a way to avoid exactly that. This isn't even close to enough."

"No, but, what?" Guy said. "You told me, you said that, that we—people—would have encounters and fall in love, even, and get better. That's what I thought you meant, that you'd go, and I should expect you to go."

"I might have meant that," Philip said. "I have entirely failed to consider any of this properly, and I'm sorry, but I haven't fallen in love since I was eighteen or so, I didn't even notice I'd done it, and I didn't expect you to fall in love with me either, and—"

"Wait! *What?*"

"Aren't you?" Philip said, with a distinctly cold sensation. "That is, I thought— If I am labouring under a misapprehension, now would be a good time to tell me before I make an even bigger fool of myself."

Guy's mouth moved slightly, then he waved a hand. "Could we tackle this one part at a time? Did—did you say you'd, uh, fallen in love?"

"Yes."

"With me?"

"Obviously with you."

"Well, it's not really obvious, because you hadn't mentioned anything about it!"

Philip twisted round, dropping to his knees on the warm stone, so that he could take both Guy's hands and see his face. "Guy. I suspect I have been falling in love with you since you came through my doors, terrified of everything and still fighting for your sister. You've given me your trust and your innocence and your body, and if I had any sense at all I would have spent the last week telling you I adore you, instead of trying not to face up to the consequences. Which…are real, and difficult, and we are going to have to speak about them, unless you want to give me my marching orders. But we should perhaps spend a moment on the fact that I love you as I have never loved anyone."

"You said you loved Lord Corvin."

"I do, but when I fell in love, I was a boy, and a damn fool one at that. As a man, I have never once fallen in love, still less found it returned." His chest with tight with tension, but he made himself say it. "Until now?"

"Until now," Guy said and lunged forward.

It was several moments until Philip came up for air, and he didn't want to. He'd rather have drowned here, with Guy warm and frantic in his arms, their legs tangled together, Guy's fingers in his hair and his mouth on Philip's with devouring need. It was everything of which he might have dreamed, and he eased back anyway, because it was time to wake up. "Guy."

"Mmm?"

"I love you," Philip said again. "And I can't simply move to Yarlcote, or come visiting every month. Can I?"

"Ugh," Guy said. "If it were me—but it's Amanda."

"You don't think she might marry, at all?" Philip suggested. He couldn't break David's confidence but there was no harm in a general enquiry.

"I can't see how. We don't have a penny put by for a portion, and—well, she's always said, she won't conceal her past from any suitor."

"She isn't the only woman to make a mistake of that nature."

"I know. But after Mother, and with her, uh, indiscretion having been awfully public… She wouldn't lie about that. And she's right not to. It would ruin everything if a husband found out afterwards."

"A sensible man would understand." David would be highly unlikely to blame a woman for behaving with a fraction of the licence permitted to men, Philip thought, although he'd seen worse hypocrisy in more unlikely places.

"If only we knew any," Guy said. "The fact is, you're right. I think if you came visiting us, everyone would assume the worst of Amanda. But I could come here, couldn't I? To see you?"

"For a few days every few months. Yes. Or you could come to London."

"We can't." Guy shut his eyes. "We haven't any money. Really, we have none. Aunt Beatrice gives us enough of an allowance to pay Mrs. Harbottle and Jane, but we've saved nothing. It's been bad enough for Amanda to be trapped in Yarlcote without scrimping every penny. And Aunt Beatrice is quite serious about us staying here. We're not even allowed to pay visits, not that we've anyone to visit, since she's our only family."

"That isn't much of a way to live."

"It's the only way we have. We've talked about it. If we dismissed Mrs. Harbottle and saved for a couple of years and I found a position— But we can't come to London that way."

"No."

"I don't imagine Amanda wants to go anywhere near Society again in any case. But suppose we did, and then something happened to me? Aunt Beatrice would be all Amanda had left. We can't burn that bridge."

"Granted, but it's been five years since Amanda's indiscretion. Surely your aunt could loosen her grip?"

"Her second daughter is on the verge of making an excellent marriage to an earl-in-waiting," Guy said. "We can't make ourselves a nuisance now. And my aunt is strict but, you know, she was truly horrified by my mother's behaviour, and Amanda's scandal was really dreadful. She's so very respectable herself, I can't blame her for not wanting people to remember we exist."

"You're more charitable than me. Damn your mother. And my half-brother," Philip added hastily. "The pair of them."

"I don't know if I can blame them either," Guy said, adjusting himself to lie more comfortably on Philip's chest. "My father didn't concern himself with anyone else's happiness, and if Sir James was anything like you, I don't blame my mother for running away with him. If she felt as I do, if she saw happiness and love and the alternative was a lifetime with a man who didn't care—"

"She left you in his charge."

"We'd have been in his charge whatever happened. If she'd tried to take us, he'd have had the law on her. No, the only question was whether she shared our misery or reached for her own happiness. And I'm not saying I'd have made her choice, but I do think I understand it better now. I hope she was happy while she had the chance."

"Christ, I love you," Philip said. "And, to return to that subject—"

"We can't go to London," Guy said again. "Aunt Beatrice has a third daughter, who is sixteen. Once she's married, perhaps—"

"Guy, this is years of your life!"

"I know. What am I to do about it? It's not as though Amanda could live here without me. She'd die of loneliness, and in any case, Aunt Beatrice would cut her off. I couldn't do that."

Philip considered his next remark. He was almost certain it was a foolish one, but he said it anyway. "I'm well off. Well off enough for three."

"No," Guy said flatly. "Don't be absurd. You can't be seen to keep Amanda."

"I would avoid being seen."

"And what would happen if you decided you no longer wanted a little country innocent?"

Philip bit back his first response. It was a fair question. "I would hope I should behave decently, but I don't expect you to wager both your futures on that."

"I couldn't."

Naturally he couldn't. Amanda would always be first, of course she bloody would, with Guy never claiming his own happiness at her expense, and Philip wasn't sure if he loved Guy more for that or simply wanted to shake him.

"Then we return to visits," he said. "I am quite sure I could show more interest in my lands, you know. Come up every few months."

"Yes. We could have that."

Philip didn't want that. He wanted Guy in his bed, waking up with him, not given time to brood and worry and wait. He didn't want to roam England on his own, wasting time, snapping at his friends, counting the days till the next visit. And, very probably, sleeping with Corvin or John to take the edge off, or not doing so because he wasn't sure what Guy would think. "Ah, hell. There's something else."

"There can't be."

"I fear so." He rolled away and sat up, hugging his knees. "I told you about Corvin, and John, and myself. I'm not sure I told you everything."

"What else is there?"

"The depth of it. They're my best friends, and my lovers, and the closest thing to family I have ever had. It has been the three of us, and sometimes only the three of us, for close on twenty-five years. We've been fucking since we were sixteen, in pairs or all three together, and that may not be the kind of love about which the poets write, nor the kind I feel for you, but it's still as real and true as anything in the world. And when John married—well, he made his vows truly and sincerely, and he kept them, and it was an appalling mistake. His wife didn't understand why he wanted to spend time with people she despised. She was a radical, she'd have happily seen my and Corvin's heads in the guillotine basket, and she thought him a hypocrite for his friendships given he shared her political beliefs. And she never came to understand because he couldn't tell her the truth of us. Or perhaps he could have, but he didn't, and it destroyed the trust between them. The damned fool thing was that he truly loved her. But he loved us too, and it was extremely hard for everyone. For us without him, and him without us, and him without her, and I imagine for her throughout the whole damned business."

"Right," Guy said slowly. "That sounds rather dreadful."

"It was. She left him after two years for a fellow radical who didn't have unwanted aristocratic connections. They emigrated to the Americas, which seems extreme but who am I to criticise, and that's gone some way to assuaging John's guilt, but you will understand why I don't want to repeat his mistake. The question is how to avoid doing so."

"I'm not quite sure what you're asking of me."

"Nor am I," Philip said. "Perhaps simply that you hear me out and consider what you think, and we start from there. I'm not going to ask you to accept Corvin and John in your life as they are in mine. But they are in my heart and always will be. I'd be lying if I said otherwise."

"You mean, as lovers?"

"I don't know. In all honesty, that's scarcely the most important part of it for me, and given our history, I don't know if our ceasing to fuck would make a great deal of difference to you. Not if what you wanted was my undivided devotion. John didn't share our beds when he was married and that didn't help at all."

"No. I see that. Um, what do they think about me?"

"They want me to be happy," Philip said. "Whatever that may mean. I'm hoping this conversation may lead, somehow and by circuitous paths, to that end. I'm trying very hard not to present you with a fait accompli, still less an ultimatum. If you want a heart-whole man without encumbrances—"

"I wouldn't have a great deal to offer one, even if I found him," Guy said. "I wouldn't be heart-whole either and then we'd all be in trouble. Is there a particular difference between what you feel about me, and about them?"

"Christ, yes," Philip said. "Corvin's a prick, and John's an obstinate swine, and they both drive me to incoherent fury on a regular basis."

Guy spluttered. Philip grinned at him. "And Corvin has a heart so big I don't know how he carries it around, and John plants his feet against the world and stares it down, and they both loved me before I understood what the word meant. Whereas you trusted me with your truth, and took me to your tree, and found words in Latin when you were afraid to say them any other way, and your eyes hold all England. It's like asking me if there's a difference between fine wine and poetry. Of course there is, but it's hard to make useful comparisons. I love you; I also love them. And that leads me to say that if you felt the need, or desire, to take other lovers, well, I couldn't and wouldn't object. You probably should."

"I—don't think I want to."

Guy reached out, a tentative movement. Philip took his hand feeling his muscles relax. "Perhaps not, or not now. But I can't offer you what you deserve. I can't ask you to be entirely mine, and pledge my own disreputable self to you in return, and I shouldn't if I could. We won't see one another for months on end, and I am neither making nor holding you to promises that stretch out over months till they snap. That kind of thing sounds wonderfully romantic at the time, and then we have to live. And I certainly shan't ask you to accept my friends before you've had a chance to consider what it means to be—let's say, primus inter pares."

Guy thought for a moment. "I've got Amanda. Which isn't the same, but—"

"She will always come first. I know."

Guy's hand tightened on him. "First among equals. Philip, you didn't conceal this. I knew you loved them. I'm just not sure how it works that you love me too."

"Corvin's lesson. The more love you give, the more you are capable of giving. It's only when you shut off the source that it dries up. Or, at least, that principle works for us. Others would disagree."

"I'm going to have to give this some thought, if you don't mind," Guy said. "I don't want to say anything until I'm sure what I think. It's all quite far from my experience."

"I'm sorry to make this so complicated. You should probably have had some simple, straightforward amour for your first, and instead you find yourself with a bastard baronet in what Corvin insists on calling a four-sided triangle."

"Triangles don't—"

"I know."

"I'm sure he says these things to annoy you," Guy said. "It is complicated, but thank you for being honest with me. I would much rather know where I stand, even if it's a bit— Oh my goodness."

"What?"

"Before she met you, Amanda was asking if you had orgies, and I said I was sure you didn't. Well. I do hope she doesn't ask that again."

"I haven't had anything that I'd call an orgy in years," Philip said. "That's quite a different thing, and requires more than three people. Also more organisation than you might think, and a great deal of tidying up afterwards. Three of us is just a rather crowded bed."

Guy choked. "I dare say. I don't even know how you'd manage with three."

That sounded like a hint. Philip cocked a brow. "I could tell you, beloved, if you'd like to hear about it. You might find it quite shocking, or then again you might not. Sometimes it's nothing but making love with extra hands. Two people you adore, stroking and kissing and telling you they want you." Guy shivered. Philip grinned. "And other times—let me see, how does one express *Pedicabo ego vos et irrumabo* in the passive voice?"

Guy opened his mouth to answer, and then his brows shot up as meaning caught up with grammar. "You mean, uh, one person for each verb?"

"Indeed."

"At the *same time*?"

Philip had a powerful memory of John's hands on his head, Corvin gripping his hips. "Very much so."

"Philip!"

"I will tell you such a bedtime story tonight," Philip promised him, delighting in the betraying wash of colour. He wondered briefly if Corvin had a point, what it might be like to see Guy writhing under his hands, or John's, or both. "And you will think about all this, as long as you need, and we will find some sort of answer between us. But whatever that answer is, I love you. Hold to that?"

"Always," Guy said, and buried his face in Philip's chest.

The others left the next day. Corvin kindly deputised four members of his staff to keep the Hall running, so that Philip didn't have to live with Yarlcote servants and the inevitable creeping around that would entail. He'd have to face that when he visited in the future: people in the house who could not be trusted, looking for secrets and guilt. He hoped Sinclair wouldn't rebel at the thought of enforced rural seclusion without Cornelius to entertain him. The last thing he needed was to find a new valet.

The following week was one of the happiest he'd known, if he'd been able to shake the sense of the end of Arcadia approaching. Rookwood Hall was an echoing place with his noisy group whittled down to himself, David, and the Frisbys, but the days were still sunny. David decreed that it was time for Amanda to put weight on her splinted leg, and she hobbled up and down the corridor with him and Guy hovering in attendance. The four of them ate together, in nonstop, laughing talk, and if Amanda had any suspicions about Guy's private activities, they didn't show.

There were a lot of private activities. Philip could have stayed in bed with Guy all day, for the closeness and the look in his eyes, and because when it was just them there was no self-consciousness, no fear of observation, no hesitant restraint or shame or flinching in anticipation of hurt. He needed nothing more than Guy's happiness; as it was he got plenty more, because Guy was warm and eager and had a lot of lonely nights for which to make up.

"Philip?" Guy asked, on the third night. He was sitting on their— Philip's—bed, stripping off his stockings with joyous unselfconsciousness.

"Beloved?"

"I'm not suggesting anything, as such," Guy said carefully. "But, well. Would I like sodomy?"

"That is without a doubt the best question that has ever been asked. English was invented purely so that you could ask that."

"Seriously, though," Guy said, blushing but grinning. "You made it sound rather enjoyable when you were telling me all about what you'd got up to with the others."

Philip had done that with Guy's prick in his hand, his own pressed between Guy's thighs. It had been highly effective. "It can be marvellous, but not everyone finds it so."

"Why not?"

"Some people find it painful. Some find the concept distasteful. And even when one enjoys it, it's not always easy for a man to admit he likes to be fucked, the world being as it is. Some feel it to be unmanning."

"Oh." Guy looked as though he hadn't thought of that.

Philip could have kicked himself. "I think that's arrant nonsense, myself," he went on. "It makes you no less a man than ever you were—no, that's not true, actually."

"Isn't it?"

Philip stroked his hair. "No, because it's the opposite. There's nothing brave about hiding from one's desires. It takes far more courage to know yourself. But other than that, the act has no significance at all. It's purely a matter of taste."

Guy nodded. "All the same, you haven't suggested it."

"A month ago, you'd never been kissed. I thought we might take our time."

"But Amanda's walking," Guy said. "We don't have much more time. *Do* you think I'd like it?"

"I don't know, beloved. If you would care to try, I am at your disposal, in either part."

"I think I'd like you to do it," Guy said, barely above a whisper. "I don't know really—or if it would hurt—but I can't stop wondering what it would be like if you did it to me."

"*With* you. It will hurt a little, inevitably. And if it isn't to your taste, we'll stop."

That won him, unexpectedly, an eye-roll dramatic enough for Corvin. "I *know* that, you idiot. For heaven's sake, we've been doing this for weeks."

"Well, you haven't had much practice in asking me to stop. Barely any. In fact, you've been as ripe for every sort of ruin and debauchery as my most sordid imaginings could have hoped. Who knew that pose of virginal innocence hid such a shameless sensualist?"

Guy was blushing fiercely. "I *was* virginally innocent, and everything else is your fault. Tell me, these sordid imaginings—"

"Have involved you bent over a bed pleading for me, yes. Now and then."

"I thought they might. Debauch me, Philip?"

Philip pushed him gently onto his back. "I will educate you, my love, and I will strive to please you. And, yes, I will also debauch you like the eager little wanton you are. If I absolutely must."

"Not if it's an imposition," Guy assured him, and they were both giggling as Philip went looking for the oil.

That was mostly what he remembered of that night, afterwards: the easy happiness. He'd had a superstitious fear, against all his experience, this might feel significant, as though it would be some final act of deflowering that changed things. That Guy would hate it, that he'd feel it a sin, that something would go wrong. In the event Guy followed instructions with no more than little gasps and a few pauses to get it right, and took Philip with a determination that ripened quickly into joy. Philip held himself back for longer than seemed possible, concentrating fiercely on Guy's pleasure, making sure every slow stroke counted, until Guy was moaning under him, clutching the sheet.

"I want you to spend," Philip whispered. "I want you to spend while I'm in you, fucking you. I want you to like it."

"I love it. Touch me," Guy panted. "If you— God! Yes."

Philip had a hand on his shoulder to brace himself. The other, oil-slick, he slid round to circle Guy's prick, sliding his hand up and down in time with his thrusts. "Tell me how it feels. Speak to me, beloved."

"It's—you're— Oh God, it's good, you're good, it's marvellous, I can't say. *Me pedica*, Philip. Don't stop."

"Tell me in English. You know the words."

"Fuck me," Guy said on a breath. "I love you, keep fucking me, *please*."

And Philip did, driving into him, feeling Guy's whole body tense as he spent and finding his own release in a near-painful rush that left them both in a wet, shivering, tangled heap.

"Christ," Philip said after a while. "Latin imperatives in bed. I had no idea. Well, now we know why the Roman empire declined and fell."

"They were declining the wrong verbs." Guy snuggled into him. "Do you remember telling me I might enjoy being ruined?"

"I remember being an unnecessary prick to you, yes."

Guy kissed him on the collarbone, presumably since that was where his lips were. "You had a point. Thank you for debauching me, Philip. You've done it beautifully."

"I should probably feel guilty about taking your virtue."

"But I don't think you have. I feel more—more loving, in all the different ways, than I ever have in my life. I feel as though, while you love me, I could be better and kinder to the whole world. If that's not virtue, I don't know what is."

"Nor do I," Philip said, and pulled him close.

Chapter Eleven

Two days later, the carriage came up the drive.

They weren't expecting visitors. They were, in fact, so far from expecting visitors that Guy was in their bedroom, braced against a table, legs wide, with Philip's oiled fingers sliding and probing inexorably against his backside. He'd been kissed into delirium and stripped naked with agonising slowness, and he was anticipating this with a combination of some nerves—last time had been the most overwhelming experience of his life—and mounting pleasure. Philip was going to bend him over the table and fuck him in broad daylight, the window uncurtained because they were too high up to be seen, and Guy was lost in delicious anticipation when he heard the sound of horses and the crunch of wheels on gravel.

"Who the hell is that?" Philip muttered.

Guy looked up and saw the coach, a vividly memorable shade of blue. It was coming up to the house and it swept out of his line of sight after a second, but that was quite long enough.

"Oh God. Oh my God. Philip!"

"What? Guy?"

"It's my aunt," Guy said, lips numb. "Lady Paul Cavendish. My aunt, here!"

"Christ's balls," Philip said. "All right, don't panic. Dress, quickly, remembering that you have done nothing wrong. *Calm*, Guy. I will be with you."

Guy grabbed for his clothes, hoping they could be rendered decent. His stand had wilted, not surprisingly, but Philip had been thorough in his caresses, and Guy knew he must look a dreadful, criminal mess. "I'm sticky. Oh God, my face!"

Philip rang the bell then returned to dressing himself, which he was doing very quickly. "Right. Do what I say. Get your drawers on, taking deep breaths as you do it. Do not try to speak."

Guy heard noises from below. The door, the tortured vowels of an extremely well-bred voice that he'd heard dispensing measured denunciation all too often. "It's her. What's she doing here?"

"We'll find out."

There was a quiet knock, and Sinclair slid in. Guy, not even half-dressed, froze in horror. The valet did not. "You rang, sir?"

"Get Mr. Frisby dressed and groomed," Philip said shortly. "I want him downstairs in five minutes looking like the perfect gentleman."

Sinclair gave Guy a swift but gloomy once-over. "Five minutes. You don't ask much, do you?"

"If you were bad at your job I shouldn't pay you. I certainly don't have you around for your personal graces."

"Yeah, well, same," Sinclair assured his master. "All right, Mr. Frisby, why don't you stand up?"

"Do what Sinclair says," Philip told Guy. "He is competent if you can look past the manner." He hadn't stopped dressing throughout. Guy wondered, in a dizzy sort of way, if he was used to this urgency. By the time Sinclair had Guy's waistcoat buttoned, Philip had shrugged himself into his coat, tied an adequate knot to his cravat, wrenched his boots on, and run a comb through his hair. "Right. I'm going down. You have been, uh, out for a walk. Get him out the back, Sinclair, without anyone seeing him. Hold fast, beloved."

He departed with a long stride. Sinclair shook his head. "Always something, ain't there? One thing after another with this lot. Well, never mind, it'll all be the same in a hundred years. This neckerchief won't do at all, sir, let me fetch a fresh one."

Guy followed Sinclair downstairs and was whisked out of the Hall unseen. He strolled round the side of the house, attempting to keep his countenance, and entered by the main door, where Sinclair met him.

"Mr. Frisby, sir," the valet said with a solemn bow. "Lord and Lady Paul Cavendish have arrived and request your presence in the Yellow Drawing-Room."

"Good heavens, really?" Guy tried, which was met with a ludicrous wink. "Um, thank you."

Sinclair preceded him to the door, announcing "Mr. Guy Frisby" with great seriousness, bowed, and departed. Guy stepped in and found himself faced with his relatives.

Aunt Beatrice had been the older sister and the prettier of the two. Coming from a family of some wealth but no particular distinction, she had done extremely well to secure the younger son of a marquess in wedlock. She had adopted a haughty manner even before their mother's flight, or so Guy's father had complained; afterwards, her efforts to distance herself from the disgrace had led her to become correct to the point of striking fear into all hearts.

Guy had always been terrified of her; he remembered her thunderous denunciations of Amanda's criminal misbehaviour with wincing horror. He couldn't blame her. Lord Paul was every bit as much a stickler as his wife, and they had three daughters, none of whom deserved to be associated with scandal, but the charity Guy and Amanda had had from the Cavendishes had not been given with love or understanding, and he didn't see that on their faces now.

Both sat bolt upright on the edges of chairs, as though preferring not to touch the furniture. There was no sign of tea things. Philip sat in another chair in a frankly slovenly posture, chin resting on his hand, one leg crossed over the other at the knee, with a hard light in his eyes that boded extremely ill. Amanda was on the sofa, leg propped on a footstool, face and lips very white.

"Aunt Beatrice," Guy said. "Lord Paul. I'm very pleased to see you. I had no idea you were going to visit."

"This is not a *visit*," Lord Paul said in arctic tones, handling the noun as though with tongs. "We do not *visit* this gentleman and his associates."

"Please," Philip said. "Make yourself free of the house."

"You uh, you have been introduced to Sir Philip Rookwood?" Guy said desperately.

Aunt Beatrice looked the other way. It was as close to a cut direct as could be administered, in Philip's own house. Guy didn't dare look at him. "I'm afraid I didn't expect you. May I ask—"

"Guy Frisby," Aunt Beatrice said, rolling the r. "The carriage waits. You and your sister will return to your home with us, as you should have done at once."

"But Amanda has a broken leg. That's why we're here. She can't travel, her leg is too precarious."

Amanda winced. Philip was casually tracing a finger in a line across his throat. Guy understood as Aunt Beatrice swelled. "Your sister was walking—*hopping*—on the arm of a male individual when we arrived. She is quite evidently able to return home. I cannot understand how you should have so lowered yourself as to spend one hour—one minute!—longer than medically necessary in this house. You have behaved with gross irresponsibility and your sister has shamed herself, her family, and, what I cannot forgive, *my* family with her immoral and disgusting behaviour—"

"Now wait a minute!" Guy hadn't meant to shout, and it came out more of a squeak. "Wait. Amanda has done absolutely nothing wrong. Her bone broke so badly she nearly died of blood loss and fever. She would have died if Sir Philip hadn't allowed us to stay, and she lived thanks to Dr. Martelo, who I'm very sure is the gentleman who was helping her walk. And Sir Philip has—has provided female attendance for her day and night, and I've been here the whole time, and—and—"

"And the party which has, sadly, just broken up included a young matron of the utmost respectability who acted as chaperone," Philip said, to Guy's astonishment. Amanda didn't even blink. "A Mrs. Salcombe, I will be happy to put you in touch with her. I must say in my defence that I have never in my life made such stringent efforts to avoid any appearance of impropriety."

"Then you have failed, sir."

"He has not." Amanda's voice was tear-stifled. "Sir Philip and his friends have been—the utmost consideration—"

"'Sir' Philip," Lord Paul said, the quotation marks almost audible, "has exposed you not only to the presence of an individual whose notoriety is such that I must decline to name him—"

"Lord Corvin," Philip said helpfully. "You must know him; Wrayton Harcourt is not far from Easterbury's seat. Why, he's all but your brother's neighbour, Lord Paul."

"*But also,*" Lord Paul went on as if Philip hadn't spoken, while his wife ruffled like a chicken with outrage, "to the contempt and disdain of any decent individual."

"Why?" Amanda almost shrieked. "All I did was break my leg!"

"You have been staying in Rookwood Hall for weeks," Aunt Beatrice said, voice like doom. "You must realise the interpretation that has been put on events."

"What interpretation?" Guy demanded.

"Let me guess: London is ablaze with the news that Miss Frisby has become my mistress, as her mother was my brother's," Philip said. "It is untrue, and I am surprised to see people of sense or decency stoop to such sordid chatter. If I were Mr. Frisby I should gravely resent it on my sister's account. Having not that right, I shall resent it on my own. You will oblige me by not repeating any further lies in my house."

That went down as well as Guy could have predicted. Lord Paul stood and denounced, waving his finger as though lecturing a schoolboy. Philip leaned back in his chair, legs crossed, an ugly sneer twisting his lip, replying with contemptuous scorn. Guy wished he'd be quiet. He slid over to Amanda and sat by her, grabbing her cold hand.

"It's all right," he whispered.

"It's not."

It wasn't. Aunt Beatrice cleared her throat loudly, putting an end to Lord Paul and Philip's exchange of compliments. "Excuse me. I *will* have silence, Sir Philip. Your denials and assertions notwithstanding, the fact is that my unfortunate niece's whereabouts for this period are common knowledge. Her reputation has been entirely marred, her name, already tarnished by her mother's reprehensible actions, brought to contempt. This is the result of her sojourn in your house, sir, and there is only one means of redress available."

Guy thought for a blank moment that Lord Paul was going to challenge Philip to a duel, and then he realised. Amanda said, loudly, "No," and Philip's lips curved in a smile as nasty as any Guy had seen on him.

"And now I grasp the game. Yes, that *would* be a convenient means by which to rid yourself of both an unwanted niece and a financial obligation. Never mind that you have denounced me as a disgrace whose chairs are not fit to be sat upon by the decent: you would hand over Miss Frisby's person and future to my notorious and disgusting self to maintain your family respectability. I wish I were surprised by that. No."

"I beg your pardon?"

"No," Philip said again. "No, I will not offer my hand to a lady who neither needs nor wants it for the sake of your propriety. Not a chance."

"Sir, you are no gentleman," Lord Paul said furiously.

"I believe that fact is also notorious."

"Perhaps you will do us the favour of allowing my family private conversation," Aunt Beatrice said, each word dripping ice.

"Certainly." Philip rose. "Mr. Frisby, Miss Frisby. Should you wish for me, or indeed footmen to escort anyone out, you know where the bell is. And allow me to reiterate that you are welcome to remain my guests as long as you care to do so."

He strolled out, shutting the door. Amanda gripped Guy's fingers convulsively.

"Well," Aunt Beatrice said. "I had heard the worst, but *that*—"

"He is a very kind and generous man," Guy said, voice shaking.

"How can you say such a thing in the face of that appalling rudeness?"

"I think you were rude to him first," Amanda said. "And it was not kind to—to attempt to force— How could you? What a dreadful thing to say!"

"You may not speak to your aunt in that manner," Lord Paul said. "The disgrace you have brought on our family— Lord Perivale himself heard the rumours!"

"Who?" Guy asked.

Amanda gave his hand a punitive squeeze, too late. Aunt Beatrice looked sabres at him. "Lord Perivale, whose eldest son is to marry Anne, your cousin. I am disappointed you have so little interest in the well-being of your only family."

"I'm sorry, I just forgot," Guy said. "And I'm sure, uh—" He couldn't for the life of him remember the fiancé's name. "—Lord Perivale and his son won't hold silly rumours against Anne. If you tell everyone it's not true, surely you'll be believed."

"I hardly think we can argue any such thing, having cancelled several important engagements to come here to rescue you from your folly."

"Well, that's not our fault," Amanda said. "It's a shame you didn't give me the benefit of the doubt."

"You have lost that," Aunt Beatrice said, voice dreadfully measured. Amanda sucked in a breath as though she'd been struck. "You will now do precisely as I tell you or I shall wash my hands of you both, once and for all. You will leave this place at once. You will return to your own home, where I shall remain with you to discuss the future. Let me remind you, you live by my charity. If you disobey me, you will not hang upon my husband's sleeve one more day. Not one!"

Amanda was breathing through her teeth. Guy could barely breathe at all. He forced the words out.

"Yes, Aunt. We'll come at once."

Philip kicked the door open as Guy was packing. It was proving quite difficult to do that and not cry at the same time.

"Guy? What the hell?"

"Well, we're going home. That's all. We would always have had to."

"You can't let that pair of sanctimonious bullies dictate your movements."

"We don't have any choice."

"I've offered you a choice," Philip said. "And if Amanda's already being talked about as my mistress—"

"I can't stop the world thinking my sister is your kept woman, but I damned well won't give them more reasons to think it!" Guy wiped furiously at his eyes. "And if you hadn't spent your entire life in this perverse effort to have everyone think the worst of you—"

"Are you seriously blaming me for this debacle?"

"You and Lord Corvin and the Murder *want* to be talked about! Can you not imagine how dreadful this is for Amanda?"

"I'm afraid I'm rather busy imagining how dreadful it is for you, while you throw your youth on the fire as a sacrifice to the domestic gods," Philip snapped. "How will you and I see each other again? What are you going to do, sit at home with Amanda till you both dry up and blow away?"

"What else should I do? Abandon her? You said you understood!"

"I don't understand why you're clinging to the proprieties when they're pulling you down!" Philip almost shouted. "That's not a life-preserver, it's a sodding anchor, a metal weight, and you will drown if you don't let go!"

"It's not my choice! I am trying to do my best for my sister—"

"Do you even know what she wants? Did she ask you to give up your life, happiness, the man who loves you, for her?"

"She doesn't have to!" Guy shouted, and they stared at each other, the words ringing off the walls. "She doesn't have to," he said again, more quietly. "Because she comes first, I told you that, and—and first among equals doesn't mean anything at all."

"No," Philip said. "I see that it doesn't. And you did indeed tell me that. So, since I have always promised to take no for an answer, there is nothing left but to bid you good day."

"What? No, wait. Philip—"

"You've made a decision," Philip said through his teeth. "I am trying to respect it, and myself, and indeed you. That will be a great deal more easily done from a distance."

The return to Drysdale House was accomplished in a miserable silence, at least on the Frisbys' part; Aunt Beatrice and Lord Paul talked more or less continually. David Martelo was nowhere in evidence as they left, and Guy had to help manoeuvre a white-faced, silent Amanda into the carriage unaided, and then out at the end of the journey.

The house smelled stuffy and unused. It had to be aired, and Mrs. Harbottle summoned, and bedrooms made up, and a bed for Amanda in the parlour since she could not safely manage the stairs, and the kitchen fire lit, and all of that kept Guy sufficiently busy that he had no time to think. Then there was dinner, which was awful, and a solid hour of prayers for repentance and improvement, which Guy thought Amanda might have walked out of, were it not for her leg. He didn't seek Amanda out for private speech that night. He didn't want to leave her alone in her misery, but he was too afraid he'd break down himself, and have no way to explain why.

The next day was much the same. Guy spent it out in the vegetable garden, pulling weeds and repairing the ravages of a month of inattention. Amanda made her way up and down the path on crutches, face drawn and set with determination.

"Ought you not be resting?" Guy asked her.

"Dr. Martelo advised me to place weight on it."

No 'David', Guy noted, and didn't dare ask.

There were more prayers, more lectures. Guy had hidden the copies of *Darkdown* in a cupboard, unable to bear it if Amanda was rebuked for reading novels. He extracted one and took it upstairs in secret to read, but the first mention of the cruel Sir Peter Falconwood left him curled on his bed in agonising misery, because all he could think about was Philip's teasing voice, the touch of his hand, the warmth in his eyes.

He'd done the right thing. He knew he had, and he was sure that Philip would see that when he wasn't so frighteningly angry, but the knowledge did absolutely nothing to soothe the jagged hole in his chest, where he'd ripped out his heart and left it behind at Rookwood Hall.

There wasn't even anyone there, as they learned from Jane. Sir Philip had left the very same day as them, setting off back to London on horseback with his household coming after in conveyances. He hadn't wasted any time in going back where he belonged.

On the third day, their misery was slightly alleviated by the announcement that Lord Paul would be leaving them.

"I shall return to London in order to make arrangements to establish my daughters at the house in Bath," he pronounced. Naturally, there was no offer to let Amanda convalesce in a pleasant location where the waters would do her good. "Lady Paul has most generously agreed to remain with you in order to give you her countenance. I hope you will demonstrate your gratitude."

Guy managed some polite murmur. Amanda didn't speak, but when Aunt Beatrice and Lord Paul were busy with the apparently complex arrangements for his departure, she jerked her head at the garden, and Guy followed.

"You've been avoiding me," she said without preamble as they sat on the bench at the far end. "Please stop or I'll go mad."

"Sorry. It's just so awful."

"Isn't it. I am so tired of living under these people's thumb, Guy. So tired of it."

"So am I, but what are we going to do?"

"Sir Philip said we could stay with him."

"Don't be ridiculous. You know what everyone would think."

"They already think it," Amanda said. "And it doesn't matter anyway. Nobody will ever marry me, no decent man, I've seen to that. So why shouldn't we? I could be very shocking and scarlet and write books, and Sir Philip wouldn't care in the slightest, and Aunt Beatrice would have a *stroke*, if we're lucky, and—and you'd be happy, darling. Shouldn't one of us be happy?"

Guy could feel the blood draining from his face. "What do you mean?"

"Oh, Guy. I have watched you, and I'm not entirely ignorant, and I talked to Sherry—in confidence, you know—because I needed to understand, and he was awfully helpful and explained all sorts of things that nobody ever tells one. Do you love him? Sir Philip, I mean. Not Sherry."

Guy put his face in his hands. Amanda put her arm round his shoulders, giving comfort in the way that should have been his job. "Dearest, you know I don't mind in the slightest, don't you? If you were happy. I've never seen you so happy in my whole life as you were at the Hall, or even just when Sir Philip walked into a room. You looked—you looked *right* with him and Sherry said exactly the same about Sir Philip with you, and we both think it's marvellous, actually."

"But it isn't," Guy said, muffled. "I doubt I'll ever see him again."

"Then you're stupid. You can't just sit here in Yarlcote forever. Write to him. Please, Guy. It's such a mess, but you could be happy."

"No, I couldn't be. Not if I left you behind, and not at the price of everyone thinking the worst of you. I couldn't."

"Wouldn't it make a difference if we knew it wasn't true? Didn't you tell me that once?"

"Then I was wrong. The way Aunt Beatrice spoke to you—she had no right. And the way they both spoke to Philip, sneering at him, insulting him in his own house. It isn't tolerable. I'm not surprised he's turned his back on society, I'd like to do the same, but... I can't just ask Philip to keep us, Manda. You must see that. Look, Aunt Beatrice will go away eventually. Things will settle down."

"If you think you'll ever be allowed to see him again, you're wrong," Amanda said. "Can you imagine if she found out you'd visited the Hall? And she'd find out, she probably has spies all over this horrid place. Someone here wrote letters about me, didn't they? A nice juicy piece of gossip to people in London who were probably so thrilled by the latest on-dit that they couldn't wait to share it. It's hateful. I wish I hadn't put the Murder in my book. They're about the only people I can think of who don't deserve it."

"No, they don't. Manda, what about David?"

Amanda's mouth tightened. "What about him?"

"I thought—well. That you were getting on."

"So did I. Only, then Lord Paul arrived shouting imprecations at him as though he were a stable-boy for presuming to take my arm, while Aunt Beatrice harangued me as a common stale, and I dare say that put him off. He—he didn't even say goodbye, Guy. He just went away, and we left and—and—"

Guy twisted to get his arm round her. Amanda leaned into him and cried, and he held her, whispering promises of everything being all right that he knew very well weren't true.

Two more days passed with no sign of Aunt Beatrice leaving. She had spent much of her stay writing and receiving letters, to whom Guy didn't know or care. He wanted to write to Philip and didn't dare to. That was contemptible, in his own house. But he didn't know Philip's direction in London, and if he'd found it out he couldn't have borne the possibility that someone might report back, and anyway he didn't know what he'd say. *I'm sorry. I miss you. I love you. There's nothing I can do about it, but I love you. I hope you'll be happy. I don't think I will be ever again.*

We get better. He reminded himself of that again and again. Philip had promised him that he'd get better from a doomed love affair and Philip had never lied to him or let him down. Only Guy had done that.

On the Friday night, Aunt Beatrice announced that they would be accommodating another guest.

"My chaplain, Mr. Dent. A man of the highest moral standards and a tower of strength to the repentant sinner. There is a living in Easterbury's possession which will fall vacant imminently—it is a post for a married man, requiring a woman's aid, and the incumbent, a widower, has no daughter. The Marquess has most generously consented to let Lord Paul put forth Mr. Dent as a candidate. He will arrive tomorrow. A room must be prepared; kindly see to it."

"Yes, Aunt," Guy managed. Amanda kept her mouth shut, but her eyes were snapping, and she broke into violent speech as soon as they were alone in the garden the next day. Guy thanked heaven for the sun, which kept Aunt Beatrice indoors for the sake of her complexion.

"Are we really going to let her invite people here willy-nilly? To our house?"

"It may be ours but she's been paying for its upkeep for years," Guy said. "Yes, it sticks in my craw too, but she cannot possibly be meaning to stay much longer. She'll want to go to Bath. I can't imagine why she's invited her chaplain here, except that I suppose we can expect more sermonising—"

"Can't you?" Amanda asked. "I can. A post for a married man? A bribe of a living? A man of the highest moral standards who stoops to pick sinners out of the gutter?"

"Oh," Guy said. "Oh, no."

"I will not marry some ghastly oleaginous toad mouthing Bible verses to make other people miserable. I will *not*."

"He might be young and handsome and kind-hearted?" Guy offered.

"But he's Aunt Beatrice's chaplain, so he'll be just like her. Bowing to those above and treading on those below. I shan't, Guy. I won't."

"No, you won't. But—" He bit back *What are we going to do?* It was time to stop asking that and start deciding it. "Right. We have your ten pounds, Manda. That's enough to rent a cottage somewhere near a school, say, if I could get a job as a schoolmaster. And I don't know how long it would take you to write another book—"

"I'll be quicker next time," Amanda said with a firm nod. "And they might even give me more than ten pounds, if the first one has sold. I wish I knew if people were buying it. Lord Corvin said he was going to write to people and say how shockingly rude it was about him. But that would work, wouldn't it?"

"If I found a job before too long. We couldn't afford a maid, but—"

"I can do without."

"I can sell my books," Guy said, needing to match her sacrifice. "And some of the furniture, maybe? That's ours. We could make probably another fifteen pounds that way, and that will buy your paper and keep us afloat till I find work. And if—if we weren't dependent on Aunt Beatrice, and we weren't here, and nobody knew us, I could see Philip. He could visit, if he didn't mind a cottage. In school holidays and so on." If Philip even wanted to see him again, but since Guy was building a castle in the air anyway, he might as well include its king. "If you wouldn't mind?"

"Of course I wouldn't. That would work beautifully," Amanda said stoutly. "I could cook and clean when I'm not writing. Guy, please can we? I know it's an awful lot and most of it will fall on you, but I can't go on like this. It's not bearable."

"No, it isn't. I'll look at newspaper advertisements tomorrow, and write to schools. And I could write to my old tutor as well, couldn't I? I'm sure I'll find something, Manda. Everyone needs Greek and Latin."

"And you know so much. I'm sure you could do it."

Six weeks ago, Guy would have doubted that. He'd been quite happy in Amanda's company, keeping well away from the world's eyes. He didn't love the idea of seeking positions and the inevitable rejections, let alone the prospect of unruly boys and the drudgery of teaching. It would be long hours, poorly paid, unrewarding at best. But it would be self-sufficiency, even freedom, and he was not going to hide from the world any more. He'd taken a far worse leap into the dark and risked far more for Philip and he was blasted—no, he was *bloody* well going to do this.

"Then we're agreed," he said. "If Aunt Beatrice is arranging a marriage, we say no. Unless this chaplain is charming and eligible and you want to reconsider. Scratch your nose if you decide you'd like to get married after all."

Amanda sniffed. "I had better not catch a cold."

Mr. Dent arrived in the early afternoon. He was not charming at all. Amanda hissed, "He's a walking sepulchre!" and Guy found he couldn't improve on that description. The man couldn't be more than thirty-five but bore himself as though he were fifty. He had a face like a gravestone, long and angular and severe, and a voice to match. There was no humour in his expression, no warmth, and he nodded with funereal gravity as Aunt Beatrice introduced her unfortunate niece.

He couldn't want a wife with a reputation, Guy thought, unless he was truly desperate for a living. There were a lot of curates waiting their chance, and if this living was in the Marquess of Easterbury's gift, it might be a plum. Or perhaps he wanted someone to chastise, a fallen woman who would always be obliged to him for his condescension in stooping to pick her up. Guy balled his fists behind his back and practised courteous refusals in his head.

They endured prayers and a sermon on the subject of Redemption and Good Works, through which Amanda sat with narrowed eyes, and then Aunt Beatrice ordered tea for them all in the parlour. Mr. Dent assisted Amanda with a hand on her arm, and Guy composed a refusal that was significantly less courteous.

"Well," Aunt Beatrice said. "I dare say you may have realised that I invited Mr. Dent here for a reason beyond the care of souls. He is my chaplain of three years' standing, and he is prepared, as his vocation directs, to extend forgiveness to a sinner."

"That's very kind of him," Guy said. "But, Aunt Beatrice, I think we've had enough forgiving."

"I beg your pardon?"

"Amanda isn't to blame for the gossip about Sir Philip. Before that—it was years ago. I think if you're going to forgive someone, you should *do* it, and not keep dragging things up afterwards, or it isn't really forgiveness, is it? And I'm afraid I don't see what Mr. Dent here has to forgive us for at all."

Amanda was looking at him with an expression of glowing adoration he hadn't seen since he had mended her favourite doll at the age of ten. "*Thank* you, Guy. Well said."

"You interrupted me," Aunt Beatrice said icily. "Mr. Dent, in the spirit of his ministry, has agreed to take Amanda's hand in marriage. He will give her the protection of his name, and as his wife she will learn discretion and good conduct. There is an excellent living available, which—"

"No," Amanda said. "I'm sorry to interrupt, but I don't want to hear about the living. It's very kind of Mr. Dent to offer and I'm sorry he had a wasted journey, but I would have said if you'd consulted me. No."

"You will kindly hear me out, young lady!"

"No, she won't," Guy said.

Mr. Dent raised a hand. His features were somewhat tense, but his voice remained controlled. "Perhaps I may speak. Lady Paul intends that the proposed arrangement would suit both parties. Miss Frisby is in need of shelter and masculine guidance"—Amanda made a strangled noise—"and I require a helpmeet who is ready and willing to fulfil the many duties of a minister's wife. I have no doubt such a marriage would suit us both." He got that out with every appearance of sincerity, although Guy noticed he didn't look at his proposed helpmeet when he said it. "However, Lady Paul, I'm sure as a mother you understand that any young lady wishes to be sought for herself. Perhaps I might have a few moments alone with Miss Frisby to put my case in person."

"Your case is that you'll take a living with me thrown in," Amanda said. "No, thank you."

"Permit me a little time to speak," Mr. Dent repeated with a fixed smile. "I hope we can reach an understanding."

"Certainly," Aunt Beatrice said, rising. "Guy, with me please."

"Certainly not," Amanda said, grabbing his hand. "Considering all the fuss about me when I was constantly chaperoned in Rookwood Hall, I'm surprised you would suggest such a thing, Aunt."

"*Guy*," Aunt Beatrice repeated.

"I am a man of the cloth, Mr. Frisby," Mr. Dent said. "I assure you, there can be no impropriety in my holding private conversation with your sister."

"But she has told you no, twice," Guy said. "I think you should take it for an answer."

"I will not have this ingratitude," Aunt Beatrice said. "I cannot and I will not tolerate any further indiscretions from this side of the family. Lord Paul has borne enough at the hands of my sister and her family. I will not see my daughters suffer because of your indiscriminate intercourse with the worst elements of society. Amanda *will* marry, and learn to behave as a wife should."

"I am not yours to dispose of," Amanda said through her teeth. "And I can't get up and walk out of this horrid conversation because of my stupid leg, but if I could, I would be leaving the room now."

"Mr. Dent," Guy said, meeting the man's eyes. "You've heard Amanda's wishes. I think you've been misinformed about her availability, and suitability. I'm very sorry you've found yourself in this position, which I'm sure is as uncomfortable for you as anyone, but it would be right to withdraw your suit now."

Aunt Beatrice was going purple. "He will do no such thing if he wishes my continued patronage. You have been living on my charity for years. I have funded this worthless family out of kindness to the children of one whose career I can only regard with horror and disgust, I exerted myself to educate you and to give Amanda a Season, for which I was repaid with nothing but insult and humiliation, and now you reject the last hope your sister has of regaining her character. I will not have it. She *will* make this marriage or I shall cut you both off without a penny."

Guy squeezed Amanda's hand. "Then I'm afraid you'll have to do that. I'm sorry, Aunt, but I will not see Amanda forced into a match she finds repellent. Er, no offence, Mr. Dent."

Aunt Beatrice snorted. "And how do you propose to live?"

"Guy will find work," Amanda said. "We'll go far away. You needn't worry that I'll come to London or take up a career as a courtesan, Aunt; I should hate to cause you any more unhappiness by my existence. But I won't marry on your say-so, and that's all."

"All," Aunt Beatrice repeated. "*All*. After everything I have done for you, all the efforts I made to rescue you from the shame of your mother and the depredations of that contemptible sot your father. I bought the mortgages myself to preserve your home when your own father was prepared to see you thrown into the streets on his death. I have never charged one penny of interest. I have always striven to do right by this branch of the family despite the gross instability of character you display. And now when I have been humiliated once more, when my own child's marriage is put at risk by your wild behaviour, when I have arranged not just a means to hide yourselves but a way to restore Amanda's soiled name, you refuse my offer of Mr. Dent's hand." Her voice was rising and wobbling slightly. Guy wondered for an improbable second if she might cry. "I have had enough of you both. Too much. I shall not give you one penny more, not if you beg me. How you can be so wicked and so ungrateful— I wish I had left you to rot as your parents did! You will do as I say or I shall call in the mortgages immediately!"

Guy felt a stab of panic. He'd feared this, tried to steel himself, but the reality was still terrifying. Amanda gave a cry of protest. Mr. Dent held up his hands, speaking firmly. "Lady Paul, Mr. and Miss Frisby, please. Let us seek reconciliation if any such is possible. I think, if we all take some time for prayer and reflection——"

There was a knock at the door, so loud it resounded. Guy hadn't heard anyone approaching; he hadn't been listening. He hoped Mrs. Harbottle would get rid of whoever it was.

"We've had plenty of prayer and reflection," he said, trying to keep his voice level. This was how it would be; there was no choice. "I don't think more will help. You must do as you choose, Aunt Beatrice, but we've made our decision. And I am sorry to say this, but when Amanda has been so clear she doesn't want to marry Mr. Dent, threatening her into it is not worthy of you."

Aunt Beatrice reddened. "You will both starve in the streets. How can you possibly support yourselves? You have no more common sense than a pair of babies. And who would ever trust Guy with employment?"

Amanda drew herself upright, a martial look in her eyes, but at that moment Mrs. Harbottle shrieked, a cry of pure domestic outrage. Swift footsteps sounded in the hall, the door opened with some force— slammed, almost—and Philip walked in.

Chapter Twelve

"Philip!"

Guy had said that out loud, he realised. Also, he was on his feet, staring, with one arm outstretched. Other than that, he'd kept his countenance rather well. He pulled his hand back and tried again. "Sir Philip. Uh—what—"

"Sir!" Aunt Beatrice was swelling. "What is the meaning of this intrusion? Guy Frisby, is this individual in the habit of visiting this house?"

"Never been here in my life." Philip looked decidedly travel-worn, as crumpled as though he'd spent hours in a coach and not stopped to straighten his cravat. "Lady Paul, Miss Frisby, Mr. Frisby, sir." He sketched a very perfunctory bow in the room's general direction. "I come as postman."

"What?"

"Postman. I have a letter which Miss Frisby ought to read at once."

"You interrupt a private family gathering!" Aunt Beatrice informed him.

"What letter?" Amanda demanded.

Philip drew a paper from his pocket. "This. While you read it, I need two words with your brother. In private."

"I cannot think you have anything to say to my nephew, sir."

"Wrong," Philip said. "Mr. Frisby?"

"I, uh—" Philip's eyes were intent on his, widening slightly as Guy hesitated. Amanda put a hand to his thigh and shoved. "The situation is a little awkward. I can't leave Mr. Dent here with Amanda."

"Doubtless Lady Paul will chaperone."

"Yes, but she's just declined his very flattering proposal."

"I should hope so. Lord Paul would surely object."

Aunt Beatrice gave a gasp of rage; Amanda squeaked gleefully. Guy gritted his teeth. "No, *Amanda* declined it, and Mr. Dent is Lady Paul's chaplain and she has put forward his suit, so you see—"

"Say no more. One moment." Philip strode out without ceremony. Guy stared after him, suddenly terrified this was another abrupt departure and having to stop himself from crying out after him. But there was the sound of his shout outside, and a second pair of feet, and when Philip came back in, David Martelo was with him.

"*Oh*," Amanda said.

"This gentleman is Miss Frisby's physician," Philip said. "I'm sure he has many questions of a medical nature to ask. Oh, and the letter." He handed it over to Amanda, who didn't even look at him as she took it. "Right. Mr. Frisby, is there somewhere we might speak?"

Guy followed him out, dreamlike, ignoring the babble of voices from the room they'd left, and took him into the dining room. Philip closed the door, and said, "Christ, you look awful."

"I probably do, yes. It's been—not pleasant."

"I'm sure it has. I am sorry, Guy, extremely sorry. I was a prick of the first water, and I am going to beg your forgiveness in detail shortly, but I need to know, right now: Is Amanda inclined to David? If he proposed, would she accept?"

"Like a shot. Is—is that why you're here?"

"It's one reason," Philip said, and the look in his eyes was everything that had been missing from Guy's life. "Beloved—"

Amanda's scream cut over his words. "Guy! *Guy!*"

Guy ran, flinging the door open and crashing into the parlour. He didn't know what catastrophic scene he expected, but the room was entirely as he'd left it, except that Amanda, on the couch, was shrieking like a kettle come to the boil. "Guy!"

"What is it?"

She flapped the paper she held. "Forty pounds! Forty! Pounds! Forty!"

"*What* is?"

"My publisher! They want my next book! They'll pay me *forty*—" Her voice rose so high that it ceased to be audible.

"Book?" Aunt Beatrice demanded.

"Amanda's an author. It's not under her name, don't worry. Forty? Manda—"

"Don't, for heaven's sake, accept it," Philip said. "It's the first one we got in writing, but Theo—Mrs. Swann, the Gothic novelist, he's a crony of John Raven's—says you can use this to get a better offer elsewhere, and then use *that* to force this up. He advises you to try for sixty at least."

"*Sixty pounds?*" Amanda said at a pitch that threatened the glassware.

"It's a success," David told her. "A truly magnificent one. You've done superbly."

"Everyone's reading it," Philip agreed. "Apparently a certain nobleman considers himself to be portrayed, unflatteringly, in your villain, and his very public discontent has attracted a great deal of attention *Darkdown*'s way."

"Oh, God bless him," Guy said.

Aunt Beatrice looked positively ill. "You cannot— Another scandal— I will not permit it. I won't!"

"But it is not up to you to permit, and you can't stop me." Amanda's tone was soft, but it was not gentle in the slightest. "You washed your hands of me, Aunt Beatrice, if you recall. I don't need your permission for anything at all, ever again."

"On that subject," Philip said. "Excuse the haste, but I have business of my own to conduct. I introduced Dr. Martelo here as Miss Frisby's physician, in which capacity I engaged and paid him. Yes? Good. David, you're dismissed. Without notice, or a character, come to that. The point I am making is that you are no longer her doctor."

"Thank you, Philip." David was watching Amanda's face. "Miss Frisby—Amanda— Could I possibly have private speech with you?"

"No, sir, you may not," Aunt Beatrice said.

Amanda shot her a glare. "Of course you can."

"Amanda Frisby! I shall not move from this room."

"Oh, this stupid leg," Amanda said. "Guy, help me up."

"No, don't move," David said. He looked around at the spectators, exhaled in an 'oh well' sort of way, and went down to his knees in front of the couch. Guy squeaked. Amanda yelped.

"Amanda," David said, ignoring the audience with impressive focus. "I couldn't express myself before but I venture to hope that you understood, that you could tell—"

"Yes," Amanda said urgently.

"Er, good. But now I am free to speak, and I must tell you how ardently—"

"No, *yes*," Amanda cut in. "Yes, David. Of course I'll marry you."

He blinked. "Really?"

She reached for his hands. David grabbed hers. Guy put his own hand to his mouth, fighting back tears, and felt Philip squeeze his shoulder. Aunt Beatrice was wide-eyed and decidedly pink. She wouldn't like the rejection of her own plans but to have Amanda safely married must surely satisfy her, Guy thought.

"The only thing—no, *please* let me finish a sentence, darling, I had an entire speech planned," David said. "The only thing is, there's something we must discuss first."

"You'll want me to convert," Amanda agreed. "I don't know anything about it, so you'll have to explain, but I'm perfectly happy to, in principle."

Guy had forgotten that part. He winced as Aunt Beatrice almost shrieked, "*Convert?*"

"David is Jewish," Amanda told her. "Will I have to study an awful lot?"

"You'll have to take instruction." David looked stunned. Amanda could have that effect when she'd made up her mind about things. "If you're sure you still want to, once we've talked properly about what it means for you. Which we are going to do first," he added, with decision. Guy wished him luck.

Aunt Beatrice slumped back in her chair. "This is too much. I will not countenance it. Guy Frisby, as a Christian—"

"I will see my sister loved and happy," Guy completed. "And I'll be honoured to welcome David to the family."

"Not to mine. I will speak to Lord Paul. I will cut you off. You will be as dead to us all."

Amanda shrugged. It was a small movement, but lethally clear. Aunt Beatrice's face darkened worryingly. "You insolent baggage!"

"Lady Paul," Mr. Dent said. "I beg you to compose yourself. A straying sheep is better brought back to the path with charity than with anger."

"I'm not a sheep," Amanda said. "And I have had enough of Aunt Beatrice's charity for a lifetime."

"That's not quite fair, Manda," Guy said. It wasn't unfair either, but he didn't want Amanda to say anything she'd regret when her temper cooled, and he did not like the way his aunt looked. "Aunt Beatrice saved our home and gave us the means to live in it, and we must not forget how—" *Kind* stuck in his throat. "How generous she has been. Aunt Beatrice, I'm sorry we've been such a trial to you, but I can't let you insult my sister, so I think you should go home. I hope we can part on civilised terms, and you are very welcome to renounce us in public if that helps Anne. We won't force ourselves on your notice again until you're willing to accept Amanda and her husband."

Aunt Beatrice's mouth opened, fishlike. Guy turned to the chaplain. "Mr. Dent, I am sorry you've been caught up in this. Thank you for your consideration to my sister. I hope you find a new, er, helpmeet very soon. I really don't think Amanda and you would have suited."

"No," Mr. Dent said. He sounded funereally calm still but his cheekbones were burning red. "I cannot disagree. Thank you for your hospitality, Mr. Frisby. I believe I would be best to take my leave."

"We shall both leave," Aunt Beatrice panted. "Instruct my woman to pack."

David was looking at her. "Lady Paul, I do not like your colour. No, don't attempt to rise. Speaking as a physician—"

Guy felt a tug on his sleeve. "Our cue to exit," Philip murmured. "Come on."

Guy led the way into the garden. It was mostly taken up by vegetables, and entirely overlooked by the back of the house. They stopped in the middle of two beds, beans climbing up stakes on one side, the dark green leaves of a healthy potato crop rising on the other. Philip glanced around. "Is there anywhere private we could speak? An outbuilding?"

"Only a lean-to full of sacks and spades."

"Could we fit in there? If you wouldn't mind the squeeze."

"I wouldn't mind that at all, but it's really not—"

"No. Well then." Philip pushed a hand through his hair. Guy didn't think he'd ever seen him look like this: tired, messy, uncertain. "Beloved, I am so sorry. Of all the damn fool ways to leave you, when you were caught in the devil's own trap and I knew it. You needed me and I failed you, and I really will try not to be such a damned swine again. Without attempting to excuse myself, I will only say that to see you leaving me was more painful than I had thought possible. When you're afraid, you hide, but when I'm afraid, I hit out, and that is precisely what I did then. Corvin assures me I am utterly intolerable when in love."

Guy tried a smile. It wobbled a little. "He's wrong."

"Yes, well, *you* tell him that," Philip said. "He and John have taken turns shouting at me for four solid days. The words 'best thing that ever happened to you' have only been exceeded in use by 'stupid prick'."

"They said that?"

"Repeatedly. They have both taken up the Frisby cause, you understand. Corvin's performance at Vauxhall Gardens was spectacular even by his standards: if anyone in London doesn't know he's Lord Darkdown by now, it's not his fault. And John and his scribbler friend joined forces against London's publishing trade, which might almost make one sorry for publishers."

Guy put his hand to his mouth, needing to hide his expression. To feel as though Corvin and John cared for him and not just for Philip, as though they might be his friends too... He had to swallow to speak. "That's quite extraordinarily kind of them both. More than kind. I can't honestly tell you what that meant, to hear about the money then. We'd just been given the choice, you see, to have Aunt Beatrice call in the mortgage, or for Amanda to marry Mr. Dent."

Philip's brows snapped together. "That cadaverous piece of work? He was happy to take a wife on such terms, was he?"

"I don't know about happy. He's Aunt Beatrice's chaplain and she promised him an excellent living to do it. I can't imagine he enjoys his current position, and Aunt Beatrice would doubtless not have been pleasant if he'd refused the idea. I don't think it was fair of her, either to him or to Amanda."

"It was most certainly not. You were more generous than I would have been."

Guy could well believe that. Philip was close enough that Guy could see the tension in his stance. He wished they could touch, that he was in Philip's arms and not standing and chatting in a garden as though they were mere acquaintances. "She did her best for us, by her lights. She wasn't kind, and she was wrong about a lot of things, but we have given her a great deal to put up with, and it must be dreadful to be always so utterly consumed by what other people might think. Well, it is. I know it is because that's how I spent my life feeling, as though everyone was talking about me and I could only stop it if I hid. Because you're right. I do hide when I'm afraid, and I'm always afraid. I hid in this house, and behind a row of books, and under a lot of convention, and even in a disguise of having to look after Amanda, because while I had to look after her, I couldn't possibly do anything else. I think I'd have spent my whole life hiding if I hadn't met you."

"That would have been a criminal waste," Philip said. "Oh, curse it. Given a bit of privacy I would go to my knees, in the unexpected but effective manner David adopted. Since I can't, could you please imagine that I have?"

"Er—"

"Guy, beloved, you delight me. You're strong and kind-hearted and true as steel; you are open to knowledge and pleasure and human foibles in a way that makes me frankly embarrassed for my own limitations. I missed you painfully, I love you immoderately, and I don't want to be without you, if you can possibly tolerate the nonsense that being with me will entail."

Guy clenched his fists tight, in the hope it would help him stay upright, and still, and not hurl himself into Philip's embrace. "I, uh— Philip, that's— Were you both writing speeches in the coach here?"

"If we were, I did better than David," Philip said. "At least *my* Frisby lets a man get a word in edgewise. Is that all you have to say?"

"No, of course not. Philip, you know I love you, but what do you mean, to be with you?"

"From a worldly perspective, I thought you might consider a position with me. Secretary, man of business, whatever you'd like to call it. A real position with a salary, because I don't want you dependent on anyone's whim again, least of all mine, and the chance to put your undoubted talents to good use.

"But you've got a man of business," Guy said. "You've got Mr. Lovett."

"Lovett thinks I'm a lunatic and can't persuade the men otherwise. I need someone with the patience and understanding to sit down and persuade a pack of labourers to put their backs into sugar beet, when I would throw my hands up and walk out after five minutes. Someone with the capacity to see other points of view, which I have never made any great effort to develop, and from which my affairs would benefit. If I'd paid more attention to that, I shouldn't have walked out on you, an act for which I have spent the last days kicking myself in the intervals Corvin and John weren't kicking me. And I have learned damn all, I may add, because merely listening to that conversation just now, I wanted to leave that room a pile of smouldering wreckage. Whereas you didn't, despite far greater provocation. You thought; you were kind; you at least made a reconciliation possible in the future."

Guy was blushing again, he could feel it. "That's nothing. I don't like arguments."

"I know you don't. But you stood your ground, you did not let either fear or anger drive you, and you were marvellous. With you at my side, my life would be not just immeasurably improved but more intelligently conducted. And now it sounds all this is a sensible business proposal, and perhaps it is, but what I'm actually trying to offer is a way for us to be together. For you to leave here and come with me, no more hiding. There is a world outside."

"You don't think people might guess?" Guy asked, almost a whisper.

"Some might speculate. I could very easily arrange the appearance of a passionate affair with a lady, if you like. And I am not known as a diligent manager of my own affairs. It is entirely within character for me to take a secretary."

"But me, though? After Sir James and my mother, and if everyone thinks the worst about you and Amanda—"

"Amanda will marry her doctor and disappear from Society's notice. Your position will demonstrate to anyone reasonable that there was nothing in that rumour, and that I am making amends for past sins. Plenty of people won't be reasonable, needless to say, Lord and Lady Paul will doubtless be livid, and I am already notorious. I can't prevent any of that, so the question is whether you are prepared to accept a certain amount of unwanted attention or ill-natured gossip as the price of us. I don't say that lightly, my love. I know you loathe it, and that you don't want to distress your aunt even if you are prepared to defy her. I will do what I can to shield you, but in the end, there will be a price, and it is your choice if you think it's worth paying."

Philip's voice was controlled but the tension was visible in his eyes and fisted hands. Guy was almost glad for the foot or so separating them, the invisible barrier of observation that meant they couldn't touch. He wouldn't have stood a chance of making this decision sensibly in Philip's arms. He wasn't sure he was making it sensibly now, but at least he wasn't trying to think through a blizzard of desire and sensation.

"Right," he said. "About Corvin and, uh, John—"

"They want my happiness, and that depends on you."

"I want your happiness too," Guy said. "I know perfectly well you wouldn't be happy without them in your life. And they loved you first. I'd never try to take that away from you. I'm not sure what it all means and we'll doubtless need to talk about things, but I don't feel as though you love me any the less because of them. And if they don't feel that about me, then I dare say we'll all get on."

Philip shut his eyes, something in his face relaxing. "Thank you, beloved. Thank you."

"Am I still imagining you kneeling down?"

"I could very well be kneeling."

"Could we imagine that you stood up and kissed me?"

"Thoroughly," Philip said, "and passionately, with one hand on your wonderful arse and the other in your hair, bending you backwards and ravishing your mouth until you have no choice at all but to say, 'Yes please, Philip'. I hope."

"I love you," Guy said again. "And I have no idea if I'll be a good man of business or what-have-you but I do want to be one—really, I mean, and do it properly. And I dare say I can learn not to mind being talked about, if you don't mind trying to be talked about a bit less. I know you can't help the reputation you've already got, but I don't want to end up a Gothic villain in someone's book."

"I am quite sure you'd be the hero, but that is entirely reasonable," Philip said. "I could very well become at least as well known for sugar beet as blasphemy. I can't do anything about Corvin, though."

"Can anyone?"

"Not so far. I don't wish to press you in the slightest, but I should like to point out that I asked you a question in a formal sort of way and you haven't given me an answer, and I'm not so arrogant as to assume your response. So if you happened to have one to give—"

"Yes," Guy said. "Yes, please, Philip. I'd love to be with you. And I'd like you to imagine I'm kissing you back as hard as you've ever kissed me."

"I truly am. Good. Good. Might I get back on my imaginary knees? I have work to do there."

They were simply standing in a vegetable garden, not even touching, looking at one another, and Guy could feel Philip's touch all over his skin. He licked his lips and saw Philip's eyes track the movement. "I think you might have to save that for later. If Aunt Beatrice starts shouting for me, I'd like to be able to walk."

"A fair point, albeit one that reminds me we have unfinished business. Never have I resented an interruption so much."

"Oh God, I could have cried. Are you staying at the Hall tonight?"

"I had the place closed up in a fit of childishness. I don't suppose we could stay here? Assuming Amanda—"

"She knows about us."

"That, yes, good, but there is the matter of my presence in the Frisby house. I'll take myself off if either of you is concerned."

"I don't see there should be a problem, with her brother and her fiancé present," Guy said. "But for heaven's sake make sure Aunt Beatrice doesn't find out you'll be staying. I don't want her death on my conscience."

Aunt Beatrice seemed significantly less close to expiry when they returned to the house, walking shoulder to shoulder, not touching except in their imagination. The place was a chaos of packing, and Guy retreated to sit with Amanda in the parlour while Philip went to have a word with David and check the disposition of his horses.

"David read her a lecture," Amanda whispered, wide-eyed. "He said she clearly indulges both her appetite and her temper beyond what her constitution can support, and that she needs to take a great deal more care, and have more taken of her. He said she must cease to assume responsibility for others until she has first attended to herself, and that her family must consider her health far better, and he wrote her out a diet to follow and the name of a physician in London who would be strict with her and *ordered* her to summon him. I honestly thought she might cry."

"I think I might have. She let him say all that?"

"Guy, she was thrilled. Well, she said he was talking impertinent nonsense, but honestly, I don't think anyone's ever told her she ought to be cared for, or treated her like she needs help. One doesn't really think of her that way."

"No. I'm sure Lord Paul doesn't."

"Maybe we should have. Mr. Dent was taking notes, if you ask me. Do you know, I think once she's got over not having her way, she might not be so *very* angry."

"Well, I'd rather she didn't hate us, but we'll be all right even if she does. You're a success. I am so proud of you, Manda."

"It's such a relief," Amanda said. "Having people like my book, but also knowing I won't be quite penniless for David. Thirty pounds, if I get it, isn't a huge portion, but it's better than nothing, and I can write more books."

"Sixty pounds."

"Thirty. Of course it's halves and don't argue with me, I'm too happy. Where was I? Writing books. I did ask if David was expecting me to act as a nurse as well, and he said no, he'd rather have someone who knew what she was doing, so that's all right."

"Probably for the best," Guy agreed.

"But what about you?" Amanda asked. "You aren't going to stay here, are you?"

"I, uh, I'm going with Philip. He's offered me a sort of post as his secretary, for—for the look of things, but—yes. So you can keep your bridal portion, and I might even be able to afford a wedding present."

"Oh, Guy. Are you happy?"

"So much it hurts. You?"

"If it wasn't for my stupid leg, I'd be dancing. Ugh. Being trapped on this couch all splinted up while that ghastly man insisted he'd talk to me—really, you have no idea what a miserable thing this is."

"But if you hadn't broken your leg we'd never have gone to the Hall. And if we hadn't—"

"Oh, don't," Amanda said with a shudder. "Just imagine, we might have sat here with everything we wanted four miles away, and never known."

"I think a broken leg is a small price to pay," Guy said sententiously, gave it a second, then added, "So long as it's yours."

Amanda hit him. "Idiot. But you're right. It is all thanks to this stupid leg, and I won't ever complain about the scar, or if I limp, or at least I'll try not to. But I am so tired of the splints. Honestly, Guy, have you *any idea* how it feels to see the most wonderful man in the world walk in, and not be able to throw yourself into his arms?"

"Yes."

"Oh," Amanda said, face stilling. "Yes. Yes, of course you do. Oh, Guy."

Guy nudged her. "I nearly did anyway. That would have put the cat among the pigeons."

"Wouldn't it. My goodness. Except you nearly didn't, because Philip is only the *second* most wonderful man in the world. David is the most wonderful."

"He isn't, you know. He's marvellous, I couldn't be happier for you, but Philip—"

"David. The most wonderful. That's all."

"Is not."

"Is so."

"You're going to have to be a great deal more grown up when you're a doctor's wife, you know."

"Shan't," Amanda said, and they both collapsed in giggles.

It was an intolerably lengthy time before Aunt Beatrice and her chaplain departed, with sighs and head-shaking but less high dudgeon than Guy had expected. Mrs. Harbottle was told of Amanda's engagement, which she received with rapture, and of Philip's intention to stay the night, which went down significantly less well. And then, finally, they were alone. The four of them ate a hastily constructed dinner, and separated without discussion into pairs. Amanda and her fiancé had the parlour, naturally.

"We could sit in the dining room, or go into the garden," Guy suggested.

"Or we could go upstairs."

"Let's do that."

Guy had what had once been their parents' bedroom. He'd considered replacing the large bed, which took up too much space, several times, but never thought it worth the cost, for which he was now grateful.

Philip closed the door. "Alone at last, as the Gothic novels say. Come here."

Guy stepped into his arms. He was rather expecting the sort of overwhelming embraces that Philip had promised in the garden, but instead Philip cupped his face, not moving to kiss him, running his thumbs along Guy's jawline, eyes searching.

"My love," he said quietly. "You do look tired, and I put some of that there."

"It wasn't your fault," Guy said. "Or, not entirely. I had to put Amanda first, but really, I ought to have faced up to Aunt Beatrice years ago. You were angry because I was in an intolerable situation, but I had allowed myself to be in it."

"We all build our own prison walls," Philip said. "Not all of us have the courage to dismantle them, even if we have the chance."

He did kiss Guy then, leaning forward, bringing their mouths together. Long and slow, reacquainting themselves, sealing a bargain, kissing without thought of more because the closeness was what mattered, until Philip grunted and slipped his hands down to Guy's arse, after which thought of more became rapidly pressing.

"God, I've missed you," Philip mumbled against his mouth. "It was lucky we were so damned busy over the last days, or I shouldn't have slept. Let me make it up to you in tangible form. How may I please you, my virgin?"

"I'm quite sure I'm not virginal any more."

"Not in the strict sense of the word, perhaps, but there is a delightful purity about you even when I'm debauching you in the worst ways. Especially then, in fact. And I do like debauching you, and I should hate to stop."

"So should I."

Philip brought up a hand to stroke his face. "Tell me what you thought of when you missed me and your hand strayed to your prick for comfort."

"Oh God. You really do want to ruin me, don't you?"

"Utterly."

"When you told me about how you, you were with John and Corvin together," Guy whispered. "And you held me, and fucked me, and talked to me, until I felt as though there was nothing in the world except your voice and your hands and you. Tell me another story like that."

"I taught you language, and my profit on't is, you will soon be bringing me off by words alone," Philip said. "My God, I want you."

They stripped each other with reasonable finesse under the circumstances, and fell onto the bed in a tangle of limbs that resolved into Guy on his side, cradled by one of Philip's arms, a thumb teasing at his lips, the other hand wrapped around his stand, and Philip's own hard length fitted close between his thighs. It felt like more of a possession than anything else they'd done, as though Philip owned every part of him, held it dear, and wouldn't let him go.

He kissed the thumb at his mouth. "I love you."

Philip stroked his lip, and kissed his ear, sending shudders down Guy's skin. "It's odd," he said thoughtfully. "I am well aware I should treat such a precious gift as you with the greatest delicacy and respect, but what I'm actually going to do is torment you in the most carnal and degenerate ways I can think of until you're writhing to spend in my hand. A story, you said. Suppose I tell you how I occupied a very long and lonely night thinking of you, and the depths of depravity to which my imagination descended in that time. It has several acts, and a cast list."

Guy swallowed. "That sounds, uh. Yes. Does it have a happy ending?"

"Of course it does, beloved," Philip said. "And always will where I am involved. I promise you that."

240

Author's Note

Sugar beet was developed in Silesia, now Poland, in the mid-18th century. The first beet-sugar factory was opened there in 1801, and the industry grew extremely swiftly across Europe, particularly in France and Germany. Britain didn't actually establish domestic sugar production until the 1920s, but it could easily have been done at the time of this book.

I owe big thanks to Sarah Slocum for pointing out a problem I'd missed, and Tamara Gal-On for immediately supplying the solution. You two can do that any time.

**For more Regency gentlemen by KJ Charles
try the Society of Gentlemen series
starting with *A Fashionable Indulgence*.**

A Fashionable Indulgence

A young gentleman and his elegant mentor fight for love in a world of wealth, power, and manipulation.

When he learns that he could be the heir to an unexpected fortune, Harry Vane rejects his past as a Radical fighting for government reform and sets about wooing his lovely cousin. But his heart is captured instead by the most beautiful, chic man he's ever met: the dandy tasked with instructing him in the manners and style of the ton. Harry's new station demands conformity—and yet the one thing he desires is a taste of the wrong pair of lips.

After witnessing firsthand the horrors of Waterloo, Julius Norreys sought refuge behind the luxurious facade of the upper crust. Now he concerns himself exclusively with the cut of his coat and the quality of his boots. And yet his protégé is so unblemished by cynicism that he inspires the first flare of genuine desire Julius has felt in years. He cannot protect Harry from the worst excesses of society. But together they can withstand the high price of passion.

Praise for the Society of Gentlemen

"KJ Charles writes some of the most inventive historical romances around, and *A Seditious Affair* is one of my favorites. ... The stakes are high and deeply felt, and once you start, there's no way to stop reading this one." Courtney Milan

"Many congratulations to KJ Charles proving that it can be done. Romance can incorporate meaty socio-economic and political context into the story-telling. And the resulting tale can be riveting and most definitely hot." Smart Bitches, Trashy Books

"The realities of class, societal mores and politics heighten the tension in this emotional, deeply romantic look at the remarkable lengths we will go for love." Washington Post

"Everything I enjoy in a historical romance can be found in *A Gentleman's Position*. Accurate, confident and luscious, the writing brings Lord Richard Vane and his 'fox', David Cyprian, to glorious life." All About Romance

Wanted, a Gentleman

Theodore Swann is a jobbing writer, proprietor of the Matrimonial Advertiser lonely hearts gazette, and all-round weasel. He's the very last man that Martin St. Vincent would choose to rely on—and the only one who can help.

Martin is a wealthy merchant who finds himself obliged to put a stop to a young heiress's romantic correspondence in the Matrimonial Advertiser. When she and her swain make a dash for Gretna Green, Martin drags Theo on a breakneck chase up the country to catch the runaway lovers before it's too late.

Theo guards his secrets. Martin guards his heart. But as the two of them are thrown irresistibly together, entanglements, deceptions, and revelations come thick and fast...

Get the free story that introduces Theo Swann to John Raven by subscribing at

http://kjcharleswriter.com/newsletter

About the Author

KJ Charles is a RITA®-nominated writer and freelance editor. She lives in London with her husband, two kids, an out-of-control garden, and a cat with murder management issues.

KJ writes mostly romance, mostly queer, frequently historical, and usually with some fantasy or horror in there. She is represented by Courtney Miller-Callihan at Handspun Literary.

Find me on Twitter @kj_charles

Pick up free reads on my website at kjcharleswriter.com

Join my Facebook group, KJ Charles Chat, for book conversation, sneak peeks, and exclusive treats.

Made in the USA
Monee, IL
27 September 2021